DIAMOND LIFE

DIAMOND LIFE

Sheila Copeland

sepia
★BET
BOOKS

BET Publications, LLC
http://www.bet.com

SEPIA BOOKS are published by

BET Publications, LLC
c/o BET BOOKS
One BET Plaza
1900 W Place NE
Washington, DC 20018-1211

All Kensington Titles, Imprints, and Distributed Lines are available at special quantity discounts for bulk purchases for sales promotions, premiums, fund-raising, and educational or institutional use. Special book excerpts or customized printings can also be created to fit specific needs. For details, write or phone the office of the Kensington special sales manager: Kensington Publishing Corp., 850 Third Avenue, New York, NY 10022, attn: Special Sales Department, Phone: 1-800-221-2647.

ISBN: 1-58314-236-3

First Printing: November 2003
10 9 8 7 6 5 4 3 2 1

Printed in the United States of America

For
my very special sister friend
ETGUINA BERNICE NEWMAN HOLDNESS.
An angel who received her wings
and upon them into glory gone.

What good is it for a man to gain the world
And then lose his soul?
—Mark 8:36

PRELUDE

In this life money and women
It's easy to lose sight of the right type of livin'.
Love, life, swimmin' and sinnin'
Pool parties, liquor and drugs and much more
I ain't comfortable mentionin'.
I can't imagine my kids growin' up and wishin'
They can get in this business
'Cause it's so, so vicious.
The media all up in your business
Look what they're doin' to Mike
Pick one the one who sings, balls or fights.

All I'm tryin' to do is bring y'all the Light
'Cause the King might call tonight.
I don't want to see y'all fall but fight.
And don't believe the hype behind this Diamond Life.
You might lose your life
Tryin' to prove that your rhyme is tight.
You'll succeed if the time is right,
But more than the time
Make sure your mind is right
Eyesight focused toward the Light.
'Cause you can move forward
Or get left behind
In this Diamond Life.

You can ball or fall
You can lose everything
Or leave with it all
In this life fast money, women and cars
But it cost tryin' to be a Chocolate Star.

Xtreme

Chapter 1

The Pacific was radiant and roaring that day. Nina Beaubien Ross sat cross-legged on her favorite rock soaking it all in . . . the smell of the salty air, the sound of the waves as they rushed in and out. Seagulls called to one another as they darted through the surf as though they were playing an imaginary game.

Nina stretched like a cat in the sun, barely noticing the hardness of the stone. For hours, she would sit perched like a beautiful bird, absorbing every inch of her waterfront Malibu Colony estate. It had become a daily ritual for her after a year of traveling throughout Europe and Asia with her husband, Kyle. Nina had just completed her second novel, and she relished the time off to spend as she pleased.

"Hello, beautiful wife." She felt Kyle's strong arms embrace her, and he gently kissed her neck. Kyle had joined her and broken the spell of the ocean. Nina smiled as she relaxed against his body. Although they had been married for more than two years, they still felt like newlyweds.

"Hi, baby." He sat down behind Nina, and she snuggled into his arms. "Isn't this beach the most magnificent thing in the world?"

"It is spectacular." They waved as a neighbor jogged by with a gorgeous jet-black Labrador. "Come on. Let's go inside before the tide comes in any farther, or we'll have to swim."

Nina placed her arms around Kyle's neck as he lifted her off the rock that she had lovingly christened Pride Rock. It reminded her of the one in the *Lion King*, the play they had seen in New York on their first date.

"Look, Simba. Everything the water touches is our kingdom," Nina recited as he carried her toward the house.

"Yes, Nala." Kyle carefully put her down once they reached the stone pathway that led up to the house and took her by the hand. "Everything the water touches is our kingdom."

She noticed the baby monitor that was stuck in his shirt pocket. "Did Nicki finally settle down for a nap?"

"Finally. After I turned on some music. She won't go to sleep without it."

"No, she won't. You know she loves music." Nina smiled as she thought about the couple's pretty golden-eyed toddler who was a joy but a handful to keep up with when she was awake. "You're the one who spoils her, Big Daddy."

"I can't help it. When she looks at me with those eyes of hers, I melt," he confessed.

"You and everyone else. I've seen those eyes in action. She knows how to work a brother."

"She sure does." Kyle laughed.

Nina's thoughts were on her daughter, Kendall Nicole Ross, until she noticed the U.S. Mail truck parked farther down Pacific Coast Highway. "I'm going to check the mail. I'll meet you inside."

She let go of her husband's hand and sprinted toward the mailbox stuffed with an assortment of letters and magazines. She sifted though a stack of envelopes as she slowly walked back around to the rear of the house past a bubbling fountain that flowed into an aquamarine swimming pool.

Nina entered a huge kitchen where Kyle was watching *Dr. Phil* on a plasma-screen TV installed over the fireplace in the family room. She plopped down on the sofa next to Kyle and handed everything to him except for two letters addressed to Nina Beaubien and Nina Beaubien Ross. She still smiled at the sight of her husband's last name *Ross* next to hers and opened that letter first.

"The Pierce Academy for Girls announces the ten-year reunion of the class of 1993," Nina read from the invitation. It included details for a weekend in June that included a dinner and a picnic. "My goodness, has it been ten years already?" she asked out loud.

"Has what been ten years?" Kyle forgot about Dr. Phil and focused on his wife.

"It's been ten years since I graduated from high school. There's a class reunion next month."

"Those are always fun. Are you going?"

"I sure am. I can't wait to show off my gorgeous husband and daughter and my *New York Times* best-selling novel." She grinned impishly.

Kyle picked up the invitation and looked at it. "You can show off your gorgeous daughter and your novel but your hubby has a big meeting in New York that weekend."

"No way." Disappointment clouded Nina's pretty face. "You can't get out of it?"

"It's a biggie. Sorry, baby."

"Then I'm not going." Nina pouted.

"Yes, you are. You'll have fun. I know I did. You'll get a chance to see what's been going on with your classmates. Who got fat, who's successful, who's not."

"I do have a couple of friends that I haven't seen since graduation. After Topaz came to California, my life changed drastically, and I lost track of so many people."

"Then it's settled. You're going."

"I guess." She still looked skeptical.

"I'll try and make it back for the picnic on Sunday but I can't promise you I'll be there."

"If you try, that's good enough for me. You're my best friend. I don't like going places without you." Nina cuddled up next to him.

"Why don't you see if Jade or your cousin want to go?"

"Topaz won't go. She never wants to do anything anymore. She's glued to Germain."

"What about Jade? She'll go with you."

"I'll think about it." Nina still hadn't spent any time with Jade, her sister-in-law who had been begging her and Kyle to spend a weekend at the ranch in Santa Barbara. Every since Nicki was born it had become difficult for Nina to spend time with Jade. "You know we really should go see Jade and Sean."

"I've seen my brother several times. We had breakfast in the marina with Eric before he went to a Lakers shoot-around."

"Eric . . . I wonder if Keisha's still in Atlanta. She went down there to check on the house they're building. I don't see anyone anymore. It seems strange. All of our lives are going in separate directions."

"It may seem like that, but we're all family. And we'll always be friends." Kyle was so reassuring.

"You're right, sweetie." Nina took the letter opener and carefully slit open the second envelope. "What's this?" She removed a metallic silver passport from the envelope.

"What's what?" Kyle put his chin on her shoulder and looked at the passport Nina held up.

"That's tight. Open it, woman. Don't keep me in suspense," Kyle demanded.

"Suicide Records invites you to its launch party at the Highlands featuring entertainment by the label's premiere artist, Xtreme," Nina read out loud as she looked over the invitation several times. "Suicide Records?" She was puzzled.

"What's Suicide?" Kyle searched her for a response as she handed him the invitation. He read over it and laughed. "Your tired ex-boyfriend invited you to a party." He picked up the envelope and laughed even harder. "I guess I wasn't invited because my name isn't on this anywhere."

"This is from Jamil?" Nina seemed even more puzzled.

"Who else?" Kyle was still laughing. "I said it was your tired ex."

"I helped Jamil set up this label. It wasn't called Suicide."

"What was it called?"

"We named it after his production company Just Jam. Remember Just Jam underwrote the cost of Chocolate Affair?"

"That's right. He sure did." Kyle had handled the finances for the big fund-raiser that Nina and Keisha had done to raise money for sickle cell disease research. It had been a huge success, and Jamil's company had been a major sponsor. Kyle looked at the logo, the letter *S* enclosed in a circle, and handed it back to Nina. "Your boy has gone hard. Maybe he thinks he's a thug or something now."

"Jamil was never like that." Nina didn't know why she was defending him.

"Then maybe success has gone to his head. He's making serious paper. He can make a hit record."

"He sure can. He blew up Topaz and everyone else he ever produced." Nina sat there staring at the envelope and the invitation several more minutes before she got up and went into the kitchen to use the telephone. She placed the announcement in front of her on the black marble counter. The phone rang several times before someone finally answered. "What are you doing?"

"Baking cookies with Baby Doll and Chris."

"Wait . . ." Nina stifled a giggle. "The superstar, the diva . . . Topaz is in the kitchen baking cookies?"

"What do you want, Nina?"

She could hear the frustration in her famous cousin's voice and doubled over with laughter. "You can't cook. You burn water."

"All right, smartie. I think I can handle this. They're the kind you break off and place on a cookie sheet. Chris begged, and I couldn't tell him no."

"Wait . . . you were in the supermarket?"

"Yes." Topaz finally laughed.

"What for?" Nina couldn't believe what she was hearing. She couldn't remember when or if Topaz had ever set foot in a supermarket.

"The kids needed some juice and milk so I stopped at the store after I picked Chris up from school."

"Wonders never cease . . ."

Topaz pressed a button on the phone as if to beep her out, and Nina screamed with laughter.

"Nina, what do you want?"

"I almost forgot." Nina finally stopped laughing. "Did you get an invitation to Jamil's launch party for the label?"

"You mean that passport thing from Suicide Records?"

"Yes."

"I got it."

"Are you going?" Nina traced a pattern in the marble counter.

"Baby, don't burn yourself. Here, let Mother help you. Hold on, girl."

Nina waited patiently while Topaz went to help Chris with the cookie sheet. Her cousin had turned into a very domesticated housewife and mother since she remarried Germain. Topaz had really changed while Nina was away.

"I didn't want Chris to burn himself," Topaz explained. "Now what were we talking about?"

"I wanted to know if you were going to Jamil's party."

"It's on a school night, and Chris has lots of homework," Topaz offered.

"Listen to you." Nina still couldn't believe what she was hearing. "You know Germain helps him. Are you going?"

"I don't want to."

"Me neither, but don't you think one of us should go?"

"Considering everything . . . one of us should go," Topaz agreed. "I'd go but Germain hates those parties."

"Jamil didn't even invite Kyle. My invitation was addressed to Nina Beaubien."

"He's still got it bad for you." Topaz laughed. "Unrequited love."

"That's not funny." Nina was very serious.

"Oh, Nina, chill out. You know Jamil's got a string of women, and he won't tell—"

"I wasn't even thinking about that," Nina interrupted.

"So what's the problem?"

"Something about this Suicide thing bothers me."

"What?"

"I don't know. It's just weird." Nina tapped the invitation on the counter. "Kyle said Jamil probably thinks he's a thug or something."

"Jamil was never like that. Bring Mother one of those cookies, baby."

Nina ignored the sound of Topaz crunching in the telephone and continued. "That's what's so strange about it. It's so unlike him."

"Don't worry about it, Nina. He probably thinks it's cool or something. You know how everyone in hip-hop tries to act like they're so hard."

"Yeah, you're probably right," Nina agreed reluctantly.

"So are you gonna represent?"

"I'll do the honors."

"Cool. Germain just walked in. I'll call you later." Topaz was off the phone in a matter of seconds, and Nina slowly returned the handset to the receiver.

Nina gave the invitation one last glance before she stashed it and the reunion announcement in a drawer in the kitchen where she kept important papers before transferring them to her office.

Chapter 2

The phones never stopped ringing at Suicide Records located on the sixth floor of the new Music Group building in Burbank. The edifice, etched between the network studios and the San Fernando mountains, was only minutes away from Hollywood or "over the hill" as Angelenos coined it, referring to the elevation that separated Los Angeles from the San Fernando Valley. The temperature automatically increased or decreased by ten degrees, depending on the destination, because the valley was completely cut off from any hint of an ocean breeze. In the city, one could get away without air conditioning on hot summer days. In the valley, the streets were eerily empty, air conditioners ran incessantly, and you could literally fry an egg on the sidewalk.

Jamil's two-way blinked bright shades of blue as his cell phone beeped a medley of notes programmed from an original tune. He ignored the two-way and picked up the cell phone.

"Holla."

It was amazing that he was even able to hear with one of his latest tracks blasting through a state-of the-art sound system. The time code ran beneath footage of a rapper dressed in a Negro League baseball jersey on a thirty-five-inch plasma-screen TV. Countless platinum records and plaques lined the walls of his office. A life-size cutout of Topaz stood in the corner behind a neatly organized desk.

"Holla," Jamil repeated as the two-way continued to beckon for his attention. He picked it up, flipped it open, quickly read the message and typed in a response.

"Can you hear me?" a warbled voice replied through the phone.

"Barely." Jamil picked up a remote and lowered the volume of the music.

"You could if you'd cut down that music, playa."

A beautiful smile lit up Jamil's handsome face, and he laughed. "That's you, but I'll cut it down. That 'I'm Hot' track is tight."

"Naw, man. Don't turn it down then. Cut it up!"

Jamil pointed the remote again and increased the volume to a deafening level as he bounced in place behind his desk. "You's a wicked boy." He laughed when the music ended. "You ready to blow the music industry apart?"

"Hell yeah." The caller laughed. "Just like I blew 'em out on the field today."

"Where you at, dog?"

" 'Bout to take off and head your way. We just finished a game, and I'm ready for da ladies."

"Did you win, playa?"

"Is my name Xtreme?"

"Hell yeah," they both replied in unison.

"Whatcha got lined up for me?"

"A few prime-choice cuts of booty are waitin' at the crib and anything else you might want to partake of."

"I'm on my way."

Jamil closed his cell phone and smiled as he restarted the track. Moments later, a beautiful young woman with braided hair down to her waist, wearing tight stretch denim jeans faded on the thighs and a black T-shirt with *Suicide Music* written across it in metallic silver graced the door of his office.

"You got a minute, boss?"

It was India, the woman who kept his life in order and ran Suicide like a well-oiled machine. With her at the helm, Jamil could still spend hours in the studio doing what he loved best—making music— knowing that the business side of things was being handled. Nobody messed with India.

"For you, always." Jamil cut off the music as she closed the door and sat on the black leather circular sofa in front of the television where he and India met at least once a day. He watched her walk across the room, enjoying the aroma of the African oil she wore. Intoxicating and delightful, it announced her presence or departure. One always knew when India was around because of her signature fragrance. He watched her walk across the room to the sofa. She was sexy as hell.

Jamil held a weakness for smart, beautiful women. He had promised himself when he hired her not to get involved because his last interlude with beauty and brains had rewarded him with a broken heart. He constantly battled with thoughts of Nina Beaubien, his first real love.

It had been more than two years since that banker playboy wannabe stole her right out of his arms and married her. Jamil still had the diamond engagement ring he had given Nina tucked away in a drawer of baubles and trinkets he used to dazzle women. He never had the heart to return it. Fortunately, for his sake, India was engaged, and now he limited his romantic escapades to mindless hoochies.

India sat on the sofa beside him with a legal pad of notes. "I've been working on Xtreme's showcase. You've gone slightly over budget."

She leaned back on the sofa, crossed her legs, and met his eye.

"By how much?"

"Ten thousand." Her response was cool and firm, and for some reason India was turning him on more than usual today.

"Ten thousand? Does that cover the food and Cristal I requested for VIP?"

"Yes."

"And everything we need for Xtreme's performance?"

"Yes."

"Okay. It'll be worth it. Have you heard his track?" Jamil got up for the remote and restarted the music.

"All day long. I could barely hear in my office." India smiled, and Jamil hoped his body wasn't giving off any telltale signs of his intense attraction to her.

"You should have asked me to turn it down."

"No, I couldn't. Whenever you play music like that, it goes through the top of the charts. I'm not going to interfere with anything that helps you make those hit records. I just used the telephone in the conference room."

Jamil felt himself reeling from her compliment and most importantly, because she understood him so well.

Suddenly, the sound of a helicopter drowned out everything.

"Uh-oh, looks like Suicide's latest and greatest is here." India gathered her notes and stood. "Everything else can wait until tomorrow."

Jamil took India's hand and stopped her as she passed him on her way out of the office.

"What?"

He carefully examined her left hand and saw the small black diamond on her ring finger.

"I just wanted to see if it was still there."

"What?"

"That ring."

"Jamil." India laughed as she pulled her hand away.

"A brother can always hope, can't he?"

She simply smiled and squeezed his shoulder as the door opened and Xtreme exploded inside the office after the helicopter had deposited him on the roof. A platinum diamond-shaped medallion designed especially for him by Jake, the jeweler of the chocolate stars, dangled from his neck. The heavy piece flaunted his name and more than thirty carats of diamonds. It was blinding as it reflected the late-afternoon sunlight. Xtreme reeked of cockiness and arrogance, but there was a playfulness that made him boyish and charming. He was also extremely handsome.

"In fact, just put extreme in front of any word and that's him," his bio read.

"Take care, sweetheart." Xtreme had been talking to one of India's assistants who like countless other young women, hoped the superstar pitcher and hitter for the California Angels would give her some play.

"Hey, Miss India." Xtreme couldn't resist flirting as she passed him by, hoping to at least get a small feel of her perfectly round derriere. "You're looking beautiful today as always."

"Hello, Xtreme." The consummate professional, India extended a hand. He took it and kissed it.

"Um, um, um." Xtreme looked her up and down as though she was good enough to eat before he moved toward the sofa.

"Thank you, India," Jamil called out as he stood to greet his boy and the label's first artist. She nodded and closed the door behind her.

"Are you hitting that correctly, playa?" Xtreme looked toward the door and then at Jamil.

"No way, man. She's my business partner and much too valuable to play games with."

"Don't tell me you're going soft on me. Booties like that were made for hitting."

"I get my share." Jamil laughed.

"I know you do." Xtreme flopped on the couch beside him and took out a plastic sandwich bag filled with cocaine. "I'm ready to get my party on." He spread some lines out on a magazine and snorted them quickly. "You gonna hit this, man?"

He looked at Jamil who was searching his desk drawer for a box of blank CDs so he could burn a copy of the track he had mixed for Xtreme. Jamil paused when he caught sight of a framed photograph of him and Nina. The sight of her beautiful face immediately caused him pain.

"Jamil."

"Yeah, man." Jamil slammed the drawer closed and stuck a CD in the burner.

"I said do you want to hit this?" Xtreme pointed to the freshly sprinkled lines on the cover of a hip-hop magazine.

"No doubt." Jamil moved back to the sofa and quickly sniffed up the lines Xtreme had made for him. "Let's bounce."

"Ready when you are." Xtreme sprang from his seat. He was already wired. He had been doing lines during the short flight from Anaheim Stadium to Burbank. He watched Jamil gather his communication devices and quickly scribble on a CD and place it in a case.

"You hungry, man?" Jamil checked around his office to ensure he had brought what he would need for the evening.

"Hell yeah."

"Want to stop downstairs for some chow?"

"Hell no. I want some In and Out burgers and fries."

Jamil could only laugh. The drug had already kicked in, and he was feeling a buzz. They headed toward the elevator, ignoring the secretaries who called "good night" after them. Inside the garage he turned the alarm off on a shiny black Hummer. The young men jumped inside and Jamil pulled out of the garage into heavy traffic on Olive Boulevard. The sun was beginning to set, and it resembled a rose-colored ball of fire as it traveled across the heavens, toward the horizon, easing the heat of the day.

"Here, fire this up." Jamil tossed him a nice-sized blunt as he cranked the volume on Xtreme's track. Simultaneously, both of their heads began to bounce with the music.

"Turn up the air, playa." Xtreme exhaled a thick stream of smoke and passed the marijuana to Jamil. "It's hot as hell in here."

Chapter 3

At least twenty or thirty people stood waiting to cross the street at the intersection of Wilshire and Westwood boulevards. After five minutes of watching every car imaginable zip by, UCLA students and staff scurried across, heading in a myriad of directions—some toward bus stops, restaurants, and office buildings, while others disappeared inside the numerous apartments and condominiums that lined the quiet residential streets south of the boulevard that provided housing for the UCLA community.

Charetta Jackson stepped off the curb after the "do not walk" sign started to flash and cursed when she was nearly run over by a Mercedes SUV. She fought back the Compton attitude that tried to rise up out of her and continued sipping a large Jamba Juice as she headed for her apartment. A wrinkled black bandanna and a baseball cap covered the kinky red hair that always looked as if it needed a good pressing. She had tried to twist it into dreds but Charetta's hair had always had a mind of its own. She removed the baseball cap and the bandanna now that class was over, took a final sip on her drink, and tossed the empty cup into a trash can. She had purchased the drink to celebrate—school was finally out. She would graduate from UCLA's law and business schools with a JD and an MBA.

She shifted her book bag and tried not to think about the school loans that she would have to pay back as she unlocked the front door of a well-kept modern building. She could hear J.Lo's latest single escaping through an open window. She knew her roommate was the culprit, and it immediately shifted her focus to music, her one true love.

Charetta entered the apartment and managed a feeble smile for the strikingly beautiful Mexican-American woman singing and dancing around the dining room. Her jet-black hair was drawn up into a thick ponytail and her deeply set alluring eyes sparkled with mischief.

"Congratulations, my sister." She smiled as she patted a director's chair at a small circular table for two.

"Toni, what did you do?" Charetta eyed the feast of enchiladas, tacos, chips, salsa, and guacamole covering the small table. There was also a bottle of her favorite red wine.

"I cooked." Toni pirouetted across the small dining room and pulled out a chair. "Here, sit."

Charetta tried to find the words as she dropped her book bag by the door and followed instructions. Montona Mena was her closest and dearest friend. They had met in high school, and once Charetta had been able to handle Montona's beautiful, sophisticated exterior they were inseparable. Both ladies had been minorities in pursuit of higher education at Pierce Academy where they had bonded despite Charetta's rough edges and Toni's enormously wealthy family.

"It's time to celebrate, girl. A juris doctorate and a master's in business administration. You're my hero." Toni's laughter was sparkling and infectious.

Charetta finally laughed, forgetting her money problems for the moment. "Yeah, girl. You're right. It is time to celebrate."

She filled her plate with her favorites and dug in. Toni was good about cooking when she wasn't choreographing some music video or dancing in one herself just to make ends meet. Every penny of Charetta's money had been invested in graduate school, and a few stipends and savings from a summer internship helped her pay her half of the expenses in the tiny, overpriced one-bedroom.

"I got the J.Lo video." Toni smiled and poured herself another glass of wine.

"Cool." Charetta leaned back and ran a hand through her thick red hair. "Now that I've finished school, I'll turn you into the next J.Lo."

"Whatever, girl. As long as I'm dancing, I'm happy."

"Spoken like a true artist."

Toni smiled and shrugged. "A true starving artist. I guess I'm still trying to prove something to my father."

"You think? I couldn't believe it when he wouldn't pay for you to attend Julliard. That was so unfair."

"He thought cutting off the money would make me do what he wanted me to do. Julliard couldn't give me a scholarship because of my family's money. There ought to be some sort of fund for kids who refuse to be controlled by their parents."

"I agree." Charetta lifted her wineglass to Toni. "I'll establish one when I make you a star."

"Char . . ."

"Toni . . ."

The ladies smiled at each other through the candlelight.

"You think I did all this work to become an entertainment lawyer? I'm going to be the toughest manager to be reckoned with in this business."

"You sure will. Not to mention your songwriting skills," Toni added.

"No doubt. I have a brain, and I can write a song." Charetta stood from the table and sat at her keyboard which was sitting on the opposite side of the room. She put on a pair of thick glasses before she clicked it on, pressed a few buttons, and began to play to a hip-hop beat she had already programmed.

"I like that." Toni danced as she tossed their paper plates in the trash and put away the remainders of their feast.

"I feel so free." Charetta stopped playing and focused on Toni.

"You should feel free, girl, after all that school."

"I thought my brain was going to explode at times." Charetta rubbed her head, and her hair stood on end when she removed her hand.

"Char, you have got to do something about that hair." Toni laughed and Charetta joined in.

"It won't dred; it won't stay straight."

"It's strong, like a crown, and it represents your strength." Toni pulled the rubber band off her hair and wrapped it around her roommate's.

"Thanks, Toni." Charetta was the only girl in a family of five brothers. Rough and tough was the only way that she knew how to be. She looked at Toni's beautiful figure clad in a colorful skirt and blouse that complimented her swarthy complexion and wished for the zillionth time that she could be a little more feminine. While Toni had a steady stream of male callers, Charetta had none. She was much too focused on her career to think about the opposite sex. She restarted the track and continued playing.

"Hey . . ." Toni cut on the lights and blew out the candles. "I almost forgot. I have a surprise for you."

"Now what did you do? Like you haven't done enough already." Charetta watched Toni leave the room and return with an envelope, which she dropped on the ivory and black keys.

"What's this?"

"Did you forget how to read?"

Charetta made a face and pulled a letter out of the envelope and read it. "So . . . Pierce Academy is having a reunion."

"And we're going. I mailed in the check today."

"I don't want to see those people." Charetta made a face at the thought. "I promised myself I would never set foot on that campus again. All those stuck-up rich people."

"That place is where we met," Toni reminded her. "And I think it's time to go back. Besides, you can show off with your new degrees."

"Thanks, but no thanks." Charetta folded the letter, returned it to the envelope, and handed it back to Toni.

"You're kidding, right?"

"No," Charetta repeated firmly. "It isn't our class reunion anyway."

"That's true, but I still think we should go."

"No."

"I don't understand why you're being so difficult about this. We had lots of fun there."

Charetta sighed but she still looked determined. "I just don't feel like I represent what a Pierce woman stands for."

"Girl, you are the epitome of a Pierce woman. You've got those degrees and—"

"And I don't have any money. I don't even have a car," Charetta fumed. "I'm real important and successful riding MTA. You know how people act in LA when they find out you don't have a car. You're like the dregs of the earth or something."

"You're tripping. No one there will know you don't have a car because we're going in mine, and you're going to have all sorts of job offers now that you've finished grad school," Toni pleaded.

"I'm going to be a manager in the music industry. It's going to take time for me to find talent and get a business going. You're my only act. When it's our ten-year reunion, I'll be ready for those snobs at Pierce. You understand, don't you, Toni?"

"No. That's completely ridiculous."

"Whatever, girl. I'm still not going." Charetta began playing again.

"I spend my hard-earned money, and you have the audacity to tell *me* no?"

"Read my lips, I said no."

"Are you *loca, chica*?" Toni's voice went up an octave, and she began speaking in rapid Spanish. She rarely spoke it unless she was angry, and Charetta burst into laughter.

"All right, already. We'll go."

Toni continued mumbling in Spanish, and Charetta couldn't stop laughing.

"I said I'll go."

"Don't do me any favors, girlfriend." Toni stood in front of her sipping a glass of wine.

"And they talk about sistas getting attitudes and popping their necks. Either you've been hanging out with me too long or there's a little sista in every woman."

Toni finally laughed too. "I was just playing. I had to do something to get you to go."

"Drama queen."

"Bitch."

The roommates smiled at each other and laughed.

"Call me names all you want, Charetta Jackson, but we're going to that reunion."

Chapter 4

The Pierce Academy for Girls in Bel Air, California, prides itself on preparing young women for life. Students are educated to become independent thinkers and intellectual scholars. A Pierce woman is confident in her abilities and herself. She is a leader, has integrity and character, achieves academic excellence, serves her community, and believes she can do anything.

Nina smiled as she removed her sunglasses and read the familiar school motto printed on her reunion registration materials. It was a sparkling Sunday morning in June, and the weather was warm, and the sky was cloudless and vibrant. She looked down at the orange linen sundress that she had topped off with a black straw hat and sandals and hoped it hadn't wrinkled during the drive in from Malibu.

"She is so adorable." A woman handed Nina nametags and smiled at Nicki who was sitting in a stroller similarly dressed and wearing star-shaped sunglasses.

"Thank you." Nina, ever the proud mother, smiled warmly.

"Is she singing?" The woman's face registered shock as she looked at Nicki and then Nina.

"Yes." Nina laughed. "She's my little song bird."

Nina pushed the stroller across the campus filled with sprawling verdant lawns that were as smooth, flawless and as plush as carpet. A throng of people had gathered under a tent in the middle of the green. Conversation and the sound of children playing peppered the air as Pierce alumnae and their families mingled and reunited. Some stood and sipped iced beverages while others were seated at tables under white umbrellas. Smoke from barbecue grills ascended into a picture-perfect sky.

Nina took Nicki out of her stroller and led her daughter to a table. She helped her into a chair and sat down next to her. When Kyle was unable to make it back from his business trip, she had elected to make it a mother-daughter weekend. One day Nicki would be a Pierce woman, and Nina chuckled at the thought. A waiter brought them lemonade and potato chips. Nicki carefully picked up her cup and took a sip while Nina scanned the crowd for familiar faces.

"Nina Beaubien, is that really you?"

Nina looked up and screamed when she saw the beautiful Latino woman. "Money Mena." She sprang from her chair, and the two women embraced.

"Money." Toni laughed. "No one's called me that since you graduated."

"After we spent spring break on your grandfather's cattle ranch in Mexico, what else was I supposed to call you?"

"Toni . . . like everyone else."

"No way. I'll never forget that place. It was a small country with lakes, waterfalls, and stables and all that cattle. I'll never forget those barbecues. That was some of the best steak I ever had in my life. It makes me hungry just to think about it."

Toni could only laugh. "It's so good to see you, Nina. You haven't changed a bit."

"How's your horse? I think his name was Julio?"

"You remember that too? I had the biggest crush on Julio Iglesias when I was younger."

"So what do you think about his fine son, Enrique?"

"I think I need to sit down." Toni pulled out the chair next to Nina and spotted Nicki who was eating potato chips very daintily, one at a time. She clasped a hand to her face and squealed. "Nina, is this your daughter?"

Nina smiled as she looked at the brown hair with very distinct golden highlights, the cocoa skin, full pouty lips, and golden eyes.

She lovingly brushed a lock of hair that had worked itself out of Nicki's ponytail.

"Yes, this is my daughter, Kendall Nicole, but we call her Nicki." Nina's voice was filled with pride and love. "Say hi to Miss Toni, Nicki."

Nicki stopped eating potato chips and looked at Toni. "Hi, Miss Toni." She picked up her lemonade and took a sip. "More chips, Mommy."

"No, sweetie, we have to save room for lunch. We're going to have hot dogs and a little salad."

"Okay, Mommy." Nicki climbed out of her chair and into Nina's lap.

"She is absolutely beautiful." Toni, who had been holding her breath, finally exhaled. "Nina and Nicki, how cute."

"Thank you. She's my little honey bear." Nina hugged her daughter and covered her face with kisses.

"Where did she get those beautiful eyes? Does your husband have them?"

"No. She reached back and found them from somebody." Nina smiled and kissed the little girl again.

"Is your husband here?" Toni looked around for some sign or evidence of his presence.

"No, he wanted to come, but he had to go to New York on business. He's in international finance." Nina hoped she didn't sound like she was bragging but she was proud of her man.

"You go, girl." They slapped a high five and smiled.

"So how are things going with you? Are you still dancing?"

"Yes. I'm doing the struggling artist thing right now but I'm dancing. I choreograph and dance in music videos. I just got the new J.Lo video."

"That's wonderful, Toni. I know how hard it is to get jobs like that. I still remember all those dance recitals you were in. You got skills, girl."

"Too bad my father didn't think so when I got into Julliard."

"Why? What happened?"

"He refused to pay. He wanted me to go into politics like him."

"Aw, Money. I'm so sorry."

"It's no big deal. I'm still dancing. Hopefully, this J.Lo video will lead to a tour. I'd love to go on tour."

"You will." Nina spoke encouragingly. She knew getting into Julliard was a big deal for Toni. "Don't go anywhere. I'll be right back. I've got to take her to the bathroom and get lunch." Nina picked up Nicki and looked back at Toni. "Don't move."

Toni smiled as Nina strutted off across the green carrying Nicki. The two of them were simply beautiful in matching outfits. She noticed others turn to admire the striking pair as Charetta slipped in the seat beside her.

"And where have you been?" Toni smiled at her roomie who was wearing a pink strapless sundress. Toni had given her money to get her hair braided, and the style was quite becoming. Charetta was wearing contacts, and her hazel eyes were sparkling.

"Mingling." She handed Toni a blended margarita. "I'm having a great time. I'm so glad you made me come."

"See . . ." Toni smiled. "I hate to say I told you so."

"Then don't." Charetta made a face. "Why are you sitting over here all alone? You're the social one."

"I'm not alone. You'll never guess who I ran into."

"Who?" Charetta took a sip of the icy margarita.

"Nina. She looks wonderful."

"Nina Beaubien?" Charetta's eyes grew wide with surprise.

"Yes." Toni wondered why she was being so dramatic.

"Do you know who her cousin is?"

Toni shook her head. "No. Should I?"

"Girl, I can't believe you. You never know anything because you're always somewhere dancing, and you never read."

"Whatever, girl."

"Topaz."

"What about Topaz?"

"That's Nina's cousin."

"Topaz the singer is Nina's cousin?" Toni repeated just to be sure she had heard correctly.

"Yes," Charetta whispered sharply.

"Oh my God . . ."

"Nina used to be her assistant. There were always pictures of them at some Hollywood party in magazines. Do you know who Sylk Ross is?"

"The basketball player?"

"Yes. Nina is married to his brother. The girl has bank."

"Get out."

"Shush," Charetta whispered firmly. "Here she comes."

Nina returned to the table carrying Nicki and a plate of food. "Little girl, you are heavy. Your daddy needs to be here so he can carry you around." She spoke as she was seated. The women watched her quickly pray over her food and feed Nicki some salad.

"Nina Beaubien, I can't believe you're going to ignore me like that." Charetta finally spoke up.

"Char . . . girl, when did you get here?"

"Miss Thing was mingling." Toni laughed. "I had to practically beat her up to get her here."

Charetta cut Toni a sharp glance before she spoke to Nina. "I had a lot on my mind. I just graduated from UCLA with a combined JD and MBA, girl."

"That's wonderful, Char. I know that was a lot of work."

"It sure was. But I'm all done now, and I plan to use my to degree to help me set up my management firm. Did Toni tell you she's my first client?"

"No." Nina was very focused on feeding Nicki who could be a very picky eater at times, but the little girl seemed to be enjoying the hot dog and salad.

"I'm going to turn her into the next J.Lo," Charetta boasted.

"That's certainly ambitious." Nina cut into a grilled chicken breast.

"Your cousin is right out there with her."

"Yes, she is, but Topaz needs to do some film. Today's artist needs to be multi-dimensional."

"You certainly seem to know your stuff." Charetta finished her margarita and wanted another but she didn't want to walk away from the conversation.

"I'll always love music, but I no longer work with my cousin. I just completed my second novel."

"That's wonderful, Nina." Toni was back in the conversation. "I am so proud of you, girl."

"Thanks." Nina finished feeding Nicki and smiled at the girls. "God certainly has blessed me."

"She certainly is a blessing." Toni held her arms out to Nicki, and the child reached out to be taken.

"She never does that." Nina laughed. "You like, Money, don't you, pretty girl?" Nina stroked the child's head and smiled at Toni who was talking to her.

"Money." Charetta laughed. "I haven't heard that since forever."

"Nina was the one who started calling you Char, remember?" Toni smiled at Charetta.

"I started that?" Nina looked from Charetta to Toni.

"Yes. We little freshmen thought Nina Beaubien was da bomb. We all wanted to be like you." Toni helped Nicki with her strawberry ice cream.

"Really?" Nina laughed. "Why?"

"You were smart and beautiful, always knew where the best parties were and managed to graduate suma cum laude for starters." Charetta joined in their walk down memory lane.

"Oh no." Nina laughed. "I was so wild back then. I was nobody's role model. And you guys wanted to be like me? That's funny."

"We still want to be like you." Charetta's tone was serious.

"Yeah, Nina. You've done well for yourself. This beautiful little girl, a successful career, and I'm sure your husband must be absolutely divine. What's your secret?" Toni was sincere.

"Yes," Charetta chimed in. "Can you hook a sista up?"

Nina shook her head and smiled. "I can't take credit for the way my life has gone. I wouldn't be anywhere without the Lord in my life."

"That's wonderful, Nina." Toni gave Nicki back to her. "I'm so happy for you."

Charetta smiled in agreement.

"So . . . I remember you always had some tight beats, Char. When am I going to hear some of your music? When am I going to see you dance, Toni?"

"When do you want to hear it?" Charetta couldn't believe Nina wanted to hear her music.

"Maybe I'll come by one day, and we can hang out, do lunch or something," Nina suggested.

"That would be wonderful, Nina." Toni smiled warmly.

It was late afternoon and the air was slightly cooler. Nina put a sweater on Nicki and stood.

"Well, I'm going to have to get this little lady home. It's really been great seeing you."

"Let me help," Toni offered. She picked up the stroller and Nicki's bag.

"Thanks. She was awake when we arrived. She gets so heavy when she's sleeping."

Nina headed for the parking lot and the girls followed her, both of them wondering what type of car Nina was driving. She stopped at the passenger side of a Bentley the color of champagne, unlocked the door, and carefully placed Nicki in the back inside her car seat.

"You rolling like that?" Charetta spoke without thinking. "Damn, girl."

"It was a gift from my husband." Nina placed all of the things in the car and accepted Toni's card.

"Ah-ight, Money. Char." She gave them both a hug. "It's really been good seeing you."

"You, too, Nina." Toni hugged her again.

Charetta was still in shock over Nina's Bentley. They waved as she drove out of the parking lot and down the winding hill away from the school.

""She is livin' seriously." Charetta finally found her voice.

"She sure is. Did you see that diamond on her hand?"

"I didn't notice. Was it big?"

"As a rock. I wonder what her house looks like. Damn. She's probably living in some Beverly Hills mansion." Charetta was still regrouping.

Toni unlocked the door of her Honda and the girls climbed inside.

"She is not going to call us," Charetta blurted out.

"She said she would." Toni drove east on Sunset Boulevard toward Westwood.

"She was just being nice. Nina's big time now and she's got no time for us."

"Nina's not like that. She'll call," Toni defended.

"I bet she doesn't, and I'm not going to hold my breath waiting," Charetta insisted. "People like that always say things they don't mean just to get rid of you. You'll see."

Chapter 5

It was intensely hot in Encino, a Los Angeles suburban community with no sidewalks and sprawling ranch homes in the San Fernando Valley. Jamil had purchased several acres of undeveloped land on a hill and built a seven-bedroom split-level house with a recording studio and rehearsal area underneath. The estate, south of Ventura Boulevard and less than a mile away from the compound where Michael Jackson and his famous siblings grew up, flaunted tennis and basketball courts and a sparkling pool and Jacuzzi.

Jamil stood on a deck outside his bedroom, which overlooked the pool. The gardener had already come and gone, and now sprinklers shot streams of water across the rolling hillside while others hydrated the floral landscape decorated with intricate patterns of some of Southern California's finest—birds of paradise, zinnias, marigolds, pink and yellow roses, and calla lilies. He stamped out the purple cush he had smoked to get him hyped for the day's activities and jumped into the shower. It was going to be a long, hot day.

Downstairs in the kitchen one of his boys was stocking the freshly cleaned fridge. MTV's *Cribs* production crew was setting up in the living room. They had already taken footage of the grounds, and they were ready for him. He walked into the great room where a makeup artist applied the smallest amount of makeup and another young woman hooked him up with a mike. He thought she accidentally brushed against his crotch, and when she did it a second time he almost slapped her.

No one touches the jewels without my permission. Especially white girls. I can't stand their silly asses. Now a sista would be bold with her stuff. She'd just tell you what she was going to do and do it. No questions asked, Jamil thought as he eyed the young woman carefully.

Jamil made sure Suicide hired black people. He would always take care of his own.

"Jamil, are you ready to get started?" the director for his segment asked.

"Let's do this." He walked over to the front door and waited for his cue. The smell of barbecue sauce wafted inside the house through an open door, and he was immediately hungry. He pushed the thought aside for the moment and focused on the camera in his face.

"What up, MTV? I'm Jamil and welcome to my crib." He flashed a brilliant smile for the camera and began the tour, walking through the living room past a grand piano, pointing out various pieces of furniture. He stopped in front of a framed black-and-white photograph. "This is my house where I grew up in Compton. I keep it here because I never want to forget where I come from."

He saw his mother beaming with pride. Janice Winters was in her late forties, and she was still beautiful. Sometimes she'd be at the house when one of his girls came over, and they immediately copped an attitude the moment they laid eyes on her. The only female who hadn't was Nina. The three of them had ended up going shopping and to the movies.

Janice had sacrificed and worked two jobs to pay for Jamil's music lessons. Now she was living in the first house Jamil had purchased on the Miracle Mile. She had redecorated it completely. Janice drove a 600 series Mercedes and knew how to shop until she dropped. She had made potato salad, baked beans, and macaroni and cheese for the pool party.

"These are all my Grammys, American Music Awards, Billboard Awards, MTV Video Music Awards, BET Awards, and my most favorite"—he picked one up and held it up for the camera—"my NAACP Image Award because this represents the struggle of my people. I think I remembered them all." Jamil smiled and looked at his mother who gave him a thumbs-up.

He led the cameraman through a dining room that seated twelve and into a large kitchen with windows on both walls that looked out on the pool and the grounds. There was a big bowl of fruit on a granite countertop. He opened the refrigerator door. "Believe it or not, I love me some Capri Sun and there's always a big container of Kool-Aid, some lunchmeat for sandwiches, milk for my Cap'n Crunch. I love In and Out burgers so I usually eat there or go to Mom's when I want a real meal. Popsicles, Coronas for the boys, and some Cris for the ladies." He held up a magnum of the expensive champagne. "Fellas, you always want to keep a bottle of Cris on hand."

He closed the refrigerator door and went upstairs to the master bedroom and bath, then back down to the game and billiard room, the audiovisual room with a flat screen covering an entire wall, the recording studio, and finally outside to the five-car garage.

"These are my girls, and they're all very sweet. My Hummer, an Escalade for my escapades, the Bentley, my Mercedes coupe, and the Ferrari." He turned around and made a face at the camera. "Ah-ight, MTV. It's time for you to get up out of here 'cuz we're 'bout to set it off correctly up in here. My dog Buffalo's been over there barbecuing all morning. See ya." He went back inside the house through the front door and closed it as the director had instructed.

India and his publicist were in his face chatting excitedly about the piece as soon as he walked back inside. India had insisted he do the show, and despite his initial protest, he had enjoyed showing off his crib.

"You hangin' out for the party?" Jamil smiled at India.

"For a minute, and only because I want some of that barbecue." India checked her two-way and closed it.

"Buffalo's hooking it up correctly. You can go upstairs and chill out until it's ready if you want to." Jamil wished he could get rid of that silly grin on his face.

"I'll hang out for a while."

Jamil watched India run up the stairs and wished she would stay forever. He'd call off everything if he had a woman like her around all the time. He shook her from his thoughts and went into the kitchen where Buffalo had brought in some of the meat he had barbecued.

"Can I fix you a little something, sweetie?" Janice fished around in the pan until she found a hot link. She also served herself from the side dishes she had prepared.

"No thanks, Mom. Just make sure you save some food for the party." Jamil grinned.

She picked up a dish towel and slapped him on the behind with it. "Don't think you're too grown for me to spank just because you have your own house now."

"I used to change your diapers," mother and son repeated together and laughed.

"Any ribs done yet, man?" Jamil looked at Buffalo.

"I thought you weren't hungry." Janice took a soda out of the refrigerator.

"I'm not. India is." The doorbell rang and Jamil went to answer it. "Ladies . . . welcome."

A string of beauties in an assortment of sizes, shapes, and colors entered the house. It wasn't a pool party without women, and Dime, their pimp, was known for having the best. Maybe because he was absolutely gorgeous himself with a body like Adonis. The fact that his girls worked all the best parties may have also been why.

"Yo, dog, where's the Hypnotic?" Dime and Jamil watched the women head down the hall toward the downstairs bedroom. They knew the routine.

"Right here." Jamil went to the bar in the billiard room. Dime sat on a barstool while Jamil splashed the blue alcohol into glasses with ice. "Take this to the girls." He took out a chilled magnum of champagne and placed it on a tray with flutes.

"Dog, you be spoilin' my hoes. You ain't got no Moet? That's good enough for those bitches." Dime read the label on the champagne.

"Man, take this to the ladies. I paid for it." There were a lot of things that had become a part of hip-hop culture that Jamil didn't like, especially calling women bitches and hoes. If his mother ever heard him say something like that, she'd kick his behind.

Dime finished the last of his drink and picked up the tray and grinned. "It always takes them a day to get back in line after they come here. Cristal."

Xtreme had arrived when Jamil went back into the kitchen.

"I didn't hear no helicopter, playa." Jamil laughed.

"I drove the Hummer." Xtreme traded pounds with Jamil and slapped him on the back.

The doorbell rang nonstop until the backyard was filled. Dime's women were swimming naked in the pool. Xtreme dove in with them, and they gathered around in hopes of time alone later. Music played and people danced. The smell of marijuana permeated the air. There was food and alcohol everywhere but no one was interested. They didn't want to ruin their temporary highs. Jamil stood at a window watching all the activity.

"Here are your ribs, boss." Buffalo brought in a pan of ribs swimming in sauce. He was a recent addition to Jamil's ever-increasing staff. Buffalo's main duty was protection. He lived in Jamil's guest house and was in charge of security at Jamil's estate and office. Buffalo, a man of few words, was also a very good cook.

"Thanks, Buffalo." Jamil took a real plate out of the cabinet and placed a healthy portion of ribs on it along with his mother's side dishes. He picked up silverware and napkins and walked with Buffalo around to the front of the house.

"Anybody else allowed upstairs, boss?" Buffalo looked up at Jamil who paused to think.

"Xtreme, but not with any of the women." Jamil sprinted up the stairs and hoped that India was still waiting for her barbecue.

Chapter 6

Charetta carefully retied a scarf around her head and looked at Toni who was still in bed sleeping. She was up early for a Saturday morning. There was work to do. She pulled on a pair of overalls and a T-shirt, walked into the living room, and sighed. The small apartment had always served as a place for them to eat and sleep . . . not to entertain. The girls had never really purchased any furniture or even tried to decorate. They owned only a hodgepodge of dishes.

She stuck a finger under the bandanna and scratched her head. She could feel the thick new growth of hair on her scalp. It had taken hours and a lot of money to have her hair braided, and it needed to be redone.

"Toni. Wake up, girl."

Toni pulled the heavy comforter up around her neck and rolled over. Charetta always had to have the room freezing because of her allergies. "It's too early."

"No, it's not." Charetta pulled Toni's linens to the foot of the bed. "Come on, girl. Wake up."

Toni sat up and squinted at the clock. "Eight? You woke me up at eight on a Saturday morning? Call me when it's ten." Toni pulled her covers back up onto the bed and was under them in seconds.

"Toni, wake up." Charetta sat on the bed next to Toni who sat up.

"I can't believe you. Why do you have to trip about every little thing?" Toni asked as she rubbed her eyes. Her hair was done in two thick braids.

"Because this is important." Charetta took off the scarf and went into the bathroom for the oil she used on her braids. She sat on her own bed and carefully rubbed the oil into her scalp. "We need to clean up, and we don't have any furniture. You should have never told her it was okay to come here."

"We've never had any furniture. It's your turn to clean the bathroom. And I told Nina to come to our house because she's our friend. Now leave me alone." Toni fluffed her pillows and gave Charetta a look that said she meant business.

"Well, you don't have to get all snippy." Charetta turned on some music and scoured the bathroom thoroughly. She tackled the kitchen next and wished again that they owned more furniture. When she walked back into the bedroom, Toni stepped out of bathroom with a towel wrapped around her.

"Good morning, Char." Toni smiled as she looked inside a small chest of drawers for underwear.

"Oh, so now you're ready to talk." Charetta pulled the bandanna from her head.

"We don't have time to talk. You'd better hurry up and get dressed. It'll be noon before you know it," Toni warned.

Charetta was in the bedroom straightening up her bed when she glanced out of the window and saw a black Range Rover pull up and stop in front of the building. She stood there watching until she saw Nina hop out. "Toni, she's here."

"Oh, goody." A beautiful smile lit up Toni's face.

"She's driving a Range Rover today. How many cars do you think she has?" Charetta demanded.

"Whatever, Char. I'm just glad she's here. And you said she wouldn't come." Toni went to open the door.

"Well, she won't come back again when she sees how we're living. I still don't understand why she didn't invite us over her house," Charetta fired back.

"Char!" Toni glared at her as she opened the door for Nina.

"Hey . . ." Nina walked in with a shopping bag, dressed in faded stretch denim jeans and a red bustier.

"Look at you." Toni gave her a hug. "You look so cute."

"Thanks. I brought lunch." Nina smiled as she held up the bag. "I hope everyone likes Thai."

"Hi, Nina." Charetta finally managed to smile.

"Hey, girl." Nina gave her a hug as she made her way over to the small table and began taking out cartons of food. "Is that your keyboard? Play something, Char."

"Yes, play something, Char." Toni gathered serving utensils from the kitchen as Nina took out the last carton of food.

"This ain't a cabaret. I'm hungry. I want some Thai food too." Charetta grabbed a plate.

"I heard that." Nina laughed. "There's plenty of food. I didn't know what everyone liked so I just bought all my favorites."

Charetta gasped when she saw the spread of stuffed chicken wings, beef and chicken satay with peanut sauce, pad Thai noodles, cashew nut chicken, and shrimp fried rice.

"Let's eat in the living room," Toni suggested.

"And sit on the floor?" Charetta was appalled.

"The television's in there, and I want Nina to see my videos," Toni explained.

"Good idea." Nina picked up a cup of Thai iced tea and followed Toni into the living room where the only furniture was a beanbag, a television set, and a VCR.

"Nina, you're the guest of honor. You take the bean bag." Toni handed Nina her plate after she was seated and turned on the VCR. "I have everything on one tape for my auditions."

"Perfect. I can't wait to see everything." Nina smiled fondly at Toni while Charetta plopped down on the floor.

Toni's reel was very impressive. It contained footage of her performing with some of the industry's brightest stars.

"You did that too?" Nina pointed at a popular commercial.

"Yes. That was my first big paycheck," Toni offered proudly. "I still get a residual check every now and then."

"I don't understand why you were never asked to do anything for Topaz. She would love to work with you."

"I'm available." Toni smiled.

"But now Topaz isn't."

"Why do things always turn out like that?" Charetta grumbled. She ignored the warning glance Toni cast.

"She took some time off to spend with her family, but she's supposed to start working on her next CD soon." Nina carried her empty plate into the dining room.

"Is she looking for some music?" Charetta was hopeful. "I've got lots of songs."

"So are you ready to let me hear something now?" Nina smiled at Charetta.

"What kind of music does Topaz like?" Charetta sifted through a box of CDs.

"Don't worry about Topaz. Just let me hear something, Char." Nina cut into a strawberry cheesecake.

Charetta finally selected a CD and placed it in the player.

"Hey." Toni was up and dancing and Nina joined her. A genuine smile finally eased its way onto Charetta's face as she watched them.

"That was da bomb, girl," Nina declared. "You got skills."

"Do you think Topaz would like it?" Charetta demanded.

"That's not really her flavor, but it's a great song." Nina chose her words carefully. "So let's see all of this talent you're going to manage."

"I haven't had the time to invest in looking for talent, yet. You know I just finished school," Charetta explained quickly. "I've just started to get the paperwork together for the business."

"I understand." Nina was sincere.

"Char, what about the kids? Show her the kids," Toni said.

"What are you talking about, Toni?" Charetta looked puzzled.

"The girls . . . your cousins." Toni dug in a box of videotapes.

"She doesn't want to see that," Charetta snapped.

"What is it?" Nina looked at the roommates.

"Char has some cousins in New York who have been begging her to help them. I think they have a lot of potential." Toni glanced around the dining room. "Now where is that videotape?"

"It's not very good. It's just a bunch of silly teenagers playing with a video camera," Charetta protested.

"Char, why are you being so difficult? Where's the tape?" Nina laughed.

"Here it is." Toni held up a large manila envelope. Nina joined her as she dumped the contents on the floor. Toni stuck the cassette in the VCR as Nina picked up a photograph and a sheet of paper.

"They're gorgeous," Nina exclaimed as three teenage girls graced the screen singing and dancing to a muffled strain of "Say My Name."

Charetta was silent as she sat on the floor between Toni and Nina.

"Aren't they cute?" Toni smiled at Nina.

"Char, you need to let them sing that song you played earlier. Money, you need to do some choreography. And then you ladies would definitely have a hit group." Nina quickly read over the sheet of paper that was included with the cassette. "Shawntay 16, Sabre 16, and Sky 15. They're teenagers, and they're called So Fine. I love it." Nina finished reading and looked at Charetta. "What are you waiting for, girl?"

"Oh, that's just great. We can make a lot of hit records on opposite sides of the country, and don't forget the fact that none of us have any money." Charetta jumped up and went into the kitchen, and Nina followed her.

"Are you really serious about this management thing?" Nina watched Charetta as she inspected the leftover Thai food.

"Yes." Charetta met Nina's eye.

"Then get your cousins out here. With the right grooming, we can get them a deal." Nina picked a slice of cucumber out of the fried rice.

"We?" Charetta could barely get the word out.

"We," Nina replied coolly. "I know some people, and from what I saw, I'm willing to pay for them to come out here and cut a demo of your song."

"Are you serious?" Charetta was in shock.

"Yes, Char. I'm very serious. A Pierce woman can do anything." Nina picked up her purse. "You're the attorney. Draw up some paperwork for a management partnership between the three of us and So Fine. If the group is as good as I think they are, I'll make my investment back in no time, and all of us will get seriously paid."

Chapter 7

Nina placed a vegetable tray in the center of the patio table overlooking the ocean. There were also turkey wraps, tortilla chips with a wonderful mango salsa, and chocolate-covered strawberries. Boxes of pizza from the California Pizza Kitchen were warming on the grill. Kyle dumped a bag of ice over an assortment of Evian and sodas.

"Do you think we bought enough food?" Nina looked up at her husband.

"With everything you have out here and inside, I would say yes." Kyle brushed a wisp of hair around Nina's ear.

"Okay, baby, but maybe you'd better thaw out another package of Nicki's hot dogs. Teenagers can be very picky eaters. The girls are from New York. They might not like all of this California food."

"Just chill, baby girl. Your girls will love everything. And if we don't have something that one of them wants, I can always go to the store."

Nina wrapped her arms around Kyle and buried her head in his chest. "What would I ever do without you?"

"You'll never have to know." His reply was always the same whenever she asked that question.

They were still hugging when the doorbell rang. "That must be them." Nina dashed around to the front of the house where Toni and

Charetta stood with three very beautiful young girls. "Hey, everybody. Come on around back."

"I guess we weren't good enough to walk through the house," Charetta whispered so only Toni could hear.

"Sky, Shawntay, and Sabre. I know you guys from your pictures. I'm Nina, and I'm so excited to meet you." She introduced Kyle and invited everyone to sit down.

Toni grabbed Nina by the arm and pulled her aside. "Girlfriend, where did you find him, and does he have any brothers? He is absolutely gorgeous."

Nina laughed. "My best friend is married to his brother, and she introduced us. But my husband does have an identical twin."

"You're kidding." Toni was practically drooling.

"But he's married too." Nina laughed.

"The good ones always are. You're terrible." Toni laughed as they joined the others at the table.

"I wasn't sure what everyone liked so I got a little bit of everything," Nina explained. "Please, help yourselves to appetizers. There's pizza warming on the grill. We'll have dinner later."

"Appetizers?" Charetta mumbled. "This is dinner. At least for those of us in the real world."

Toni pinched Charetta hard on the arm. "If I didn't know you better, I'd swear you were jealous."

Nina, who hadn't heard a word of Charetta's comment, sat down at the table with the girls. "I'm so excited to meet you, and I can't wait to get to know each of you personally."

"Thank you, Mrs. Ross." Shawntay, the lead singer for the group, replied. "Everything looks real good."

"What is that?" Sabre wrinkled her nose as she pointed at the turkey wraps. There were only chocolate-covered strawberries on her plate.

"That's a turkey sandwich wrapped in pita bread and . . ." Nina began.

"Whatever happened to a few slices of turkey on white bread and potato chips?" Sabre demanded. "Where's the pizza?"

"It's on the grill warming." Nina was shocked by Sabre's impudence. She watched Sabre walk over to the grill and turn on the charm for Kyle who opened several boxes of pizza for her before she finally selected a slice.

"I like to try everything at least once." Sky, the youngest member of the group, smiled warmly at Nina as she served herself a little of everything. "My cousin Charetta said you were responsible for bringing us out here. None of us have ever been to California. Thank you so much."

Nina watched Sabre join the others at the table before she went over to the grill where Kyle was preparing to barbecue. She looked inside the boxes until she found her favorite.

"What's wrong, baby?" Kyle attempted to wipe the charcoal dust from his hands.

"Attitude." Nina took her pizza and joined the others.

"Everything is so delicious, Nina, especially this mango salsa." Toni pulled the bowl of chips and salsa closer. "Wherever did you find it?"

"It's an old family recipe of Rosa's, my daughter's nanny. I've tried to get her to tell me. I've even tried sneaking in the kitchen while she's making it." Nina laughed.

They watched the ocean and ate until Nina interrupted the silence. "I'm anxious to hear So Fine. Let's go inside. We've got some microphones set up in the family room. We can take the food inside too."

Nina led the way inside. She noticed Sabre make a detour to the grill—and Kyle.

"Sabre," Toni called out. "We need you inside now."

"Are you going to come watch us sing, Mr. Ross?" Sabre smiled coyly at Kyle before she swung her narrow hips and went inside.

Three microphones had been set up in the family room. Shawntay was in the middle and Sky was to her right. Sabre stood behind the remaining microphone as Kyle slipped in and sat down on the sofa beside Nina. The girls were dressed in jeans and cropped tank tops in different colors. All three of them had pierced their belly buttons with an assortment of jewelry.

"Okay, you guys. Do something a cappella and sing like your life depended on it because it does," Charetta commanded. "Mess this up, and you'll be on the first thing smoking back to Brooklyn."

Sabre made a face and sucked her teeth as Shawntay counted off the beat.

"I swear I'll snatch her little half Puerto Rican ass before this is over," Charetta whispered through gritted teeth as the group began "Say My Name."

They sounded wonderful. They sang like angels, and their voices blended beautifully. They eagerly searched their perspective managers' faces when they finished. Nina and Kyle applauded fervently.

"Can you guys dance?" Nina questioned as Topaz, Germain, Baby Doll, and Chris entered the house through the kitchen. "You were supposed to be here an hour ago." Nina jumped up and gave Topaz and Germain a hug.

"I'm sorry. Chris had a softball game and his daddy is the coach so it's not like we could run right out," Topaz explained while everyone gawked at her.

"I didn't know *she* was coming," Charetta whispered to Toni.

"Nina probably wants Topaz's opinion about the girls," Toni whispered back.

"She still should have told us she was coming. We're supposed to be her partners," Charetta grumbled.

Nina picked up Baby Doll and kissed her. The four-year-old was the spitting image of Topaz, right down to the golden hair, eyes, and pouty bottom lip. "How's my fat turkey?" Nina asked.

"I'm Baby Doll now, Auntie Nina." The little girl seemed exasperated. "How many times do I have to tell you that?"

"She's so cute." Sabre was in the midst of the family. "Can I hold her?"

"Baby Doll's really funny about strangers," Germain explained. But to everyone's surprise, she allowed Sabre to hold her.

"Diva recognizes diva." Nina laughed as she led Topaz and her family over to the group.

"Excuse me, Mother, but may I go swimming now?" Chris looked at Topaz through a set of identical amber eyes. "Daddy and Uncle Kyle are going outside to barbecue."

"Me too, Mommy." Baby Doll motioned for Sabre to put her down and ran over to her brother.

"All right as long as your daddy keeps an eye on you." Topaz looked at Germain and smiled.

"Please. Those two swim better than me." Germain laughed as he and Kyle ushered the children outside.

"I'm sorry." Topaz smiled at the visitors. "My kids can be quite demanding."

"No need to apologize. You have a beautiful family," Toni offered. "My name is Montona but all my friends call me Toni."

"I call her Money, and she's a fabulous choreographer," Nina declared proudly. "She just did the new J.Lo video."

"You did?" Topaz was obviously impressed. "We'll have to talk about you doing my next video. I'm going to start my next album and—"

"I thought we were here for So Fine," Charetta interrupted.

Topaz took a step back and looked Charetta up and down.

"Topaz, this is Char, and that's So Fine—Sky, Shawntay, and Sabre." Nina jumped in the conversation quickly. "Girls, why don't you sing for us again? I wanted my cousin to take a look at you too."

The girls took their places at the mikes as Nicki paddled into the family room barefoot, dressed in her bathing suit and sunglasses.

"Hi, sweetie. Did you have a good nap?" Nina picked up the little girl and cuddled her in her arms.

"Oh, look at her," Topaz cooed. "She's so precious."

"We're never going to get anything done around here," Charetta groaned. Toni elbowed her in the ribs as Topaz gave her a look of death.

"Want to go outside with Daddy, Nicki? Baby Doll and Chris are here." Nina smoothed her daughter's hair as she talked.

"I want to see them sing." Nicki pointed at So Fine standing patiently behind the microphones.

"Well, I'm glad someone around here wants to hear them sing," Charetta barked.

"Sorry you guys," Nina began.

"But we do have children, and their needs come first." Topaz looked directly at Charetta.

"Go on, So Fine." Nina smiled at the group. "Do your thang."

Shawntay counted off, and the group sang again.

"Do they dance?" Topaz asked when the performance was complete.

"Yeah, Money. Give them a routine and let's see how fast they learn it," Nina suggested.

"We need some music." Toni opened her bag and flipped through a selection of CDs until she selected one. "Never leave home without them." She smiled as Aaliyah's "Rock the Boat" started. "I danced in this video. Fatima is an incredible choreographer."

Toni demonstrated a combination and looked at the girls. "Now you try it." She stood in front of the girls and danced while they attempted to follow. Sky and Shawntay were having a difficult time but Sabre picked it up immediately.

"She's good," Topaz whispered to Nina, referring to Sabre.

"I agree," Nina whispered back.

When Toni restarted the music, Nicki climbed down off the sofa and started dancing. There was no question that Nicki was trying to do the routine.

"Look at her." Topaz giggled. "She's trying to do the routine, and she's so cute."

"You go, baby," Nina said, laughing. "She just loves Aaliyah. Where's the camcorder? I've got to tape this." Nina went for the camera and Charetta groaned. "Topaz, go get Kyle, please. He has to see this."

Nicki began to sing while she danced, and everyone forgot about So Fine. Sabre and Toni danced along with her.

"That's right, baby girl." Kyle laughed. "You work it." Nicki danced and sang until the music ended, and everyone applauded. Sabre picked the little girl up and kissed her on the cheek.

"There's burgers, dogs, and steaks outside if anyone's interested," Kyle informed them.

"So what about our business, Nina? What do you think about So Fine?" Charetta demanded.

"Excuse me for one second." Nina smiled at Charetta and grabbed Topaz by the arm. "What do you think about the group?"

"If they work really hard, and I mean hard—you saw how two of them struggled with those dance steps—and if you get a great song and make Sabre the lead you could have the next Destiny's Child on your hands."

"But Shawntay is the lead." Nina glanced at the girls who had come back inside with their food.

"You asked for my opinion, now I'm getting something to eat." Topaz brushed a wisp of hair out of her cousin's face. "You're the smart one. You helped me get where I am today. You know what to do."

Chapter 8

The conference room at Suicide Records offered a tremendous view of the San Fernando mountains. Wednesday morning was Suicide's weekly creative and marketing meeting when Jamil and his entire staff would gather around the huge glass-topped table to discuss the status of the company's current projects. India placed an agenda on the table in front of each chair. Roscoe's Chicken and Waffles provided their famous fried chicken and waffles along with scrambled eggs, grits, biscuits, and sausage for the breakfast meeting that could last for hours. Starbucks and Jamba Juice provided beverages.

India looked around the room to ensure everything was in place before she went over to the credenza and opened a box of Krispy Kreme doughnuts.

"Caught you." Jamil stood beside her and pulled several of the gooey glazed doughnuts out of the box for himself.

"I love these things." India laughed and took a healthy bite out of a doughnut.

"I don't know why we order all of this other stuff. Just give me a box of Krispy Kremes and a gallon of chocolate milk, and I'm straight." Jamil walked out of the conference room and back into his office and India followed him.

There was a full bathroom complete with a steam shower and tele-

phone behind a specially concealed door. India opened it and pulled
Jamil inside. There were fluffy embroidered towels and a matching
bathrobe as well as an assortment of toiletries and soaps. "Come over
here, Jamil." India squirted liquid soap on his hands and turned on
the water in the sink.

"If you insist on smoking that stuff before meetings, you're really
going to have to do something about the smell." India cut off the
water and sniffed his hair. As usual she was driving him crazy.

"I love it when a woman takes control." Jamil grinned at her.

India squeezed toothpaste onto a toothbrush and handed it to
him. "Brush."

Jamil couldn't stop smiling the entire time. She dabbed astringent
on a cotton ball and cleaned his face. Then she rubbed in moistur-
izer, poured some of his favorite aftershave in her hands, and rubbed
it gently into his hair. She was about to apply the aftershave to his face
when he took her by the hands and held them, forcing her to look
him in the eyes.

"Jamil." India's voice and hands were trembling as he pulled her
closer and stared into her eyes for several moments before he gently
kissed her.

"Jamil." One of India's assistants, Anita, was knocking at his office
door. Inside the bathroom India moaned softly with pleasure as his
kisses grew in intensity. "Jamil." Anita was inside his office now.

"You'd better go see what Anita wants," India finally managed to
whisper.

Jamil flushed the toilet and left the bathroom. "You looking for
India?"

"Yes." Anita looked around the office as though she expected India
to pop out at any moment.

"I haven't seen her. Did you check the copy room?" Jamil sat down
at his desk and picked up the telephone. "She may be in there running off the agendas for the meeting."

"I already did that for her and they're in the conference room on
the table. Everyone's waiting for you guys."

"Well, I haven't seen her. Maybe she ran downstairs for something."
Jamil picked up his two-way and followed the young woman out of his
office. "Let's get busy."

He went into the conference room where an assortment of young
men and women were seated at the table with plates of food. Buffalo

was sitting by the door, and Jamil acknowledged him before he got several more doughnuts and a big glass of chocolate milk.

"Good morning, people." India breezed into the room with freshly applied lipstick. Conversations slowly faded as everyone focused on her. "Let's get this meeting started. We've got a lot to accomplish today."

Jamil smiled as he looked at India and reflected on what had almost happened in his executive bathroom. India had done a good job of covering her feelings but when she had looked into his eyes that morning, he had seen everything he needed to know.

The meeting opened with the video department showing the completed version on Xtreme's video. It was already slated to go into heavy rotation on MTV. "I've already booked Xtreme on *TRL* and *106 and Park*. He'll be a household name in a matter of days." Cookie had come to Suicide from Virgin Records. She personally knew every music editor and TV talent coordinator in the world. She had worked with Janet Jackson, Madonna, and Aaliyah. "I've already started putting together a promotional tour for him too." She passed around a tentative itinerary.

"Great work, Cookie." Jamil smiled. "Did I tell you that I want to make love to you?"

Everyone laughed for several minutes. Although Cookie was a gorgeous blonde, it was no secret that she preferred women to men.

"I'll see if I can arrange something for tonight, boss." She grinned.

India got up and went over to the credenza for food. Jamil loved watching her walk. She was wearing a skirt with splits up the sides. Even though she had sprayed one of his own fragrances on him, Jamil could still smell her signature African oil on him. A few more minutes in the bathroom would have been heavenly.

"Is that right, Jamil?" His A&R guy looked at him along with everyone else in the room.

Busted . . . he had been so busy thinking about India, he hadn't heard one thing.

"Yes, that's right. We're looking to sign at least two additional acts this year, especially with the runaway debut success of Xtreme's "I'm Hot" on radio this week. The numbers are through the roof." India had come to his rescue yet again.

"Have you guys come up with anything yet?" India looked across the table at Danny, the head of A&R who had yet to produce talent worth recording. Jamil had discovered Xtreme. They had been best friends long before Jamil put him in the recording studio. If basketball players were signing recording contracts, why not a baseball player?

"India's right. Xtreme is going to put Suicide on the map, and we're going to need someone just as hot to follow up with." Jamil was back at the helm and ready for business. He looked at his A&R staff.

"I hear Foxy Brown might be looking for a new deal." Danny was the newest addition to Suicide, and for a white boy, he knew his stuff. No deal went down in the industry without Danny knowing every detail.

"Get me some numbers, Danny." India didn't look up once as she typed away on her laptop.

"What's going on with Topaz? Although she's signed to Populartis you discovered her." Danny looked at Jamil.

"I'm working on it," Jamil lied. He hadn't spoken to Topaz or Nina since Nina's housewarming and wedding reception.

"She is joining the team?" Danny wanted answers.

"I've got it covered. Now let's move on." Jamil took a sip of India's orange juice. She reached under the table and squeezed his hand for support.

The creative team produced a batch of photos to be considered for Xtreme's press kit and CD cover. The main one had already been selected and worked up with graphics. Xtreme was bare-chested and glistening. His well-developed pecs commanded your attention. The platinum diamond pendant sparkled. Oh, to be that piece of jewelry, fortunate to lay against his taut, smooth skin. There were no tattoos but talk about honey dip. All of the women on the staff were swooning.

Jamil pounded on the table. "Can I get some order up in here? Damn, I can't believe y'all acting like that over a photograph."

India giggled. "You're not jealous, are you, boss?"

"Hell no. I just want to get this damn meeting finished so we can get out of here. It's almost noon." He looked at his diamond Rolex to be sure.

"I just need to bring everyone up to date on the launch party that's less than two weeks away, and then we can jet." India looked at Jamil.

"There's already a buzz throughout the industry about the label since Jamil has created and produced hits for the who's who of the music industry," Cookie added. "I've got every major entertainment television crew covering. Everyone loves the invitation, India. The passport idea was so cool. Good job."

"Thanks, Cookie. You did a great job with the press." India smiled.

The party was India's special project, and she had overseen everything down to the smallest detail.

"The RSVPs have been pouring in. The voice mail is full every morning," Anita added. "I can't wait to get my party on."

"You got that right," the others chorused as the room buzzed with conversation.

"Listen up, everyone. This party is not for you. It's an extremely important night for Suicide, and everyone has got to pitch in. A&R, and of course publicity, are the only teams with permission to mingle." India was running the show now. Every staff member had to have India's stamp of approval. India hired and India fired.

"Even though Jamil's been in the business for years, we're a brand-new label, and we need product. People are going to be there with tapes and all sorts of offers, and we're going to be professional. I don't want to see any of those Hollywood attitudes. We aren't Def Jam, Murder Inc., Roc-A-Fella, Priority, Bad Boy, or anyone else who's already got it going on. We're Suicide and we'll earn our respect by the quality of our artists, not with a bunch of hype and bling-bling."

India paused and looked around the room at every staff member. The conference room was completely silent. "Ah-ight?"

"Ah-ight," everyone replied in unison.

Jamil stood at the head of the table and folded his arms across his chest. "Meeting adjourned. I'm out."

Chapter 9

Everyone was silent as Toni headed west on Sunset toward Pacific Palisades. The Honda was barely big enough for Toni, Charetta, and the girls but it was transportation. As they continued driving, the Pacific Ocean came into view as a vibrant blue strip of ribbon against the horizon.

"Do all these people have to live on the ocean?" Charetta asked as she changed the radio station.

"Stop drinking that Hatorade, chica." Toni laughed.

"Yeah." Sabre leaned over the front seat. "I like it out here. I'm going to own a house at the ocean, too, one day. Right, Sky?" Sabre smiled at Charetta's youngest cousin. The two of them looked more like sisters than Shawntay and Sky.

"Right. We can be roommates until we get married, and then we can live next door to each other." Sky laughed as her sister, Shawntay, grunted.

"Y'all gonna be livin' in the projects just like the rest of us." Shawntay took out a fresh stick of Juicy Fruit and popped the gum loudly as she chewed.

"Projects?" Charetta turned around and looked at her cousin. "Is that how you feel?"

Shawntay rolled her eyes and continued cracking her gum.

"I said is that how you feel?" Charetta repeated.

Shawntay sunk down in her seat. "No."

" 'Cause I ain't goin' back to no damn projects. And if you're not willing to do the work, I'll take your little ass to the airport now and you'll be out of here on the next thing smoking." Charetta glared at Shawntay. "Ain't nobody playing with your ass . . . none of y'all." Charetta looked at all the girls. "You think Nina put a hundred thousand dollars into this project for you to think that it's not going to work and you're going back to Brooklyn?"

Shawntay just stared out of the window. Charetta grabbed her by the arm "Don't you hear me talking to your little silly ass?"

"Yes." Shawntay stuck out her mouth.

"Then answer me before I knock your little ass out."

Char, just chill." Toni rubbed her roommate on the leg. "You didn't mean it, did you, Shawntay?" Toni looked at Shawntay through the rearview mirror. Sabre, who sitting in the middle, nudged Shawntay in the ribs.

"No," Shawntay finally responded minus the attitude.

"See, Char, Shawntay didn't mean it." Toni hoped Charetta would calm down.

"Her ass is the best singer in the group and she wants to trip like that. I've been waiting for this opportunity all my life and no one's gonna screw this up for me. Just let one of them mess up one time, and I'll send all three of their little asses home," Charetta declared.

"You can't . . ." Sabre began as Sky's hand covered her mouth.

"I can't what?" Charetta turned back around. Every since Toni and Charetta had formed a partnership to manage So Fine with Nina, Charetta had become a madwoman.

"You can't send us home because your deal with Nina is with So Fine, and that's me, Sky, and Shawntay." Sabre reminded her with much attitude.

"I swear I'm gonna kick your little ass. Toni, pull this damn car over right now." Charetta was fuming.

"Hey, look, you guys. We're here." Toni sighed with relief.

All of the houses faced the ocean. It was a quiet neighborhood. The only sound was that of waves quietly lapping against the rocks. A red-bricked path led up to a pink-stucco Spanish-influenced house with a red Mediterranean roof, surrounded by lofty palms. The flawless green lawn had been recently cut and a myriad of flowers decorated the path.

"Oh, how beautiful!" Toni exclaimed. "It reminds me of Poppi's house in Mexico except there was no ocean."

"How come I never went to your Poppi's house and Nina did?" Charetta questioned.

"Because you didn't want to go, remember?" Toni started up the path to the house and everyone followed.

"Whose house is this again?" Sky whispered to Sabre.

"Topaz's," Sabre whispered back.

"Why did we come here instead of Nina's?" Sky was still whispering while Toni rang the doorbell.

"I don't know," Sabre replied. "Just be glad she invited us."

Nina, Baby Doll, and Nicki answered the door, and the teenagers rushed to pick up the little girls. Sabre picked up Baby Doll and Sky had Nicki. Shawntay followed them cooing after both little girls.

"Hello, ladies." Nina laughed as So Fine sat on the sofa with the little girls, but no one responded. They were too busy talking to the girls. "Hey." Nina gave Toni and Charetta a hug. "I guess my directions were okay. You guys made it."

"Just straight out Sunset like you said." Toni smiled.

"Cool. Let's go to the playroom." Nina smiled as her business partners were about to sit on the sofa. "Only very special company is allowed in here."

It was easy to understand why. The entire room was done in different shades and textures of white. The room was split into several levels with white carpeting, marble, and bleached wood. There was a huge portrait of Topaz, Germain, Chris, and Baby Doll all dressed in white hanging over the sofa.

"Your cousin has such a beautiful family," Toni exclaimed. "And that portrait is one of the most beautiful things I've ever seen. Is it a photograph or a painting?" Toni stepped closer for a better look.

"Both. The artist wasn't cheap either." Nina stood there admiring the beautiful artwork with them.

"How much was it?" Charetta asked.

"I think Topaz said by the time she had it matted and framed, it was about a hundred grand," Nina replied thoughtfully.

"Damn!" Charetta was in shock. "It's nice but it ain't all that."

"Oh, it is." Toni was still inhaling the painting.

"I love it too," Nina agreed. "The artist is out of Atlanta. She can do it from a photograph. They did a sitting and she used a photograph.

I'm going to have her do one of me, Kyle, and Nicki as soon as she can fit us into the schedule."

"Hi, everybody." Topaz bounced down the stairs looking every bit the diva in jeans and a simple sleeveless top. "I sent the guys off so us girls could have the house to ourselves. Like a girlfriend day, huh, Nina?" Topaz smiled at her cousin warmly. Her blond tresses had been twisted, and a hint of gold sparkled on her lips and over her eyes. "My hair looks a little crazy because I've been swimming every day with the children."

"I like it like that, cuz. I wish mine would do that, but it's too straight," Nina complained. Her hair was pulled up into a simple ponytail.

"Topaz is so beautiful," Toni whispered to Charetta. "We were just admiring that wonderful portrait of your family."

"Thank you. I love it too." Topaz led them down a small winding staircase to the playroom. "There's sodas for the kids but I thought we might have a little Cristal to toast your new venture."

There was a huge bar decorated like an old-fashioned soda fountain in an ice cream parlor and a flat-screen TV. Baby Doll was running the show. She had everyone watching her DVD of *The Lizzie McGuire Movie* and drinking various flavors of Crush. There was an antique popcorn popper, a Coca-Cola machine, and a jukebox. A billiard table was on the other side of the bar.

"Playroom?" Charetta whispered to Toni. "Damn. Talk about lifestyles of the rich and famous."

"I wouldn't mind playing in this room," Toni whispered back.

"Now do you understand why I'm so hard on those little heifas? They're our ticket to the big time." Charetta was still whispering as she eyed the teenagers curled up on the sofas with the little girls. "Those little girls will never have to work a day in their lives. This is all they've ever known. The playroom."

"I know, Char, but the girls are still little girls too. You shouldn't curse at them like that." Toni voiced her concern.

"Those little things aren't that innocent. Don't let them fool you. I talk to them in the language that they understand." Charetta stopped whispering and smiled at Topaz who was walking toward them with a magnum of champagne and four flutes.

"Let's go upstairs to my suite. The clothes are up there too." Topaz led the women up a winding staircase to the top floor.

When she and Germain had remarried, they had built another floor on top of the house. Topaz's wardrobe had taken up the entire old master bedroom. The new bedroom was done in gold and cheetah print. Toni and Charetta caught a glimpse of it as Topaz led them to a sitting room that had a fireplace and books and looked right out on the ocean. There was a dance studio and exercise room. Topaz sat down on a bright red circular sofa. Nina sat on one side and Toni on the other.

Topaz uncorked the bubbly and Nina giggled as Topaz poured the golden liquid into each flute. "Don't start, Nina." She didn't look at her cousin as she handed the first flute to Toni. Nina's giggles turned into laughter as Topaz continued pouring. By the time she finished pouring the champagne, Nina was howling with laughter. Toni and Charetta look at each other, puzzled. "I used to drink a lot of this stuff," Topaz explained.

"She used to drink it every day." Nina wiped the tears from her eyes. "Cristal please." Only Nina could imitate Topaz.

Toni and Charetta smiled as they looked at the cousins.

"Would you be quiet?" Topaz handed Nina a glass and pretended to be mad.

"Thank you, cousin." Nina stifled a giggle as she leaned over and kissed Topaz on the cheek. "You know I love you."

"Are you going to make this toast?" Topaz crossed her leg and looked at Nina who was laughing again.

"Yes," Nina whispered through her laughter.

"Thank goodness Keisha isn't here." Topaz's comedic timing was incredible.

"You guys don't know Topaz. She can really act. She's acting right now. In fact, if she were to do a film, people would say who's J.Lo? She's a triple threat. My cousin can sing, dance, and act but she's so in love she hasn't got time for her career," Nina taunted.

"Nina, I appreciate the accolades, but if you don't make this toast, I swear I'll knock you out." Topaz looked like she meant business and now all of the women were laughing.

"Okay." Nina picked up her glass. "To So Fine and the diamond life."

"I heard that." Charetta lifted her glass, and the ladies gently tapped their glasses together.

"What's the diamond life?" Toni questioned as the ladies sipped their champagne.

"In *Billboard* when you sell ten million CDs you get a diamond next to your title," Topaz explained.

"And the life is the lifestyle that goes along with the sales like the lovely Topaz." Charetta smiled. For some reason she genuinely liked her.

"That's right," Topaz agreed. "And selling ten million units of one CD isn't easy."

"Most artists are happy to get one million. That's platinum, and two million on up is multi-platinum," Nina further explained.

"But So Fine is headed toward the diamond life," Charetta declared.

It was as if the girls heard their names. Baby Doll led them all into the sitting room.

"Let's go check out the clothes. I know I've got things in all sizes that I'll never wear again. After three babies, I'm happy to be a size six. I've got tons of zeros, twos, and fours, and you're welcome to take all." Topaz smiled.

"I thought you only had two kids?" Charetta questioned.

Nina held her breath and looked at Topaz.

"Did I say three? I meant two. Give me a little champagne and I don't know what I'm talking about." Topaz giggled. "Doesn't take much for me." She refilled everyone's glasses.

Nina sighed with relief. "Come on, everyone. Let's go shopping."

Baby Doll and Nicki ran down the hall screaming with laughter. They ran into Topaz's bedroom and climbed up on the huge bed and started jumping up and down.

"I'm going to tell your father, Turquoise. You know how he feels about you jumping on the bed." Topaz walked into a gold-and-tan marble Romanesque bathroom and opened her closet door.

"Daddy isn't here." The little girl laughed. "And my name isn't Turquoise, it's Baby Doll."

"Nicki, get off that bed before you fall and hurt yourself," Nina commanded. Nicki obeyed her mother promptly. "Turquoise, didn't your mother tell you to get off the bed?"

"My name's not Turquoise, it's Baby Doll," she chanted as she continued jumping on the bed.

Nina climbed over on the bed and pulled the child toward her. "Now you're getting a spanking."

"No, Nini, don't spank. Please don't spank."

Nina found a ruler and tapped her lightly on the legs several times, and Baby Doll screamed as though someone had tried to kill her.

"Hush, before I really spank you." Nina was serious.

"No, Nini, don't spank. Please don't spank me anymore."

Topaz came out of the bedroom and looked at Baby Doll. "I told you not to jump on the bed, and you were disobedient. Disobedient little girls get spankings." Baby Doll went to Topaz for her to pick her up. "No, I'm not picking you up. Your father and brother have you so spoiled it's ridiculous."

Baby Doll started crying again, stormed back into the room, climbed up on the bed, and cried. She covered her face but everyone saw her peeking to see if anyone was watching her.

Nicki climbed up on the bed next to Baby Doll and rubbed her on the back to comfort her. "Don't cry, Baby Doll."

Baby Doll sat up and Nicki put her arms around her.

"Oh, that's so sweet," Toni exclaimed. "Someone needs to take a picture."

"Aah," the teenagers cooed.

Nina tried not to smile. Somehow whenever Baby Doll and Nicki were together, Nina did the spanking and it was Baby Doll who got spanked.

"Those two look just alike," Charetta remarked. "That's amazing how much those two look alike."

Topaz walked into the bedroom with a stack of pants, tops, and dresses for the girls to try on. She saw the two little girls hugging and smiled. "Isn't that sweet?"

The teenagers dove into the clothes, pulling for items that caught their eye.

"Nicki and Turquoise, why don't you two go get your dress-up clothes. You can put on lipstick," Nina suggested.

"Come on, Baby Doll." Nicki helped her of the bed.

Baby Doll lifted her hands to Nina, and Nina picked her up. I'm sorry, Nini. I love you." She puckered her little lips and kissed Nina on the lips.

"I love you, too, Baby Doll." Nina placed her on the floor, and Baby Doll and Nicki ran into Topaz's closet for the clothes she allowed them to play dress-up in.

"You guys want to just come in the closet?" Topaz suggested. I'm tired of carrying things out. "Nina, is there any more Cristal?"

"See." Nina looked at Toni and Charetta who were laughing. "Yes, your highness."

Everyone was speechless when they saw Topaz's closet. It was the size of a small boutique. Everything was very neatly organized and separated by item and color—dresses, coats, shoes, hats, pants, and blouses.

"Damn," Charetta exclaimed. "Talk about diamond life."

"All the stuff on that side, I'm giving away." Topaz pointed to a large assortment of various items. "Whatever you don't take, I'm giving away, so take as much as you like."

Everyone had a ball trying on clothes and primping in the mirror. Charetta wouldn't admit it but she had never had so much fun in her life. Nina finally went for a second magnum of champagne. Sabre and Sky consumed a good portion of it by sneaking sips out of everyone's glasses, but no one noticed.

The little girls were going through a big box of costume jewelry.

"What's this, you guys?" Sabre sat down with them and fished through the box until she picked out a pair of topaz earrings.

"My jewels." Baby Doll was wearing a rhinestone tiara. "I'm a princess."

"Are you a princess too?" Sabre asked Nicki.

"Yes," Nicki replied.

Sabre fished in the box until she found an ankle bracelet, necklace, and bracelet that matched the earrings. When no one was looking she slipped the items in a little clutch bag Topaz had given her. She walked over to the side of the closet that Topaz had declared off-limits.

"Is it all right if I just look at these things?" Sabre asked politely.

"Sure, sweetie." Topaz and Charetta were engrossed in conversation.

Sabre sifted through the dresses, admiring all of Topaz's beautiful things. She gasped when she came across a hot red dress that was simply to die for in a size two.

She looked at Topaz who was at the other end of the closet giving Charetta a pair of shoes to try on and slipped the dress off the hanger and quickly folded it up. She had stolen things from department stores. This was a piece of cake. She had no security guards or sensors to worry about.

Sabre slipped out of the closet and stashed the dress in a shopping bag with her other things and then went down the hall to the dance studio. Toni was choreographing a routine to Charetta's song that So Fine was going to record. Sabre studied her reflection carefully in the mirror as she began her stretches.

"I'm going to be bigger and better than you ever were, Topaz, because you're nothing but an old, stupid, ugly has-been, and I'm young and beautiful and fresh," Sabre whispered to herself.

Chapter 10

Nina, Charetta, and Toni sat in front of the mixing board with the recording engineer listening to the playback of "First Kiss." Charetta had done an amazing job laying down the tracks and programming all the instruments with her keyboard and drum machine. It was nearly midnight, and the group was just getting ready to lay down the vocals. All three of the girls were in the booth wearing headphones, awaiting Charetta's instructions.

"Okay, let's do this." Charetta spoke to the girls through their headphones. The engineer started the track and the girls sang in harmony. The vocal track was clear and sweet, and the girls sounded like angels. Nina and Toni smiled at each other.

"That was da bomb, y'all. Sabre and Sky, come on out of there. We're gonna lay down Shawntay's vocals now," Charetta commanded.

The smile faded from Sabre's face as she took off her headphones.

"Come on, Sabre. I'm hungry. Let's go order a pizza or some shrimp fried rice," Sky suggested. "Plus, we can go see if those cute guys are still working in the studio next door."

"I'm not hungry, and I don't want to see those dumb boys. They weren't all that." Sabre flopped down on the sofa in front of the mixing board.

"We could use some food." Nina took out her cell phone and placed an order for Chinese. The food arrived and everyone was eating while Shawntay was still in the booth attempting to lay down a lead vocal track to Charetta's satisfaction.

Shawntay sighed as the engineer rewound the track for the umpteenth time." Can I have something to eat?"

"No." Charetta crunched on an egg roll. "We don't have time for you to take a break. You have to get this vocal down tonight."

Shawntay yawned, wishing for her sleeping bag and pillow back at the apartment. Sky had fallen asleep but Sabre was wide awake.

"Shawntay, would you sing like you're sixteen and stop trying to be Whitney Houston?" Charetta demanded as Sabre tried not to laugh.

"Stop singing like Whitney Houston? In her dreams." Sabre laughed.

"Yeah," Sky agreed, opening her eyes. "I want to go home."

"You think you could do better?" Charetta looked at Sabre and Sky.

"Yes," they chorused.

"Please. Sky, you're already rapping on the chorus," Charetta reminded her.

"Let Sabre try it," Nina suggested. "I know Shawntay's the lead but maybe she's not right for this song."

"Yes, let me try," Sabre pleaded. She was already on her way into the vocal booth.

"Let her do it, Char," Toni suggested. "Or else we'll be here all night arguing, and I'm sleepy, too, now."

"Yeah," Nina agreed. "What harm can it do?"

"Sabre is a background singer. Her voice is too thin for a lead," Charetta protested.

Sabre was already putting on the headphones.

"She's in there now." Nina nodded at Sabre who was already standing in front of the microphone awaiting her cue.

"Come on out, Shawntay, and take a break." Charetta looked at Sabre carefully. "We're just letting you do this so Shawntay can take a little break."

"Okay," Sabre agreed sweetly. "I just have an idea that I wanted to try."

"Do your thang, Sabre." Shawntay spoke through her headset.

"Yeah, so we can go home." Sky yawned and stretched out on the sofa.

"Sabre, just—" Charetta began.

"I know how to sing it." Sabre cut in.

Charetta folded her arms and pushed the record button as Sabre closed her eyes and moved to the beat as she felt the music down in her soul. She sang the words with the innocence and sweetness of a young girl who had just been kissed for the very first time. Nina sat up in her chair and started bouncing with the music as a huge smile covered Toni's face.

"That's it," Toni exclaimed. "I love it!"

"Me too," Nina agreed excitedly.

"It's not strong enough," Charetta protested.

"It's not supposed to be strong," Nina explained. "Shawntay was over singing. This is perfect."

"Whatever." Charetta was still not convinced. "It's your money." She looked at Nina as she headed out the door. "I need a bathroom break."

"Come out of there, Sabre," Nina commanded. She took out a notebook and wrote intently for several minutes while Toni replayed the track with all the vocals for the girls.

"We love it." The girls grinned at one another.

"But it's missing something." Nina smiled at Sky. She handed her the sheet of notebook paper. "Go in there and freestyle with this on the track."

"I can do it any way I want?" Sky was wide awake now. Sabre took the page and quickly read what Nina had written.

"Ooh, that's tight, Nina." Sabre smiled. "Girl, act like you do when you're talking to your boo."

"Ah-ight." Sky grinned and dashed into the studio. As soon as she put on the headphones, she nodded for Nina to start the track. All the girls screamed when she began the rap.

"What are y'all doin'?" Charetta demanded as soon as she entered the studio and saw Sky in the vocal booth and Nina in her chair.

"Finishing the song," Sabre replied. "Miss Nina got skills. I didn't know you had it goin' on like that."

"As many hours as I spent in the studio with my cousin and my ex-boyfriend, I ought to know a little sumpin', sumpin'." Nina grinned. "That was perfect, Sky. Come on in here and let's get you guys home and to bed. Tomorrow's a big day for us."

"Oh, so you're the producer now?" Charetta looked at Nina.

"Co-producer," Nina replied smoothly. "And So Fine deserves a co-production credit too."

"I leave the room for five minutes, and all of a sudden all of you are producers?" Charetta looked at Nina and the group.

"Yeah, your song was whack until Miss Nina told me to go into the studio and sing. Then I sang it the way I felt it should be sang and Sky freestyled. We're all sisters." Sabre pulled Shawntay and Sky to her sides. "So we, So Fine, will take a co-production credit too."

"And Nina deserves a songwriting credit for this." Toni held up the sheet of notebook paper that Nina had written the rap on.

Charetta was fuming. She had just had her hair rebraided, and the style was quite becoming but her head was throbbing. She grabbed her purse and searched for some aspirin.

"Just listen to it, Char." Toni pushed the play button and Sabre's sweet vocals filled their ears and Sky was seriously macking in her rap. "It's da bomb."

"Yeah," everyone in the studio chorused, including the engineer.

"It's a wrap, ladies." Nina smiled as the engineer handed them CDs of the track.

"She'll get over it," Toni whispered to Nina before they went separate ways.

"Thanks, Miss Nina." So Fine was all over her with hugs and kisses.

"You just made our first record a hit," Sabre whispered in her ear. "Char was jacking it up."

Nina pushed the CD into the player in her dashboard and cranked the volume. During all her time in the studio with Jamil and Topaz, it was the first time she had ever made any real input and now she had a songwriting and producing credit. She took the CD out of the player and ran into the house where she found Kyle asleep on the couch. He had tried to stay awake until she came home. She left the CD and her purse on the counter and woke him with a kiss.

"Is that my beautiful wife or am I dreaming?" Kyle smiled sleepily.

"Come on, baby. Let's get you upstairs to bed." She led him by the hand up the stairs to the bedroom overlooking the ocean. Moonlight filled the room softly so there was no need to turn on a lamp. She helped Kyle undress and got him into bed and then she lit a huge scented candle, undressed, slid under the sheets, and cuddled up next to him.

"Don't think I'm asleep for one minute," Kyle said several minutes later.

Nina could only laugh. "You big faker. I thought you were asleep."

"I bet you did," he replied. "I love it when you undress me for bed. A brother waited up all night and deserves a little sumpin', sumpin'."

"You deserve a lot of sumpin', sumpin'," Nina agreed. "But first, since you're so wide awake, I want you to hear my song that I co-produced and co-wrote for So Fine."

"You co-produced and co-wrote a song for So Fine?" Kyle sat up in bed and looked at her.

"Un-huh." A huge grin covered her face.

"You never cease to amaze me." Kyle pulled her into his arms and kissed her. "You wonderfully talented, amazing woman."

"Hold that thought, okay, baby?" Nina kissed a finger and pressed it to his lips before she jumped out of bed and ran downstairs for the CD. She grabbed Nicki's boom box and took it out on the balcony. "Come out here so we don't wake Nicki." She ran back into the bedroom for her robe.

"Were you running around butt naked all this time?" Kyle looked her up and down with a little smile.

"Yep. I was so excited I forgot to put my robe on." Nina laughed.

"My kind of woman . . . totally uninhibited." He pulled her into his arms and held her, but when the opening beats came through the speaker he began bouncing. "Hey, I thought this was going to be a slow jam. This is tight. You wrote this, baby?"

"No, it's Char's track. She's good but she wants to make everything hard. I just suggested that Sabre do the lead vocal because Shawntay over sings and I wrote the rap for Sky to freestyle. The girls loved it. They were all over me kissing and hugging me. And Sabre got the group a co-production credit too." She cut off the track and led Kyle back into the bedroom.

"That Sabre is something else." Kyle laughed.

"She's sweet. Charetta's the one. That girl has too much attitude sometime."

"Miss Sabre will show you what's she's made just as soon as you cross her. You're the writer. Check out word *sabre* in the dictionary. Fits her to a T." Kyle pulled Nina over on his side of the bed.

"What do you think about Toni?" Nina propped her head up on a pillow so she could see into Kyle's eyes. She valued his input on everything and everybody.

"I think Toni is sweet and beautiful, but sometimes I wonder if she and Char have something going on."

"Something going on?" Nina repeated. "What do you mean something going on?"

"The way you and I are about to have something going on between these sheets."

"Kyle, no." Nina was shocked.

"It wouldn't surprise me."

"Kyle, no." Nina laughed. "That's nasty."

"My sentiments exactly. There's nothing better than a man loving his woman and a woman loving her man."

Chapter 11

The sun had barely pushed itself above the horizon when Jamil opened his eyes. Heavy silk drapes hung at the windows to keep the light and heat out. He knew he wouldn't be able to go back to sleep so he flipped on the television to MTV. There was a screen on the ceiling as well as two on either side of the entertainment system built into the wall directly in front of the huge California king.

"What's wrong, Jamil? Can't you sleep, baby?" A zebra-printed sheet covered India's nude body.

"Just got a lot on my mind." He switched from channel to channel, searching for nothing in particular.

"Jamil." India took the remote out of his hand and turned off all the screens. "Do you want to talk about it?"

"Talk about what?" He smiled at her.

"Whatever's bothering you." She rolled over and sat up in bed next to him.

"I'm probably just getting a little hyped about the launch party," he confessed. "Do you really think Xtreme's gonna put us on the map in hip-hop?" There was a small refrigerator under the wet bar in the master suite. Jamil took out a decanter of fresh-squeezed orange juice and poured it. He handed a glass to India as he got back into bed.

"Thanks, babe." India drank the entire glass in a couple of gulps.

"Somebody was thirsty." Jamil laughed. "Want some more?"

"Yes, please." India smiled as she watched Jamil pour the orange juice. "Jamil, why are you second-guessing yourself about Xtreme now? You know that CD is gonna blow the biz apart."

"You're right." Jamil took the empty glass from India and kissed her. "Why did this take us so long?"

"Between Xtreme's game schedule, practices, and training camp, it was crazy but worth it."

"I'm not talking about Xtreme or business. I'm talking about you and me, woman." Jamil looked down into her eyes and gently traced the outline of her full lips.

"Oh." India pulled his face to hers and kissed him. "You know I don't believe in office romances."

"I can't believe you had me fooled for a year." He took her hand and looked at the small black diamond on her finger. "Using your brother and that ring as a decoy."

India's laughter was bubbly and sparkling like fine champagne. "I'm sorry, boss. You were such a cutie, and I knew I could like you so I was trying to be strong. But I never thought we'd end up here."

"I never thought I'd fall in love again after Nina wouldn't marry me," Jamil confessed softly.

"I am so glad she didn't marry you. I'm sorry she broke your heart, but I'm glad she didn't marry you or else we wouldn't be together." India held him tightly.

"I don't know what I'd do without you." Jamil took her hand, slipped off the small black diamond, reached into his nightstand, and handed her a blue velvet ring case.

"Jamil, babe . . ." India looked at him and then the box.

"Did I ever tell you how much I love that little accent of yours?" Jamil watched her carefully.

"Accent? You can still hear it? I thought I had lost that." India had been born in Barbados but raised in New York and Los Angeles.

"Don't you ever lose that accent, India. You and it give Suicide a lot of class. He watched her open the ring box and gasp at the brilliant seven-carat black diamond in a platinum setting.

"Jamil!" India looked at the ring and then at him.

"What? You don't like it?" He was genuinely concerned.

"No, I love it, but what's it for?" India took the ring out of the case.

"I want you to be Mrs. Jamil Winters," he declared proudly.

"Your wife?" India couldn't believe what she was hearing. "I'd run Suicide without being your wife."

"I want you around for more than business." Jamil was starting to get a little nervous. He wasn't going to be turned down again, was he? "I trust you, and I need you. I want to be there for you the way you always are for me."

"Jamil . . ." India looked up at him with eyes filled with tears. "I don't know what to say."

"Say, yes, baby. Say yes."

"Yes." India smiled. She took the ring out of the box and handed it to him, and he slipped it on her finger. "Yes. Yes. Yes." She jumped on him and the two of them rolled across the bed and onto the floor.

"Alright. Yes!" Jamil shouted. "You know I had that designed especially for you. That black diamond was flown in from Europe."

They were interrupted by a knock at the door. "Holler," Jamil yelled.

Buffalo stuck his head in the room. "Just wanted to make sure everything was okay, boss."

"It's more than okay." Jamil was grinning from ear to ear and India, wrapped up in the bedsheet lying on top of him, was also grinning. "India said yes."

"Congratulations, boss. Congratulations, Miss India. Y'all want some breakfast?"

"No—" Jamil began.

"Yes," India cut in. "Thanks, Buffalo. Now that I'm going to be Mrs. Winters, I have to make sure my man is well-fed."

"Okay, boss lady." Buffalo smiled, something people rarely saw him do.

"We're gonna keep this engagement on the down low, just between the three of us," Jamil declared. "There's too much going on right now. After the party we can go down to the Caribbean and do something private or do something grand like Jen and Ben. However, my baby likes."

"Okay, babe." India looked at her ring and kissed Jamil.

Buffalo nodded his agreement and began closing the bedroom door.

"Yo, Buff," Jamil called after him.

He turned around and looked at Jamil.

"You can take your time with that breakfast." Jamil grinned.

Chapter 12

Los Angeles, constellation of the chocolate stars, was also the host city for Magic Johnson's annual Midsummer Night's Magic weekend benefiting the United Negro College Fund. It was always heavily supported by the brightest in the sports, music, film, and television industries. Superstar ball players flew in from every part of the country to play in the all-star game while other celebrities either performed at or attended the concert. This year's festivities would also serve as a wonderful opportunity to indirectly introduce So Fine to the public.

Everyone gathered at Nina's to dress for the event. She had hired a limousine for the night, and the teenagers were bubbling over with excitement. The girls had spent the day at Umberto's getting their hair done. Sabre's and Sky's hair had been flat ironed and Shawntay had gotten a crop cut that accentuated her features nicely. She had inherited extremely curly red hair like Charetta only she knew how to work with hers.

Nina had taken them shopping downtown in the garment district and to the Slauson Swap Meet. Nina's one-hundred-thousand-dollar investment had been budgeted and was being spent carefully in order for the management team to achieve its goals.

"Can't we wear the things Topaz gave us?" Sabre begged over and over. The faded stretch denim jeans and T-shirts were cute but Sabre wanted to wear more expensive and sophisticated clothing.

"Not yet." Nina was drop-dead gorgeous in a red mini dress with her hair tucked simply behind her ears. She studied the girls and ripped Shawntay's shirt a little more on the shoulder and Sabre's at the bottom. All three of the girls had lovely but different figures. Sabre was the shortest with all the curves. Shawntay had great legs and Sky had the cleavage. "I want people to know two things about you."

"What's that?" All of the girls wanted to know.

"First, that you're young, that's why you can't wear Topaz's clothes, Sabre. You'll have plenty of time to be a diva. And second, that you're a group. That's why we dress you guys alike." Nina gave them a final inspection. Toni had done their makeup and it was very natural so they were fresh and youthful.

"Everybody ready?" Nina looked at Charetta who looked wonderful in a black dress that Topaz had given her. Toni looked exquisite in pink and orange. Charetta had said very little since they had arrived.

Kyle was also attending the event. He had on a red shirt and black pants, and Nicki was also wearing a little red dress. Sean and Eric were playing in the all-star game. It would be the first time all of the friends would be together in months.

"Let's go." Nina led the way out to the super stretch white Hummer parked in the driveway. The driver got out and opened the doors for them. The teenagers climbed in first and then Charetta and Toni. Everyone smiled as Kyle assisted Nicki and then Nina into the car. They were just about to pull off when a BMW SUV pulled in front of them, honking.

"What the . . . ? Driver, please stop the car." Kyle got out just as Jade jumped out of the truck. She looked fabulous. She had let her hair grow, and it was pulled back into a ponytail with a decorative ornament.

"*She* is beautiful," Sabre exclaimed. Everyone watched with interest as Kyle kissed her and took her toddler son, Kobe. They walked over to the limo together.

"Nina, did you forget your sister-in-law?" Kyle smiled at his wife as he helped the beautiful African-American and Asian woman inside the car.

"Guilty." She touched cheeks with Jade so she wouldn't smudge her makeup. "I love you."

"Don't even go there with me, Nina Ross." Jade pretended to be mad.

"We can leave now, driver," Nina yelled.

"You sure you haven't forgotten anyone else?" Kyle smirked. "Where's your daughter?" Nina panicked and looked around until she saw Nicki and Kobe sitting with the teenagers.

"I'll take care of you later." Nina tried not to smile as she looked at her husband who was sitting on the other side of Jade.

"I can't believe you were going to leave without me, after you invited me to ride with you. Besides, I have all the tickets." Jade reached into her handbag and pulled out a small stack of tickets. "And these are very good seats. Maybe I'll just scalp them."

"Maybe if she was handling her part of the business instead of trying to write and produce songs she would have remembered." Charetta looked directly at Nina.

"Who is she?" Jade demanded. She never had a problem poking her nose into business that was not hers, and she was good for talking about people in the third person when they were present. Kyle smiled and looked out of the window.

"I'm sorry, Jade. We've been so crazy with the group and getting them dressed for tonight," Nina explained. "We want to create a buzz . . . people talking about them and wondering who they are."

"I can understand that. But does she have to be so rude?" Jade whispered.

"She's got issues," Kyle whispered back.

"Jade, I want you to meet my group, So Fine." Nina introduced each girl to Jade and then she introduced Jade to Toni and Charetta.

"This is so cool," Jade exclaimed. "This is the first time that all of us will have been together since you guys returned from that two-year honeymoon. I'm surprised you're not pregnant again." Jade laughed. "Keisha's coming. She's back from Atlanta."

"Wonderful. And I forgot you were coming." Nina gave her a hug. "I'm so sorry."

"Where's my beautiful niece?" Jade demanded.

"Where's my beautiful nephew?" Nina replied.

"Up there with the girls. Where else?" Jade laughed. "Hi, Nicki. Hi, baby." Jade waved and blew kisses to Nicki and her three-year-old son, Kobe.

"Hi, Auntie." Nicki waved back.

"She's so beautiful with those eyes like her auntie Topaz." Jade blew more kisses. "That still is so strange to me how she got those eyes."

The limo pulled underneath the Staples Center, and everyone got out and headed inside where the who's who of then entertainment industry had gathered.

Charetta grabbed the girls. "Act like you're stars, don't gawk."

"Act? I already am a star." Sabre didn't even look at her. She was too busy smiling at Fabolous who was throwing her much action.

Nina and entourage attracted the attention of the entire building. Sean and Eric had gotten them floor seats in a section where just about every other person was somebody famous. Nina was amazed at how well So Fine handled all the attention. She didn't know Charetta had threatened to strangle them if they even blinked wrong.

"Auntie Nina." Chris, Baby Doll, and Kendra, Keisha's daughter, were waving at her. Topaz, dressed in a shimmering gold pantsuit and some of her best diamonds, looked too fabulous to move sitting next to Germain. A beautiful smile lit her face, and Nina couldn't remember when she had seen her cousin look more beautiful. She seemed to glow from within.

"Hey, Auntie Nina." Keisha stood and the two of them hugged for several seconds.

"I have missed you so much." Nina wiped a tear from her eye.

"I know. I didn't realize how close we all had become until we had to part ways for whatever reasons." Keisha looked like new money with her hair in twists.

"And look at this little man." Nina picked up Keisha's son, Rick, who was only a few months younger than Nicki.

"There's my precious girl." Keisha received a kiss from Kyle as she plucked Nicki from his arms.

"Okay, everyone has got to come to my house," Nina demanded. "We'll have a barbecue or something."

"No mine." Everyone was staring at Jade who really looked like a black Barbie Doll.

"Girl, is all of that your hair or did you have some added?" Topaz was up and examining Jade's braid.

"Only my hairdresser knows for sure." Jade laughed as they settled in for the game.

"You would think Nina would introduce us to people," Charetta mumbled. "At least the girls. I thought that was the purpose us all going out together."

The girls had a ball watching the game and pointing out celebrities to one another on the down low. At the after party, Sean and Eric had arranged for the entire entourage to be seated together. The press and stars invaded them. So Fine received more attention than they could handle. Nina had them posing for photographs with Topaz, Sean, Eric, and countless other people. Topaz noticed the girls collecting numbers.

"You girls are going to meet a lot of people, especially young men, and you are not going to want all of them calling you. You can't make yourself too accessible. If one of these celebs wants to find you, they will. Trust me." Topaz winked at the girls as she sat back down with her family.

"She is so beautiful." Sky looked at Topaz adoringly. "Did you ever think we'd be kicking it with her?"

"She's cool," Sabre agreed. "But that pantsuit would look better on me."

Every man who stopped by the table to speak to the ball players spoke to every woman . . . except Charetta. They all seemed to ignore her, but they drooled over Toni. She was just as popular as Nina and her gorgeous friends. Topaz's favorite Cristal was everywhere. Charetta consumed as much of it as she could. It helped numb the fact that no one was paying her any attention. She watched everyone like a hawk.

The music was really great but people hardly danced. The women mostly stood around trying to be seen by one of the ball players or some other star, and the men stood around looking at the women.

Charetta noticed a handsome young guy kiss Topaz's hand and smile at Nina. There was something very familiar about him. He was *somebody* but she just couldn't remember who. He smiled at the others and walked to another section of the club. Moments later, Nina got up and walked in the same direction the young man had gone. Without thinking, Charetta got up and followed Nina.

"Jamil, wait a minute." Nina caught up with him by the bar. "Can we go somewhere and talk?"

Jamil stood there just looking at her for several seconds. "Sure, why not?"

There's a story here, Charetta's legal mind informed her. She followed them to an outside patio where it was a little quieter.

"How have you been?" Nina smiled.

"I'm straight." He laughed cockily. "You know me."

"I do know you, and I always want us to be friends." Nina gave him a hug and kissed him on the cheek.

"I think that would be kind of hard considering . . ." He looked away at someone passing by to avoid eye contact.

"We can try," Nina suggested. "I want you to hear something." She took the So Fine single out of her purse and handed it to him. "I'd like you to listen to this for old times' sake."

"What is it?" Jamil was trying to be nonchalant but Nina knew him too well.

"So Fine, a group I'm managing. I co-produced and co-wrote the song, and before I let anybody in this business hear it, I wanted your opinion." Nina's smile was sincere. She noticed the enormous man standing by Jamil. She had noticed him earlier but hadn't paid him that much attention.

"This is you?" Jamil finally smiled.

"Yeah, that's me."

He gave the CD to Buffalo before he grabbed Nina and kissed her on the mouth. "That was for old times' sake too."

"Jamil . . ." Nina began walking away.

"I'll let you know what I think about your little CD," he called after her.

Nina was stunned and shaken by Jamil's kiss. It had been totally unexpected and definitely unwanted. She ducked inside the powder room to collect her thoughts and freshen her lipstick. Every woman in there was on a cell phone. The one pay telephone had a line . . . sistas were making connections. There was no space in front of any mirror. All sizes and shapes of lips were puckered as liner, lipstick, and lip gloss was expertly applied. Nina made a quick touch-up with a tube of lipstick and a compact and left.

Jamil is Nina's ex-boyfriend? A brother from Compton?

Charetta sat alone at a table away from the others attempting to put the pieces of what she had just witnessed together.

I am so sick of these wanna-be fake-ass bitches using brothers for a record deal. Nina never gave my brother the time of day except when she wanted drugs. I told Bootsie's stupid ass she had money and to charge her ass, but he wouldn't listen to me. Bootsie thought she was so fine. Why are men are so stupid? Now she thinks she's gonna steal my tracks so she can impress her bourgeois-ass husband? I don't think so.

Charetta went to the bar for a shot of tequila and chased it with a glass of champagne.

I wonder what her precious Kyle would think about that little clandestine meeting with Jamil . . . the two-timing ho.

Chapter 13

It was a scorching hot day in August but the Pacific Ocean cooled things off by at least ten degrees. Nina and Topaz were oiled and tanning by the swimming pool. Both of their daughters were at Keisha's for the weekend, and Chris had been invited to spend the weekend with a friend. Kyle and Germain were both out of town on business so the ladies were minus children and husband for the first time since they were married.

"It seems strange with no husbands and no kids around." Topaz sat up and fished a bottle of water out of the ice chest.

"It does," Nina agreed.

"So, are we going out for dinner or shall we have something delivered?" Topaz drank a long sip of water and screwed the cap back on. She was wearing a white-and-gold bikini, and she was still in excellent shape after three babies.

"I don't care." Nina was wearing a metallic-gold bikini and she was also in fabulous shape. She hadn't gained one pound since she had married Kyle. *"Probably because the two of you are always working out and I don't mean with weights,"* she could hear Topaz say and she smiled.

"Nina, what's wrong?" Topaz sprinkled her face with water from the bottle.

"Did you say something?" Nina looked at Topaz.

"Is it Kyle? Girl, if you can't stand to be away from him, you should have gone with him." Topaz took a bowl of fruit out of the refrigerator by the grill.

"No, it's not Kyle. I miss him but Jamil's party is tomorrow." Nina plucked a handful of strawberries out of the fruit bowl.

"That's right." Topaz ate a cube of watermelon. "Were you able to get everyone in? You said the guest list was tight."

"I took care of that weeks ago. His assistant, India, seems really cool. Actually, she runs the label."

"Okay, wonderful. Now tell me why we aren't on our way to our favorite Japanese restaurant in the Colony for sushi or why someone isn't driving down PCH with some type of food for us?" Topaz dug another cube of watermelon out of the bowl. "I'm hungry."

"I'm sorry. Where is my mind?" Nina picked up the phone and placed an order for their favorites.

"With Kyle." Topaz laughed.

"Food's on the way."

"Thanks, Nini. Now what's wrong? This is me, Topaz, and I know something's bothering you."

"It's Jamil." Nina had finally managed to say his name.

"He looked really good the other night, didn't he? And he was very sweet. He wants to meet with me about signing with Suicide."

"I don't know about all that." Nina reached into the fruit bowl for a fork and speared an orange slice.

"All about what? You aren't telling me something."

"I think we need to watch Jamil and let things develop a little more first." Nina picked up one of Nicki's swim toys from beside the pool.

"What things, and why are you being so evasive? Did something happen?"

Nina stood and looked out at the ocean.

"Nina, you're scaring me." Topaz stood next to her cousin. "If you can't tell me, who can you tell?"

"My husband." Nina looked at Topaz sideways.

"Well, tell him. Forget you. I'm going home." Topaz stuck her perfectly manicured feet into a pair of gold sandals, snatched up her towel, and headed toward the house.

"Don't be mad, Baby Doll," Nina called after her.

Topaz turned around and looked at Nina who was laughing so hard, she could barely stand. She kicked off her shoes, ran toward

Nina, and knocked her into the pool. Nina grabbed Topaz's arm as she was falling and pulled her right into the pool with her.

"I can't believe you did that." Topaz swam toward the edge of the pool where Nina was already getting out. "You'd better run because I'm gonna kick your butt."

Nina ran around the pool screaming, with Topaz right behind her. "Stay away from me." She pointed the garden hose at Topaz.

"I wish you would." Topaz tried to reach for it.

"Be careful what you wish for 'cause you just might get it." Nina sprayed her, and both of them screamed with laughter.

"No, you didn't." Topaz was still determined to get the hose from Nina. She had managed to grab the nozzle when she noticed the delivery boy from the restaurant watching them with the biggest smile on his face.

"Ladies, don't stop on my account," he called out to them.

"I wonder how long he's been over there," Nina whispered, feeling foolish because they had been caught playing like children.

"Too long. I ought to turn this on his ass." Topaz looked at the water hose that she had finally managed to capture.

"Do it." Nina laughed. "I double dog dare you."

"I don't want to get our food wet."

"True dat."

"But I will get you." Topaz turned the spray on Nina, and the game of chase was back on.

"Time out," Nina called from the other side of the pool. "I have to get his money."

The delivery boy continued smiling while Topaz cut off the water. Nina counted out some cash and took the food. "I hope you enjoyed your tip." Nina grinned.

"Best one I had all day." He laughed.

"I'm sure." Nina handed him an extra five. "I'd get out of here if I were you. My cousin wants to wet you up."

"My kind of girls." He laughed and was gone.

"I still can't believe you pushed me in the pool." Nina laughed. "But it was fun." They sat in their robes eating Japanese food.

"It was," Topaz agreed. "Are you ready to tell me what you were trying not to tell me about Jamil now, or do I have to throw you in the pool again?"

"He kissed me." Nina used chopsticks to dip a California roll in soy sauce.

"Who kissed you?"

"Jamil."

"Stop . . . with his tongue?"

"Yes."

Topaz's eyes grew wide. "Do you still have feelings for him?"

"Hell no." Nina covered her mouth with her hand. "I'm sorry, Lord." She punched Topaz who was laughing. "Now you got me saying bad words."

"So why are you making a big deal about this kiss when you didn't feel anything?"

"He knows I'm married. He disrespected me and my husband."

"Hey . . . where was Kyle when all of this was going down?"

"On the other side of the club."

"Did you tell him?"

"No."

"Why not? I can't believe *you* would keep this from Kyle."

"Because I don't want Kyle to trip."

"Kyle wouldn't trip." Topaz tossed her empty food container in the trash. "Wait a minute, he's a man. He'll trip."

"He might try to fight Jamil or something."

"I can't see lover boy Kyle fighting but it's not like Jamil wouldn't have it coming."

"It's deeper than that. I gave Jamil a copy of So Fine's single. I wanted his opinion."

"Do you want to sign So Fine with Jamil?"

"I might, but I'm not sure now."

"Jamil doesn't have the only label in the business. I can always take it to my label and give it to Latrell. We know a lot of people at a lot of other labels too."

"But you said Jamil wants you at Suicide. He is the hit maker," Nina offered.

"It might be time for me to work with new producers. And I haven't made up my mind about signing with Suicide."

"I still don't like that name." Nina made a face.

"It's just hip-hop." Topaz laughed.

"If it's just hip-hop, why does Jamil have this enormous man who looks like a water buffalo following him around?"

"He does?"

"Yes. He was with him the other night."

"It's part of the image," Topaz explained.

"Maybe it's more than that. Remember that trip to the Cayman Islands with Gunther when he brought Reno, and Jamil asked us why Gunther was hanging out with drug dealers?"

"How could I ever forget it?" The color drained from Topaz's face.

"He said we were just a couple of Valley girls and we didn't know anything."

"We were." Topaz laughed. "Jamil was the one who gave us the 4-1-1."

"Exactly."

Well, we're not so young and naive now."

"And neither is Jamil, Topaz. But then he never was."

"So what are you saying, Nina?"

"I'm not saying anything, yet."

Chapter 14

The club was practically empty when India arrived except for personnel setting up equipment in various parts of the building for the party. India had come especially early to ensure that every single detail was carried out according to her instructions. The tri-level edifice seemed enormous now, but tonight would be different when it was filled with all of Suicide's guests.

India ran up the stairs with a huge canvas bag with contents more vital than the black Prada dress and shoes she also carried. It had taken her hours to find the right outfit. She wanted to be breathtakingly gorgeous for Jamil, but despite her efforts, she would be happy if he was able to get a glimpse of her. There was still so much to do. This would be one of the biggest nights of their lives next to their secret wedding, which would take place in Barbados over Thanksgiving weekend.

She went to a colorful room on the third floor that had been designated for VIP. All of Jamil's family and friends, celebrities, and important business associates would be entertained in this section of the club. A pressroom was set up in an adjacent room for television crews doing on-camera interviews. The most important journalists would also be allowed access to the VIP section. India, once again, had personally okayed every individual who would enter the room, and India would also be on hand to see that the requests of this group—ranging from special food and drinks to lap dances and drugs—were met and as timely as possible.

She dug in her canvas bag for her cell phone and two-way and placed them on the table in front of her. It would only be a matter of time before one summoned her, if not both. She opened a folder that contained at least a dozen copies of the guest list for the ladies working the door. She would check one last time before distributing the lists for any last-minute stragglers whose names would be handwritten on it. No one liked to be told his name was not on the list, and because of the overwhelming response to the event, the list would be strictly enforced.

There were also several copies of Xtreme's video and CD for his performance. India would hold on to them until he walked onstage, making sure the music and video were cued properly. She looked at her notes. She still needed to inspect the ice carvings, the flowers and centerpieces, the seafood for the sushi bar, and make sure the interns had assembled the goody bags properly. She could hear dishes and glasses being moved out of the kitchen to various stations. Her cell phone rang, and she jumped.

"Hello, sweetheart." She grinned from ear to ear the moment she heard Jamil's voice.

"Hi, babe."

"Everything okay over there?"

"Yes, boss."

"Is someone there with you?"

"No." India dug her makeup case out of the canvas bag.

"I thought you weren't going to call me that unless other people were around."

"It's a habit."

"I'm sending one of the guys over just in case you need something lifted or moved."

"Thanks, sweetie." She could hear him smiling through the phone.

"If tonight wasn't the launch party, I'd walk in there with you on my arm and let everybody know what's up."

"I know, baby. They'll know soon enough. I think it's fun keeping it a secret."

"Are you wearing your ring?"

She looked at the seven-carat black diamond engagement ring that

Jamil had surprised her with and smiled. "You know I never take it off."

"Well, they can look at that tonight and wonder who your man is."

"That's right," India agreed.

"It sounds like you've got everything under control over there. But I knew you did. I just wanted to hear your voice."

"Me, too, sweetie. I'll see you later, okay?"

"Ah-ight, sexy."

India hung up with butterflies. She picked up her list and clipped the pager and cell phone to her waist.

"Do we have to look like a group tonight?" Sabre stood in front of the mirror looking at the faded stretch denim jeans that she no longer liked.

"Yes, Sabre. Especially tonight." Toni was in the other side of the closet digging through piles of shoes and clothing searching for her black shoes. "There are going to be a lot of important people at this party. And we want them—"

"I know. You want them to see us fresh and youthful. I'm so sick of fresh and youthful I could—"

"You could what?" Charetta came out of the bathroom with a towel wrapped around her head.

"Nothing," Sabre replied flatly. She fussed with her hair in the mirror.

"You already used up all of the hot water. I wouldn't say too much of anything if I were you."

Sky came out of the bedroom. "Come on, Sabre. Let's go play our CD and imagine we're onstage. Come on, Shawntay."

Shawntay joined the others in the dining room, and within moments they were laughing, giggling, and singing.

"I used to like that song," Charetta commented to Toni who had just taken a very quick shower. The water was barely tepid after the four previous ones.

"It's still a great song, Char." Toni was tired of her complaining.

"I better not smell any funky underarms in the limo or guess who won't be going." Charetta was dressed in a simple black pantsuit. Her hair had been braided with extensions that nearly reached her waist.

"You look beautiful, Charetta." Shawntay smiled at her cousin.

"You do," Sky agreed.

"Thanks." It was the first time Charetta had ever heard *beautiful* and her name in the same sentence. "But don't ever call me Charetta in front of anyone. It sounds so ghetto. My name is Char."

Nina watched Topaz put the finishing touches on her makeup. "How come you changed your mind about going?"

"After our conversation the other day, I thought you could use a little reinforcement." Topaz smiled at Nina in the mirror. "You know you're the only sister I've ever had."

"I know, big head." Nina polished her copper lips with clear gloss. "Come on before I redo my makeup."

"I'm done." Topaz was wearing a white jumpsuit with white stilettos and a white cowboy hat. "I had to braid my hair after I saw Jade's." Topaz fussed with the braid. "Didn't she look incredible the other night?"

"She really did. Sabre never gives anyone a compliment, and she even said Jade was beautiful." Nina laughed. "Jade's really come into her own."

"After all her marital problems with Sean, Jade would want to get her act together." Topaz led Nina downstairs to the playroom where Germain and Chris were playing with Baby Doll and Nicki.

"No spoiling my daughter." Nina pointed a finger at father and son. "I always have to threaten to spank her after the two of you baby-sit."

"Okay, Auntie Nina." Chris got up to give her a hug. "You look beautiful, Mother." Chris wrapped his arms around Topaz.

"Thanks, baby. Can you believe he's almost as tall as me?" Chris's head came up to Topaz's shoulder.

"I can still remember when he was a little guy." Germain pulled Topaz into his arms.

"I'm going out to the car. Don't be all night, you two, or the party will be over." Nina picked up Nicki then Baby Doll and gave them each a big hug before she went out to the stretch limo that was waiting in front of the house.

Topaz slid in beside her within moments. "Let's get this party started."

* * *

At the club, people were lined up all around the building waiting to get in. India's passport invitation was unable to be duplicated so it made the entry process a little smoother. People still weren't used to being searched, but everyone forever would feel the repercussions of 9-11.

India had changed clothes, and she ran around making sure everyone was in place before Jamil and the real VIPs arrived. The club was really starting to fill up. When she arrived back at VIP a few B-list celebrities were serving themselves from the sushi bar. Jamil arrived with Buffalo and his mother.

"Hello, Janice." India greeted Jamil's mother warmly.

"Girl, you just give me a hug." Janice hugged her tightly. "Now let me see that ring."

India proudly held out her left hand and displayed the ring.

"That is beautiful. My baby has good taste, and I'm not just talking about the ring," Janice said so only India could hear.

India saw Topaz approaching the VIP section. "Gotta get back to work."

Jamil grabbed India and pulled her to his side. "Hey, beautiful." He was wearing sunglasses and she knew why.

"Jamil, let me smell your breath." He blew in her face and grinned. "I've got something for you."

"I know you do." He was still holding her hand.

"Jamil, Topaz is here."

"I see her. The girl with her is Nina. Put Nina next to me and Topaz by my mother. Put the group at Xtreme's table and the other two you can seat anywhere."

"Okay, boss."

"No, wait."

"Jamil, if you don't let me go, I won't be able to seat them anywhere," India whispered through gritted teeth.

Nina and Topaz were leading the others to a table across the room where they all could sit together when India accosted them.

"Good evening, ladies." India stepped between Topaz and Nina and took each of them by the hand. "Jamil has requested the presence of you beautiful ladies at his table."

"Oh, that won't work. I have my group and my business partners with me, and we really need to sit together," Nina explained as India led her to Jamil's table.

"Nina, it's so good to see you, girl. You look wonderful." Janice stood and embraced her.

"It's really good to see you, too, Janice." Nina smiled at her warmly.

Meanwhile, India seated Topaz on the other side of Janice and the others as Jamil had requested.

"What the hell is going on?" Charetta demanded as India's assistant ushered them to a table. "We're supposed to be sitting with them." Charetta pointed to Topaz and Nina.

"You'll have to speak with India about that," Anita explained kindly.

"Well, send her over here and I'll explain it to her," Charetta barked.

'Char," Toni whispered, "just chill. Nina will take care of it."

"She's too busy socializing to think about us. We're over here in the middle of nowhere. We can't even network." Charetta was fuming. "The girls are sitting right behind her," Charetta pointed out. "I don't trust her. She's trying to steal our group."

"If it wasn't for Nina, we wouldn't be here and you wouldn't even have a group to try and sign."

The sound of a whirling helicopter grew louder by the moment.

"What the hell is that?" Charetta yelled.

"I don't know." Toni looked around the room for some sort of explanation.

"What's going on?" Nina asked Jamil. She had finally accepted the seat next to him.

"You'll see in a minute."

A searchlight illuminated the patio, and the helicopter flew right over it. Everyone on the third level watched as a rope was tossed out. Moments later, Xtreme slid down it onto the patio. His song "I'm Hot" started playing as soon as his feet touched the patio. The entire event was filmed and viewed on screens throughout the club. Everyone clapped and cheered as he walked over to Jamil and exchanged pounds.

"That was tight." Topaz moved to Jamil's seat so she could sit next to Nina.

"That was off the hizzy for shizzy." Nina laughed as an extended remix of "I'm Hot" continued playing.

"Xtreme's going downstairs to perform a couple of songs. Y'all wanna roll with me or watch it from the screen up here?" Jamil looked at Nina and Topaz.

"Let's roll," Topaz suggested. "I want to check him out in living color."

"Ah-ight," Nina agreed excitedly. She motioned for Sabre and the girls to join her.

"We're going downstairs to see Xtreme perform. Want to come?" Nina asked.

"Of course So Fine is coming." Jamil nodded to Buffalo who escorted them through the crowd. "And y'all are some very fine sisters."

"Look at that." Charetta pointed to the group as they left the room. "Those are my cousins. Nina's up to something with that guy. That's Jamil, and this is his party for his new label Suicide Records."

"It is?" Toni was obviously impressed.

"I did a little research. Suicide is his baby. Don't you think it's strange that Nina never mentioned it?"

"I don't know. Let's just wait and see," Toni suggested. "If he's with the girls and Nina, what's so bad about that?"

"That we're not with them. Jamil is Nina's ex-boyfriend. I caught them kissing the other night at the club after the basketball game," Charetta revealed.

"What?" Toni exclaimed. "I don't believe it."

"I saw it with my own eyes. She also gave him a copy of the girl's CD."

Toni was in shock. "But she seems so happily married with Kyle and their beautiful little daughter."

"I wouldn't have believed it if I hadn't seen it with my own eyes. If she cheats on her husband, what makes you think she won't cheat on us?" Charetta motioned for the waitress to bring her another drink.

"That is true," Toni finally agreed, but her eyes were still glued to the screen.

"What the hell are you watching?" Charetta was so irritated she barely noticed Xtreme's spectacular performance.

"Xtreme." There was a little smile on Toni's face as she watched.

"Who the hell is that?" Charetta finally looked up at the screen.

"Xtreme. Baseball's first bad boy." Toni smiled. "He sure is fine."

"Have you lost your damn mind? We could be losing millions, and you're sitting here drooling over a stupid-ass rapper. I don't believe you."

"Whatever, girl."

"You're just as mindless as that stupid-ass Nina." Charetta finished another shot of tequila. "I've got to get things back under control, and quickly."

"You thought that entrance was something?" Jamil asked the girls as Buffalo led them back up to VIP. "That's nothing compared to what I have planned for you." Jamil grinned at So Fine who squealed with excitement.

"I heard your single 'First Kiss.' Y'all sounded real tight. Me, Nina, and Topaz are old friends."

"Really?" Sabre took Jamil by the hand.

"Just like family," Jamil declared while Nina and Topaz exchanged glances.

Chapter 15

Jamil's seating arrangements were forgotten as soon as everyone returned to VIP. Xtreme wanted to sit with Jamil, and Topaz wanted to be next to Nina. So Fine wanted to be wherever Jamil and Nina were. India tried her best to accommodate everyone by having Jamil's and Xtreme's tables placed together.

Jamil held on to Nina's hand tightly while India rearranged the seating. "Come with me." He led her into a very private room with Xtreme. They sat down at a table where Xtreme poured a large amount of cocaine on the table.

"Ladies first." Xtreme smiled at Nina. "Jamil, I haven't had the pleasure of meeting this fine, sweet thing." He ran a finger gently across Nina's thigh.

"You never met, Nina, dog? I thought everyone had met the lovely Nina." Jamil ran a finger across her cheek in a way that made Nina wonder if the two men had more on their minds than doing drugs. "Xtreme, this is Nina Beaubien. Nina Beaubien, Xtreme, but his mama named him Frank. Frank Hammond."

"Hi, Frank." Nina found her voice from somewhere.

Jamil suddenly started laughing. "Dog, your mama named you after a hot dog, frankfurter."

"True dat, playa. But I'm a hot dog in more ways than one," Xtreme bragged.

"You's a wicked boy." Jamil was still laughing.

Nina watched the two of them laughing over nothing and wondered how she had gotten herself into this situation. The door opened and India walked in with a tray of tequila shots. She was surprised to see Nina sitting with the guys.

"Sit down, baby. You work too hard." Jamil took the tray from India and pulled her into his lap.

"Nina, have you met my fiancée, India?" Jamil snorted some of the cocaine and took a shot. Xtreme did the same.

"Your fiancée?" Nina was totally surprised.

"I thought we were going to keep it a secret until after the wedding, babe." India snorted some of the cocaine and followed it with a shot of tequila.

"Nina's cool, baby. Nina knows how to keep secrets and so do I. Right, Nina?" Jamil gave her a weird smile and fear raced through Nina's body.

"Right," she agreed. She hoped her voice wasn't shaking. "Congratulations, you two. When's the wedding?"

"Thanksgiving." India showed Nina her engagement ring. "So celebrate with us, girl." India handed her the rolled-up one hundred dollar bill they had used to ingest the cocaine.

Nina looked at the white powder still remaining on the table. There was a time she would have partied right along with them but she was no longer that girl. "I don't do that anymore," Nina heard herself say. "I'm a Christian now."

"That basketball player's wanna-be playboy brother ruined a perfectly good woman." Jamil looked at Nina. "I remember the day when my girl would have cleaned off this entire table with one hit."

"Well, it's been great seeing you but I really have to go now. Congratulations on the marriage. Good luck with the new CD, Frank." Nina stood, and Jamil grabbed her by the hand again.

"Not so fast, pretty lady. We still have some business to discuss." Jamil brought out So Fine's CD and put it on the table next to the drugs and alcohol. "I played it for India and my A&R guy, and they loved it." India nodded in agreement. "We still have to run it by a few other staff members but this deal looks very doable."

"Well, we have several other offers," Nina lied. "The group will be showcasing soon at the teen club at the Highlands. We'll make a decision by then."

"Showcase, huh?" Jamil looked at Nina.

"That's right." Nina wanted to shout. She really wanted to leave.

"I taught you well." Jamil looked at her with the same strange little smile. "Leave that husband of yours at home and we'll be there." Jamil looked at India and Xtreme. "But when it's all said and done So Fine will become part of Suicide."

Nina got up and tried to open the door. When it opened Buffalo was standing right in her face.

"See ya," Nina managed to whisper. She practically ran back to the table where Topaz was sitting with Charetta and Toni.

"Let's get out of here now," Nina whispered sharply.

"What happened?" Topaz demanded.

"I'll tell you later. I'm going to the rest room." Nina went downstairs so she wouldn't run into anyone. Jamil and the others came out right behind her.

"Topaz, glad to see you're still here. I just offered your girl a deal for So Fine and she turned me down." Jamil pulled out a chair next to Topaz and sat.

"Well, I'm sure she had a very good reason—" Topaz began.

"She doesn't have the authority to do that," Charetta cut in.

"We haven't met." Jamil extended a hand. "I'm Jamil and—"

"I know who you are." Charetta cut him off mid-sentence. "I'm Char Jackson, and this is Toni Mena. Two of the members of So Fine are my cousins. We co-manage the group with Nina, and we know nothing about an offer from Suicide."

India was standing right by Jamil. Her body looked as if it was ready to explode out of the little black dress she was wearing.

"Must she hover?" Charetta glared at India. She was still angry about the previous seating arrangements. There was always some hoochie in her way, and she was tired of it.

"I don't hover. I'm the chief operating officer of Suicide Records. You do know what that means, don't you?" India was used to some girl getting an attitude with her over Jamil. But ever since they had become engaged she was less tolerant.

"Bitch, I'll . . ." Charetta began.

"Ladies, ladies. There's enough of me to go around." Jamil winked at India but she sauntered off to another side of the club.

Charetta folded her arms and looked at Jamil. "He's cute," she heard Toni whisper in her ear.

"Can I get you ladies something to drink?" Jamil summoned Buffalo.

"Tequila. So you want to sign my girls?" Charetta finally smiled.

"Yep." Jamil folded his arms and looked at Charetta.

"So let's do it. Set up a meeting," Charetta suggested.

"Char, have you been in this business very long?" Jamil asked.

"No."

"The music industry is a relationship-driven business. Nina and I go back a long way, and until she agrees to sign the girls, I can't do it. Sorry, ladies." He was gone before Buffalo returned with their drinks.

Charetta stormed off to the food table and Toni followed her.

Topaz had been sitting there observing the entire conversation. "Yay, Jamil," she wanted to shout.

After what seemed like forever, Nina returned. "I was down in the limo when I finally realized you guys weren't coming out."

"You should have been here," Topaz chatted excitedly.

"What did I miss?" Nina demanded.

"Charetta told Jamil you had no authority to make a decision about the girls without her and Toni," Topaz revealed.

"She did what?" Nina clapped a hand over her mouth.

"It was like she was trying to go behind your back."

"I don't believe her," Nina fumed. "Everybody's going crazy."

"Jamil really had your back. Maybe you were wrong about the other night," Topaz offered.

"He did?" Nina was clearly shocked.

"Most definitely. I was so proud of him." Topaz grinned. "He's still our boy."

"Now I really don't understand him, especially after our little round table meeting in the back room." Nina watched Xtreme walk by with a girl on each arm. "I wonder if Frank has something to do with it," she thought out loud.

"Do with what? Who's Frank?" Topaz questioned.

"Xtreme." Nina watched him carefully. "Jamil's changed. I wonder if Frank is the reason."

"What did he do?" Topaz whispered.

Nina thought about all the drugs and alcohol on the table in the back room. She had never seen that much cocaine in her life. Was it making Jamil act like Dr. Jekyll and Mr. Hyde?

"Do you think Jamil's acting differently because he has money now?" Nina looked at Topaz.

"Jamil was already a millionaire when we met him. I'm getting something to eat. Want something?" Topaz asked.

"I couldn't eat if I wanted to." Nina managed a smile for her cousin.

Jamil had remained grounded throughout all the years of his prior success. Why the big change in behavior now? And if he was marrying India, why was he kissing her?

"It has to be the drugs." Nina shook her head and sighed.

"Nina, who are you talking to?" Topaz was back with food for both of them.

"She definitely hasn't been talking to us." Charetta sat down next to Nina. "Jamil told me you turned down a deal for So Fine."

"I did for now." Nina met Charetta's eye.

"How dare you? Five of us are crammed in a one-bedroom apartment and you're turning down record contracts?" Charetta was livid. "Everyone's not living in a Malibu estate like you and Topaz."

"Excuse you?" Topaz was in the conversation now.

Nina shook her head at Topaz. "I told him we weren't making any decisions until after the showcase. We do want to do what's right for the group, don't we?" Nina looked at Charetta and Toni.

"From now on, I want to know what's going on. And I mean everything or I'll take the girls and go on my own. Don't forget that's my family you're messing with," Charetta declared.

"And that's my one hundred thousand dollars that's paid for every single thing. Until you pay me back my investment, you aren't taking anyone anywhere," Nina reminded her. "I have a lot riding on this deal too."

"Is that so? First you tried to steal my song, now you're trying to take my group. No telling what else your little sneaky ass is up to," Charetta snarled.

"Okay, everybody. Calm down." Toni looked at all the partners. "Char, would you forget about the damn song? We wouldn't be sitting here right now having this discussion if Nina hadn't changed the song, nor would we be at this party fighting about a deal we didn't know about if it wasn't for Nina. Everyone's always saying women can't do business together. And we're supposed to be friends."

Everyone was silent for a long time.

"Well, I just want to know what's going on," Charetta mumbled.

"And you will," Nina replied.

"Wonderful." Toni smiled. "Now can we all just get along?"

Finally everyone laughed. Toni ordered a round of champagne for everyone. A waitress brought them flutes of the bubbly.

"To So Fine." Charetta raised her glass.

"To So Fine," the others chorused and tapped glasses.

"Hey," Charetta looked around VIP, "where their little asses at anyway?"

Chapter 16

The Beverly Center wasn't overly crowded Wednesday afternoon. The multi-level shopping complex sat on the edge of Beverly Hills and West Hollywood. Not only did it house some of the city's finest boutiques and stores, it was also home for a chain of movie theaters, restaurants, and a private club.

"I can't believe you waited to the last minute to find something to wear for tomorrow night." Topaz paused to look in the Louis Vuitton boutique.

"It's been crazy with the girls in rehearsals, running up to Santa Barbara to take Jade the things she needed so she could work on their outfits, hair appointments, nail appointments . . ."

"It'll all be over tomorrow." Topaz laughed.

"Actually tomorrow is only the beginning. Once we sign them, there will just be more of the same." Nina took a bottle of grape juice out of Nicki's bag and handed it to her daughter.

"I bet Jade's outfits turned out really cute." Topaz stopped in front of a shoe store.

"They are too cute. Sabre kept complaining about the faded jeans. I was telling Jade and she said to let her have a go at it. She beat the jeans with rocks, used sandpaper, and then decorated them with rhinestones, lace, and air brushing. She did T-shirts, a cap for Sky, and even put their names on them."

"She really is quite talented. I'll never forget the day Sean and I wandered into her art exhibit." Topaz smiled.

"I'm sure Sean won't either." Nina laughed.

"Isn't life funny? Whoever thought that you'd end up being Sylk Ross's sister-in-law?" Topaz laughed.

"Ha, ha, ha." Nina smirked.

"I'll be glad when this showcase is over because you aren't any fun these days." Topaz went into a store. "Let's find something for you now. Why didn't you have Jade do something for you too?"

"Because I need to look like a manager, not a teenager. Once the group takes off we're going to do a So Fine clothing line."

"Sounds cutesy." Topaz held up a dress to Nina.

"Exactly," Nina agreed. "Hey, this is kind of tight. I like it. Good work, cuz." She pinched Topaz on the cheek and went to try on the dress.

Topaz looked at some jewelry and handed Nina a pair of earrings, bracelet, and necklace to go with the dress.

"You should open your own store or something," Nina suggested. "You are so good at this. That's what's wrong with my wardrobe, I haven't had you around to do my shopping."

"Your taste has changed since you got married." Topaz pushed Baby Doll's stroller toward Bloomingdale's.

"Yeah," Nina said, laughing. "It's less hoochiefied."

"So what are your co-managers wearing?"

"I'm sure Char will have on something you gave her, and Toni will look beautiful as usual."

"Have you ever wondered if Char and Toni are an item?" Topaz looked at Nina.

"Not until Kyle mentioned it. Did you suspect something too?" Nina looked sick.

"No. Germain brought it up after the basketball game." Topaz laughed. "Do you think it's true?"

Nina shrugged. "We don't know nothing. We're just a couple of Valley girls."

"I love you in this dress." Kyle zipped Nina into her outfit and stood back to admire her.

"You do?" Nina twirled around so he could see it from all views. "Yes. Now take it off."

"Why?" She stopped brushing her hair to look at him.

"You know why." He kissed her on the back of her neck.

"Don't even think about it." Nina laughed. "I still have to put on my makeup. Go see if Rosa's finished dressing your daughter since you're feeling so frisky. And check on your brother. You know how he likes to primp. We can't be late."

Jade and Sean had arrived earlier to drive in to the city with them. Jade had surprised Nicki with an outfit similar to So Fine's and she looked adorable in the denim jeans and T-shirt. Nina had brushed Nicki's hair up into a ponytail. Sean was playing with Nicki when Nina finally made it downstairs.

"Kyle and Nina, I want to thank you guys for giving me another niece. Kyrie is so big and she's on the East Coast. Remember when Kyrie was this little, man?" Sean was grinning ear to ear as he tickled and kissed the little girl.

"No problem, man." Kyle picked up Nicki and headed for the door. "Let's do this, y'all. The limo's here and the diva can't be late."

When they arrived at the club, Nina headed straight for the dressing room where a professional makeup artist was working on the girls.

"Hi, Nina." Sabre's makeup and hair were already done. "We just love these outfits."

"I'm glad. You guys look so wonderful." Nina felt a wave of excitement rush through her as she looked at So Fine. She felt like a proud mother watching her child take his first steps.

"Is Jamil here?" Charetta stood in a corner with Toni, nursing a smoothie.

"I don't think so. I rushed back here to see how the girls were doing." Nina's tone was pleasant but cool.

"Then why don't you go out front and make sure he and any other VIPs are accommodated. That is your area of expertise." Charetta smiled but her voice didn't. Ever since their disagreement at the Suicide party, things had remained civil but reserved.

"Are you guys okay?" Nina asked the group. "Do you need anything?"

"Just some tea, Nina." The makeup artist was putting the finishing touches on Shawntay.

"Okay. I'll send some back." Nina smiled. "You guys look absolutely beautiful."

The club was practically filled with teenagers when Nina went back inside. They had given away tickets on The Beat. Nina had also managed to get several of the teen actors from the UPN and Disney Channel shows to attend. Chris Stokes, B2K's manager, had promised to drop in and check out So Fine for his production company.

Topaz and her family were walking in as Nina walked up and everyone started screaming. The Lakers' season was over but Eric still received nothing but screams as he and Keisha were seated with the others. Nina always forgot how famous her family and friends were until they were in public.

Jamil walked in with India. Buffalo was right behind them.

"Hey, you guys." Nina kissed India first and then Jamil. She smiled at Buffalo as she led them to seats near Topaz and Germain.

"Babe, can you bring our A&R guy over when he arrives?" India requested.

Toni and Charetta came out of the dressing room and Jamil motioned for them to join him. Charetta's face lit up as she switched over to the couple but the light faded just as quickly when she saw Jamil's hand on India's knee and the seven-carat diamond on her finger. Nina had just seated Latrell and a few other executives who had come out when Chris Stokes arrived.

"I'm so glad to see you." She squeezed his hand warmly as she seated him near Kyle. Nina thought B2K would be perfect label mates for So Fine.

Shanice and Flex were cohosts for the night. After Flex had hyped the audience to a deafening pitch, So Fine ran out. Nina was too nervous to sit down. She cheered as the girls danced and sang their hearts out. She felt a hand slip around her waist. Kyle was there, as usual, to offer his quiet support exactly when she needed it.

So Fine performed three songs to a screaming, cheering audience. Flex introduced the celebrities in the audience before all the teenagers went to dance. So Fine and the other teenage celebs were right on the floor with them.

"So what did you think?" Charetta asked Jamil.

"I knew I wanted them when I heard the demo. Now that I've seen them perform, I really want them." Jamil was sincere but very cool.

"Who did the choreography?" India demanded.

"I did." Toni was just as cool.

"And who wrote the songs?" Danny, the head of A&R, had finally arrived.

"I did." Charetta smiled at Jamil.

"Y'all just a regular little production company. I'm impressed." Jamil laughed. "I knew my girl Nina would come correct. I gotta go somewhere where I can get a real drink. Y'all can meet me at L'Ermitage for drinks later if you want. We be out."

Charetta watched them leave the club before she ran over to Nina. "Jamil wants us to meet him at L'Ermitage for drinks later. He . . ."

"Char, we should be pursuing Chris Stokes, B2K's manager," Nina cut in before Charetta said anything further. "It would be great to set up a meeting."

"Not interested," Charetta replied flatly.

"What?" Nina was trying to understand her logic. "Don't you think we should discuss this with Toni first?"

"We're signing with Suicide. We already made up our minds," Charetta declared triumphantly. "Jamil's expecting us for drinks. Are you coming?"

Nina was totally shocked. "I still think we need to take meetings. We have quite a few offers and want to get the best deal."

"Look, this topic is no longer open for discussion. It's only necessary for two of the three partners to agree, and that's me and Toni. You can come with us or you can stay. Either way we're signing with Suicide. And if you don't like it, we'll give you back your investment and you can step."

Chapter 17

L'Ermitage hotel in Beverly Hills was an industry haunt. It was *the* place to stay while in Los Angeles on business. Multi-million-dollar deals were made in the hotel lounge where Jamil, India, and Danny were having drinks and appetizers.

"Those kids were really good, boss." Danny bit into a chicken breast strip.

"They were," India agreed, "but I think they really need to let Sabre sing all the leads. She's really magnetic."

"I agree one thousand percent," Jamil added. "She's the one you want to watch."

"Yeah," Danny agreed. "She could be another Topaz."

"I know what you mean, Danny, but she really makes me think of Aaliyah. She has that same kind of sweetness in her vocals." India took a bite out of the apple slice in her martini.

"There will never be another Aaliyah." Jamil became very solemn. "It tears me up every time I think of what happened to her. She should be here singing."

"I'd like for Toni, So Fine's choreographer, to work with Xtreme on his next video." India decided it was time to change the subject. "I've seen her work but I wasn't sure if you'd be interested in a Latina dancer."

"If I didn't believe in diversity, old Danny boy wouldn't be part of the family." Jamil grinned as he slapped Danny on the back.

"Great." India smiled at Jamil. "It's settled then."

"So do you think So Fine is going to sign with us? I saw Chris Stokes at the showcase. I'm sure So Fine's management will definitely be interested in what he has to say. Look what he did with B2K." Danny moved the basket of chicken strips a little closer.

"Are you saying we can't do the same?" Jamil looked at Danny.

"No way, boss. I was just playing devil's advocate." Danny grinned.

Charetta and Toni walked into the hotel with So Fine and stood at the entrance of the lounge looking for Jamil.

"You were saying?" Jamil got up and went to meet the ladies.

"Hey, Jamil." Charetta greeted him as if they were old friends.

"Hello, So Fine." Jamil smiled at the girls.

"Did you like our show?" Sabre was over him and the other members of the group followed suit.

"I sure did. Why do you think we're here?" He embraced the group as he led them back to his table with Charetta and Toni following them.

"Hello, ladies." India welcomed each member of So Fine as they approached the table.

"Ladies, this is India." Jamil smiled at her fondly. "She runs Suicide Records. And this is Danny, who finds artists for the label."

"Hi." The girls could barely contain their excitement.

Jamil had a waiter bring chairs for So Fine who sat between him and India. Charetta and Toni sat with Danny.

"Is Nina on her way?" Jamil signaled for the waiter.

"Nina won't be joining us tonight. By the time she takes the limo back to Malibu and drives back in, she thought it would be too late." Charetta accepted a menu from the waiter.

"That's too bad." Jamil took out his two-way and typed in a message. Moments later it signaled a response and he opened it. "Nina sends her regrets."

Charetta sighed with relief. She opened her eyes to see India's focused on her.

"I like your ring, India." Sabre, sitting between Jamil and India, relished the attention. "It's beautiful."

"Thanks, babe." India smiled and held out her hand so Sabre could take a closer look. "Can I try it on?" Sabre asked timidly.

"Sure." India pulled the ring off her slender finger and slipped it on Sabre's.

"Look, Sky." Sabre extended her hand so Sky could see the ring. "It fits perfectly."

"Give that back," Charetta ordered.

Sabre rolled her eyes as she took off the diamond and put it back on India's hand.

"That's okay, babe." India tilted Sabre's head so she could look into her eyes. "When you become a very famous singer, the right guy will come along and put something twice this size on your finger."

Sabre relaxed and smiled. "Thanks, India."

"So, Jamil, was there something you wanted to discuss with us about the girls?" Charetta asked.

"We want 'em." Jamil smiled.

"I'm listening." Charetta set her empty glass on the table.

"This is an opportunity for you guys to ask any questions you might have, get to know the three of us a little better," Jamil explained.

"Look, let's cut to the chase." Charetta looked at Jamil. "What kind of money are you talking about?"

"We have some figures in mind . . ." Jamil began.

"But we won't be discussing any of that until Nina's present," India finished.

Charetta was ready to explode when Toni calmly patted her on the knee.

"Toni, I really loved your choreography. I've seen your work. We're shooting a new video for Xtreme, and I'd love to put you on the project." India smiled warmly at Toni.

"Really? That's wonderful. How soon do you want to get started?" Toni asked excitedly.

"Wait," Charetta interrupted. "I thought this meeting was about So Fine . . ."

"It is. Jamil told you we were here for questions," India replied. "Obviously you don't have any, so I moved on to take care of some other business so the night wouldn't be a complete waste of time."

"How much money? That isn't a valid question." Charetta was embarrassed by India's response. She felt stupid.

"I told you we would discuss that when Nina was present. It makes no sense to go over it twice." India sat back in her chair and folded her arms. Jamil's arm was around the back of her chair, and without thinking he began playing with her braids.

"Jamil, you invited us here just to socialize?" Charetta was steaming.

"Char, I told you the other night that this business is built on relationships. This was your opportunity to build one." Jamil signaled the waiter for the check.

"And you just blew it." India stood and Danny followed suit.

"Wait," Sabre pleaded. "Are we still going to get a record deal?" She looked at Jamil and India.

"I don't know, sweetheart." Jamil kissed the girls and they left.

"You certainly handled that well." Toni looked at Charetta.

"What just happened?" Sabre asked. "How come they left?"

Buffalo drove Jamil and India back to Encino in the Bentley.

"How'd I do, boss?" India tried to suppress her laughter.

"You certainly scared the crap out of Char." Jamil laughed

"Let's hope so. She's going to be a handful. Are you sure you want to get into this?" India smiled into his eyes.

"I'm sure she'll be a lot more cooperative now, and we can probably get them to sign for a lot less money." Jamil yawned.

"Why don't you set up a meeting with Nina tonight for tomorrow morning before they go with Chris Stokes since you're so set on this deal?" India cuddled up beside him. "Char won't tell Nina a thing about tonight. She won't want Nina to know she blew it."

"Yeah." Jamil laughed as he took out his two-way and typed in a message to Nina. Moments later the pager blinked, signaling a reply. "She said they'll be there. How did I wind up so lucky?" Jamil kissed her gently and smiled. "Beauty and brains."

"I'm the lucky one." India kissed his cheek. "I can't wait until Thanksgiving, babe."

"I bet I can't wait more than you. India, you and I are going to rule the world."

"I know because we make such a lovely team." India sighed. "Such a wonderful, lovely team."

Chapter 18

Everyone was silent as Toni drove through Beverly Hills to West-wood. The Honda felt cramped and small compared to the limousine they had ridden in to the Kodak Center. Toni unlocked the door to the apartment, and they solemnly filed inside. There were no giggles and whispers as the girls undressed and rolled out their sleeping bags.

"I'm tired of this dumb old sleeping bag and I'm tired of sleeping on the floor," Shawntay complained. "Damn."

"We would have had a record deal if Char hadn't messed things up with her big mouth." Sabre pulled on a Lakers T-shirt.

"What did your little smart ass say?" Charetta stood over Sabre who had just gotten into her sleeping bag.

"I said you messed up our record deal," Sabre repeated through gritted teeth.

"Tonight is not the night, Miss Thang." Charetta gave Sabre a look of death but she just didn't have the energy to get into it with her. She could just taste that deal . . . but someone was always getting between Charetta and the success she desired. First Nina and now India. She turned around, went into the bedroom, and shut the door.

"I blew it, Toni. I blew it." Charetta flopped on the bed and looked up at her roommate. "Suicide Records invited us for drinks. It was right there in the palm of our hands. I could taste it. You know . . .

I've been looking at houses. With the advance money we could lease one so the girls could have bedrooms and we could get a bigger car." The tears rolled down Charetta's cheeks. "I'm tired, Toni."

"Oh, Char . . ." Toni pulled her friend into her arms. "It's not over yet. Jamil didn't say he didn't want the group."

"But India did. Damn her. I get so sick of women like that." Charetta wiped her tears with her hand, and Toni went into the bathroom for tissue.

"Women like what?"

"The Ninas, Topazes, and Indias of the world. Women who just have to show up and look beautiful and they get everything handed to them on a silver platter, and they've never had to work hard for anything in their lives." Charetta sniffed.

"So what are you going to do about it? Are you going to sit here and cry or stay in the fight and kick some ass?" Toni wiped Charetta's tears.

"Kick some ass," Charetta mumbled.

"That's my girl." Toni kissed her.

"What did I ever do to deserve you?"

"Take me in when my father kicked me to the curb?" Toni laughed.

"Thank goodness he did. He saved you from becoming a mindless member of the rich and beautiful. 'See my diamond ring, my lovely mansion, and my beautiful clothes that a stupid man bought me for allowing him to tell me what to do,' " Charetta said in a prissy voice.

"You're crazy." Toni laughed. "And all those women you mentioned work very hard."

"Please."

"It's nice to have a man around and the sex can be great," Toni continued. "You should try it sometimes."

"Highly overrated."

"That Jamil is so cute . . . I think you guys would make a great couple if you ever stopped fighting long enough to get to know each other. He's from Compton like you."

"And how did you find all this out, Montana?"

"You're the one always saying I never read, so I thought I'd do a little research. The Internet has a wealth of information. I thought I'd read up on Suicide since you are so determined to sign with them."

"Well, I guess you better keep on reading. See what you can find out about Chris Stokes."

The telephone rang and Toni reached down to answer it.

"Who is it?" Charetta demanded after she watched Toni listen intently for several minutes.

"Okay," she finally said and hung up the phone. "That was Nina."

"What did *she* want?" Charetta asked, but she really wasn't interested.

"She said . . ." Toni started hyperventilating.

"What did she say, girl? What did she say?"

"She said we have a meeting with Jamil, India, and Danny at ten in the morning. They're making us an offer," Toni screamed.

Sabre, who had been listening at the bedroom door, got back into her sleeping bag and pretended to be asleep just as Charetta and Toni ran out of the bedroom screaming.

"Wake up, you guys. We did it. We're going to sign with Suicide Records." Charetta gave them all a hug.

"For real, Char?" Sabre rubbed her eyes.

"Yes." Charetta sat on the floor with them. "I'm sorry if it seemed like I was a little hard on you guys, but I had to be tough and now it's paid off. And I'm going to be even tougher if I have to because you're winners, all of you. And we're going to be number one."

They met Nina in the lobby of the Music Group building.

"All right, you guys, let's do this." Nina smiled as she gave each girl a hug. Charetta allowed them to dress differently for once. They rode in silence up to the sixth floor.

"Char, please let Nina do all the talking," Toni whispered in her ear as they got off the elevator.

They were only in the reception area for a few minutes when India came out and escorted them inside. She took the girls into Jamil's office and led the others into the conference room where Jamil and Danny were seated.

"Ladies, good morning." Jamil stood as they entered.

"Good morning." Nina looked fabulous in a white pantsuit. Charetta and Toni were silent.

"Okay, let's do this." India looked at Danny.

"We'd like to offer So Fine a deal for three CDs but the other two are contingent upon how well the first one sells," Danny explained. The managers said nothing so he continued. "Jamil's going to oversee the songwriting and the production. Don't get me wrong, we like what you've done and this may very well turn into a co-production effort."

"Our business affairs department has outlined the financial terms of the offer in this deal memo. You'll see we've included figures for marketing and video. And the bottom figure is what we're offering as an advance." India handed them each a sheet of paper and the ladies read them over. "And ladies . . . this is our final and only offer."

"Can we have a few minutes to discuss this?" Nina smiled at India.

"Sure." Jamil stood. "Take as long as you want."

"This looks reasonable." Charetta looked at Nina.

"I think we can get a lot more." Nina pushed the paper away.

"Aren't these things supposed to be negotiable?" Toni looked at Charetta and Nina.

"We'll renegotiate after our first album," Charetta declared. "But we can't pay Nina back out of our advance. We won't have anything for ourselves."

"I guess you can't get rid of me that easily." Nina looked at Charetta.

"I say we take it. What's your vote, Toni?" Charetta looked at Toni.

Toni looked at the paper. She knew her decision was crucial. She felt the group was worth more money but for some reason Charetta was determined to work with Suicide. Should she follow her business instincts that were telling her to hold out for more or give in to the wishes of her friend?

"Toni, we're waiting for your answer." Charetta was becoming impatient.

"Looks like we're signing with Suicide." Toni smiled, hoping she had done the right thing.

"Why are you guys so set on this company?" Nina looked at the partners. "We can get so much more."

"And why are you so against it? Is there something you're not telling us, Nina?" Charetta met her eye. "I thought you and Jamil were such good friends. I'd want to work with my old friend. Wouldn't you, Toni?"

"Friendship is one thing, business is another," Nina fired back.

"There's no reason to get so bent out of shape." Charetta smiled, very aware that she had pressed some button to disturb Nina's cool demeanor.

Nina left the room and went to find the others so they could complete the deal.

"That girl is hiding something and I'm determined to find out what it is," Charetta whispered to Toni.

Chapter 19

Nina wasn't exactly sure what she was feeling when she began the drive out to Malibu. She yearned for the first glimpse of the ocean to soothe her weary soul. She fished through her CD box, and when she couldn't find anything she wanted to hear she pressed the button to see what was in the player. Donnie McClurkin's "Stand" filled her ears. Keisha had given Nicki a bunch of CDs, and this had quickly become one of her daughter's favorites. The vibrant blue ocean finally came into view as the Santa Monica Freeway turned into Pacific Coast Highway, and Nina felt herself relax as she pressed the repeat button on the CD.

"Hi, honey." Nina was glad to see Kyle in the family room when she arrived. She left her briefcase on the counter and joined him on the sofa where he was typing on a laptop.

"Hey, boss lady." He paused to kiss her. "How did everything go?"

"It went." She sighed. "We just signed So Fine to Suicide."

"What? I thought you said you guys had some much better offers."

"We did, but they weren't interested." Nina sighed and kicked off her shoes.

"I don't know if I like this." Kyle focused on Nina.

"Like what?" Nina looked up, expecting to see Kyle's dazzling smile and twinkling eyes.

"You working so closely with that tired wanna-be thug."

"Kyle! I don't believe you. Tell me you're joking." Nina laughed as she put her arms around his shoulders.

"Do you see me laughing?"

Nina couldn't remember, if ever, when she had seen him so serious. She sat back on the sofa and took a good look at him. "You're serious, aren't you?"

Kyle's only response was more silence. His eyes seemed to look right into her soul.

The thought of Jamil kissing her the night of the basketball game made her sick, and Nina felt like crying. She could never tell her husband what had happened. "Do you know how much I love you?"

He pulled her into his arms. "Yes, I know. But I still don't like it."

"You know my business is with the girls, baby, not Jamil."

"You're still going to be around him, and he might try to take advantage of you or something, and I'd have to hurt him."

"Kyle, you don't have a violent bone in your body." Nina finally laughed

"You never know what a real man's capable of when you mess with his woman or his children. Never forget that God created us to protect."

The telephone rang and Nina welcomed the disturbance. Things were starting to get a little too deep.

"I forgot to tell you Karla's been calling all morning for you. She said she really needed to talk to you."

"Thanks, baby." Nina grabbed the phone on the third ring. "Hey, Karla."

"I thought that might be her." Kyle remarked.

Nina took the phone up to her bedroom so she wouldn't disturb Kyle and to change.

"What are you doing, Nina?" Karla, Nina's sister-in-law, demanded.

"Changing my clothes and talking to you." Nina laughed.

"No, that's not what I mean. Are you involved in some kind of music venture?"

"Yes. We just signed the paperwork this morning. Did Kyle tell you?"

"No. I was praying for you this morning, and the Lord told me."

"God told you what?" Nina sat down on the bed in her underwear.

"The Lord told me you were involved in some sort of music venture and it's evil . . . demonic."

"Evil . . . I don't understand."

"Nina, I saw darkness."

"Darkness? Karla what are you talking about?"

"Spiritual darkness. Do you know what that means?"

"No."

"Okay let me back up and see how I can explain this to you."

"Please, because I don't know what you're talking about."

"Nina, your spirit is the part of you that comes from God. Your soul is what makes you Nina. It contains your will, personality, and your emotions. Your spirit and soul live in a house, your body."

"Okay, but what has all that got to do with music?" Nina scooted up on the bed and cut off the television she had just turned on.

"I wanted to give you some information on the spirit so you can understand what I'm going to tell you."

"Okay." Nina reached over to the side of the bed for the notepad and pen she kept in her nightstand. She saw her Bible and picked it up too. With all the craziness she hadn't spent as much time reading as she should.

"Now God is a spirit. There was a time when there were no humans, just angels and the Godhead."

Nina quickly began taking notes.

"Lucifer was the most beautiful angel God ever created. Girl, he was fine. He was also really smart. In heaven there's constant worship and praise to God, and Lucifer was in charge of it. That's where the music comes in. Are you with me so far?"

"Un-huh." Nina was trying her best to write down every word.

"So Lucifer was so full of himself he wanted to be even more important than God, so he rebelled against God and got a third of the angels to go along with him."

"Wow."

"Now when Lucifer tried to make himself higher than God he was kicked out of heaven and those angels with him. And Lucifer's name changed to Satan."

"Is there a book where I can read all of this?" Nina stopped writing so she could listen.

"It's all in the Bible."

"Okay."

"Now remember these were spirit beings. Now man . . . human beings are God's most prized creation. And Satan hates man because of how special man is to God."

"Karla, this is all wonderful but I really don't understand what it has to do with music." Nina was becoming frustrated.

"Well, there's music on earth now and Satan wants all of it to glorify him. He's still trying to take over. He wants to lead as many people to hell, and one of the ways he does it is through deception—letting people think something is harmless when it's not. There is a lot of deception in the music industry."

"Oh my God. Are you serious?" Nina sat straight up in her bed. "Do these people know what they're doing?"

"Some do but most of them don't. There's a spirit behind everything. That's why I explained all of that to you. The spirit world is very real. Everything is influenced by something in the spirit realm. It's either God or Satan. There's no gray area."

"So you really think I've gotten myself involved with something evil?"

"I know you have. I told you I saw darkness. What's the name of the company?"

"Suicide Records," Nina replied quietly.

"Oh my God. Nina, how could you?" Karla was very concerned. "What is suicide?"

"A record company."

"No, what does it mean?"

"It's when someone kills himself . . . it's self murder." Nina clasped a hand to her mouth. "I never liked the name of the company."

"That was God trying to warn you then and you didn't listen."

"But it's a friend of mine's company, and he's really a good person. He got into hip-hop and we thought he named the company Suicide because he thought it was cool. That's the image, rough and hard, but no one's thinking that they're doing something evil, they just want to make some money," Nina explained.

"That's why it's deception . . . they think it's harmless but it's not. Think about the violence, drugs, illicit sex, degrading lyrics, and murders that are a part of this music."

"But not all music, and Jamil's not like that. Neither are Char, Toni, and the girls. They're good people who just want to make some money."

"Are they Christians?"

Nina was silent for several minutes before she answered. She thought about all the drugs and alcohol she had just seen the other night at Jamil's party and cringed. "I don't think so."

"Well, it looks like God has given you an assignment—to help your friends. Don't sign anymore contracts with these people, Nina. I hope you can help them see the light because anyone attached to suicide has a death wish."

"Karla, what am I supposed to do?" Nina was terrified.

"First of all, don't be afraid. God will always protect you. And pray . . . cover yourself with the Blood of Jesus. Satan is afraid of It. And make sure you pray for Nicki and Kyle. Check out KRS-One too. Now that's rap inspired by God, and he's representing the culture righteously."

"KRS-One? Karla . . ."

"I gotta go. I have to pick your niece up from basketball practice. Miss Kyrie's determined to go to the WNBA."

"KRS-One?" Nina repeated.

"*The Temple of Hip Hop.* Go to the music store. Ask Kyle . . . He knows. I gotta go."

Nina slowly hung up the phone and thought about everything Karla had said. Her mind was in a thousand places. She picked up the phone to call Topaz and dialed Keisha.

"Hey, girl. What's up?" Keisha answered.

"Keisha! I thought I was calling Topaz." Nina was a wreck.

"What's wrong, Nina? I can hear it in your voice," Keisha demanded.

"Karla just called me and told me about some things I was doing. She said God told her and then she told me about all this crazy stuff going on in the music industry."

"Oh yeah. Karla is on it. When something is up with someone in her family, God shows it to her. The girl is a prophet. If she says something's going to happen, it happens. And you're part of her family now. Did she tell you about something specific?" Keisha asked.

"Not exactly. She was just explaining some things. I wrote a lot of it down. Keisha, I can't believe my friends are doing anything bad. They're good people trying to make music and make some money." Nina was on the verge of tears.

"That's what makes it so bad. A lot of innocent people get into things because they've been deceived—they think it's harmless," Keisha explained.

"That's exactly what Karla said."

"That's my girl." Keisha laughed. "And she's usually right. So what did you do?"

"Signed a deal with Suicide Records."

"Nina, Suicide? Why would you even want to be involved with something with a name like that?" Keisha demanded. "Words are very powerful. That's why you have to watch what you say. You can speak things into existence."

"Now you tell me . . . remember the guy I was dating before I married Kyle?" Nina was shivering in her underwear.

"Jamil?"

"Yes."

"What a sweetie . . . I felt a little sorry for him when you kicked him to the curb for Kyle." Keisha laughed.

"Suicide is Jamil's label. I helped him put together the business plan when we were dating, and you know he produced all of Topaz's albums."

Keisha inhaled deeply. "Nina, no. Please tell me that's not true. Not Jamil."

"I wish I could, Keisha. I wish I could." Nina rubbed her head. She was really stressed out.

"You have to talk to him, Nina. Pray for Jamil, and I'll pray too."

"Do you really think he's in some kind of trouble?" Nina was still hopeful.

"It's nothing to play with or take lightly."

Nina clicked off the cordless phone and laid it on the bed. She got up and went inside the huge walk-in closet she shared with her husband with the weight of the world on her shoulders. Nina carefully hung up her pantsuit and finished undressing. The room was too quiet so she turned on the television for a distraction, but it didn't begin to drown out Karla's words, which were still echoing loudly throughout her mind.

Chapter 20

Jamil rarely attended music video shoots but Xtreme and the director wanted him to be in this one. A large portion of Xtreme's video had been shot in Las Vegas with Xtreme and Jamil as high rollers in a casino. Another segment would feature Xtreme and Vegas showgirls. It would be shot on the rooftop of the Mirage. Toni, the choreographer and featured dancer, was also going to be in the video.

Although it was night, it was still extremely hot, and all the lighting equipment kicked the temperature up a few more notches. A makeup artist touched up Toni's red lipstick while a hairdresser worked on a section of her thick black hair with a brush and a can of hair spray.

Jamil and Xtreme were sitting in director's chairs wearing sunglasses. Xtreme had on a headset listening to a CD of Charetta's songs. Buffalo was sitting behind them under a fan.

"Yo, dog. This is dope." Xtreme nudged Jamil and handed him the headset.

Jamil put on the headphones and listened. "Damn, girl. You got skills."

Charetta sat in another director's chair appearing uninterested, as if she hadn't heard Jamil's comments as she watched the stylist slide a pair of black sunglasses over Toni's eyes. An animal trainer brought up one of the hotel's famous white baby tigers on a diamond leash as the stylist slid a full-length white mink coat over Toni's black satin Victoria's Secret lingerie.

"Yo, playa." Xtreme was nudging Jamil again. "Check baby out." He nodded at Toni who strutted up and down the roof in a pair of black stilettos to Xtreme's song.

"I didn't know Toni had it goin' on like that." Jamil continued listening to Charetta's music through the headphones.

Playback stopped and the director called Xtreme to the set. He was going to rap while Toni walked past him. He was wearing a black satin robe and silk boxer shorts. His signature diamond encrusted pendant dangled from his neck.

India came up on the roof and sat in Xtreme's chair next to Jamil. "I got that studio time you wanted. You guys can go in as soon as we wrap here."

"Thanks, babe." Jamil smiled and stroked her face. "How are my So Fine girls doing?"

"We just got back from watching the light show at the Bellagio and Fatburgers. They're at the pool now. They wanted to go swimming. I think I'll join them if you don't need me at the studio." India went to get a bottle of water out of the cooler.

"No, I've got things covered there. I just hate to think of you stuck in the hotel baby-sitting." Jamil wiped at a smudge on Xtreme's Discman.

"It's cool, babe. It's part of the territory when you sign underage artists." India laughed. "Maybe we'll have a pajama party and do each other's toes or something, which reminds me . . ." India took out her Palm Pilot. "I've got to find the girls a tutor. School will be starting soon."

"Thanks, babe." Jamil planted a kiss on her cheek. "You're the best. Char's got some really great beats and rhymes. Want to take a listen?"

Charetta focused on India, waiting to hear her response.

"No thanks. Songs and the studio are your domain and you always know best." India watched as a group of strippers dressed like showgirls joined Toni and Xtreme. "I only hope her musical abilities exceed her management skills because those suck." India watched the video shoot a few minutes more before she disappeared off the set as quickly as she had came.

"That's a wrap," the director yelled and the music ended. The strippers cast seductive glances at Xtreme and Jamil as the women left the roof. Xtreme took his spot next to Jamil while Toni slipped out of the stilettos and the mink. "I'm heading back to LA tonight. I want to get started editing so I can have something for you to look at on Monday."

"That'll work." Jamil stood and the young men traded pounds. "I'll be back late Sunday night. We're going to chill in Vegas for the weekend."

"I wouldn't rush right back but I've got a crazy schedule. This video is going to be hot, Xtreme." The director grinned.

"I'm hot." Xtreme laughed and stood to shake hands with the famous video director. "Thanks for making me look good, playa."

Toni came and stood next to Charetta. She held a bottle of chilled water to her chest, enjoying the coolness against her skin. "Come on, Char. Let's get out of here. It's hot."

"Oh, to be that bottle of water." Xtreme grinned and Toni smiled back.

"I'm going to the studio with the guys to lay down some tracks for one of my songs. Why don't you come with us?" Charetta suggested.

"Yeah, why don't you?" Xtreme grinned.

"What about the girls?" Toni looked at Charetta.

"India's with them," Jamil offered.

"So there's no reason you can't come with us unless you don't want to." Xtreme was too charming.

"Okay." Toni grinned. "We'll meet you in the lobby."

India and the girls settled down on pillows in front of the television in her suite.

"Can we order a pizza, India?" Shawntay smiled as the others chorused yes.

"You guys are hungry again?" India looked at their faces as they nodded in agreement.

"Okay, eat now but your diet will change when you start working out with a trainer." India placed an order for the pizza and hung up the telephone.

"Trainer?" Sabre stood and looked in the mirror. "I don't need a trainer. I already look good."

"And we want to keep you looking that way, Miss Thing." India pulled Sabre away from the mirror. "Now let's do your toes while we wait on the pizza. You're California girls now, and we have rules." India took out a box of various colors of nail polish.

"What are they?" Sky sat down next to her on the floor as India placed cotton balls and remover on a tray.

"We never—and I mean never—wear open-toed shoes or go barefoot without our toes done." India smiled.

"Oh," the girls chorused.

Sabre sat down on a pillow in front of India and stuck out her foot. "Me first, and I want this blue." She picked out a bottle of polish and handed it to India.

"Come on, Shawntay, I'll do yours," Sky offered.

There was very little conversation as the toe polishers concentrated on their work.

"Your ring sure does sparkle, India." Sabre watched India's hands move as she polished her toenails. "Did Jamil give you that?"

"Huh?" India looked up from what she was doing and saw Sabre grinning like a Cheshire cat.

"Yeah, India." Sky finished Shawntay's last toenail and put the cap on the polish. "Dish . . . we know Jamil gave you that ring."

"I don't know what you guys are talking about." India tried to suppress a smile as she spread clear polish over Sabre's blue toenails.

"Yes, you do." Sabre giggled and the others joined in.

"Okay, but you guys have to promise not to say anything to anyone . . . even your managers . . ." India began.

"We promise," the girls chorused.

"No, I can't tell you guys." India laughed. "Come on, Sky. What color would you like?"

"India." Sabre hated to hear no. "You're telling us. Get her, y'all."

The girls grabbed the bed pillows and started to beat India with them. India did a pretty good job of defending herself but the three teenagers eventually got the best of her.

"All right," India yelled. "Truce. I give up already."

"Are you going to tell us?" Sabre drew back her pillow ready to begin the fight again.

"Yes." India sat on the floor and looked at the girls." "Yes, Jamil gave me the ring."

"Are you guys getting married?" Sabre grinned.

"Yes." India smiled. "At Thanksgiving."

"Can we come?" Sky demanded.

"We'll see." India smiled. "Now what color polish would you like, Sky?"

"Pink . . . with the glitter," Sky replied. "Can I try on your ring?"

"Sure." India twisted off the ring and handed it to Sky. "Just tell me one thing, how did you guys know?"

"Girls can always tell when a boy likes somebody," Sabre declared knowingly as she tried on the black diamond and admired it on her finger.

At the studio, Jamil was fascinated as he watched Charetta at work. "Char, I've got to hand it to you, you got mad skills. I never knew a female who could put it down the way you do."

"Compton in the hizouse, Jamil. I take that as a huge compliment coming from you." Charetta looked up from the mixing board and smiled.

"Yeah," Xtreme agreed. "I heard at least three cuts that I want on my album."

"I thought your album was done." Charetta looked at the guys.

"Not quite." Jamil punched some buttons on the mixing board. "We were looking for something to give it an edge and you brought the noise, home girl. I didn't know you grew up in the big C. No wonder you got skills."

Charetta turned to smile at Toni who was smiling at Xtreme.

"We've got the studio until tomorrow afternoon. We'll finish the rest back in Cali."

"Tomorrow afternoon? I'm getting sleepy." Charetta yawned.

"Playa, hook a sister up." Jamil looked at Xtreme.

"Cool, dog. I was ready for a little sumpin', sumpin' myself." Xtreme went over to the sofa in front of the mixing board and picked up a magazine. He took out a bag of cocaine and spread it all over the magazine. "Ladies."

Toni looked at Charetta who grinned as she went over to the table. "I know y'all brought some good stuff." She sniffed several lines and handed the hundred-dollar bill she had used to sniff the drugs to Toni. "Come on, girl. One hit of this and you'll really be able to dance."

Toni timidly sniffed a few lines. "Wow." She smiled at Xtreme who was sitting beside her.

He did several lines and then pulled her into his arms and kissed her. "I've been wanting to do that since the first time I saw you."

"Hey, hey, hey." Jamil walked over to the table. "Get a room."

"I've got one." Xtreme laughed.

"Baby ain't goin' nowhere. Now let's do this," Jamil declared as he returned to his chair in front of the mixing board.

Together, Jamil and Charetta laid down the tracks for the song while Toni and Xtreme kissed and laughed until he went in to put down vocals.

They were all tired when they returned to the hotel around four in the afternoon. They had put in almost thirty-six hours of nonstop work between the video shoot and the recording studio. All of their rooms were together on the same floor. Toni waved good-bye to Charetta as Xtreme led her into his suite.

"Later, Char." Jamil smiled before he opened the door and went into his suite. "Good work."

"Later, JW," Charetta called back. "He is cute," she whispered to herself as she opened the door and went into suite she and Toni shared with the girls. It was empty. She knew the girls were probably at the pool, riding roller coasters, or exploring one of the other surrounding hotels. It was late afternoon and she was wide awake. She got into bed and wondered what Jamil was doing.

Toni said we'd make a cute couple. Maybe she's right. It was so great working with him.

Charetta lay there about an hour, unable to sleep. For the first time she felt lonely without the girls or Toni around. She got up and dressed and decided to go downstairs rather than lay in bed in the room alone. She opened the door and was just about to step into the hallway when the door to Jamil's room opened. Charetta watched him look up and down the hall and then walk to India's room where he opened the door with a key and went inside.

"I should have known *she* had gotten her hooks in him." Charetta sighed unhappily as she closed her door and leaned against it.

Chapter 21

Charetta had been doing her house hunting over the Internet ever since the girls arrived in Los Angeles. It had been quite obvious the first night when five females were forced to share a small one-bedroom apartment. She had always frowned at the living room without furniture but when it became a bedroom for the girls, she was glad there was no furniture to rearrange. She looked at Sabre's pink Barbie Doll sleeping bag still spread out on the floor. With the advance check Jamil had given them for signing So Fine everyone would have a bedroom and a bed to sleep in.

Nina had refused any payment on her investment into the management partnership. They had also seen very little of her lately except when she had to sign a document. Even then, she would request that it be faxed or brought by messenger to the house. With the girls in school, dance lessons, and singing lessons, very few real management decisions were being made. Charetta had been paid handsomely for her work on Xtreme's CD. She was listening to previously written songs and writing new material for the So Fine CD.

Charetta glanced at her watch. Toni had left her the car and she had to pick up everyone from the rehearsal hall. They were waiting outside when she arrived.

"Can we go to McDonald's?" Sky demanded as soon as they were in the car. "I'm hungry."

"No, Taco Bell," Shawntay protested.

"Yuck. I can't stand Mexican food." Sabre made a face.

"I beg your pardon?" Toni tried not to smile as she looked at Sabre in the rearview mirror.

"Not your Mexican food, Toni." Sabre smiled.

"Un-huh."

"We don't have time to eat right now. I'll take you guys for Thai food after our appointment."

"What appointment?" Toni looked at Charetta.

"You'll see." Charetta smiled as she pulled up in front of a house.

"Why are you stopping here?" Toni asked. They had been so busy discussing food that no one noticed that Charetta had taken Riverside Drive into a residential neighborhood instead of the Ventura Freeway, which would take them back to Westwood.

"I made an appointment with the owners of the house. Let's see if we all like it," Charetta declared excitedly.

Car doors slammed as everyone got out and looked at the well-kept, pink two-story house. It was a quiet area of Van Nuys within walking distance of Ventura Boulevard, not far from the Fashion Square Galleria.

"It kind of looks like Topaz's house." Sabre looked like an excited child.

"Not hardly." Charetta grunted.

"It's the same color," Sabre pointed out.

The lawn was nicely kept, and there was a sprinkling of flowers around a lemon tree in the front yard.

"We're going to have a house with our very own lemon tree," Sky said as Charetta rang the doorbell. "Just wait until I tell everybody back in Brooklyn."

An elderly gentleman answered the door. "Five beautiful young ladies at my door. I must be in heaven." He smiled as he welcomed them inside. "And you three must be the Supremes."

"We're So Fine," Sabre informed him proudly.

"Indeed you are." He grinned. "I'm Martin Alper. You can call me Marty."

"Hello, Marty. I'm Char. We spoke on the phone." She immediately fell in love with the beautiful peg-and-grove hardwood floors in the living room. "Can we see the rest of the house?"

"Sure." He led them through the dining room into a blue-and-white kitchen with white marble floors. There were four bedrooms, a family room, and a swimming pool. The deep end was only eight feet but it was still a pool. Marty's wife had recently passed away, and he was going to live with his daughter in Phoenix. He was anxious to leave and would lease them the house at a great price for one year.

"What do you guys think?" Charetta asked as they huddled outside by the pool. Two of you girls are going to have to share a bedroom. Everything with five bedrooms was out of our price range."

"Okay," they all agreed excitedly.

"It's better than a sleeping bag." Shawntay rubbed her backside. "I'm tired of sleeping on the floor."

Within two weeks Marty had packed up and the girls were moved in. Charetta had suggested the teenagers pull straws for the bedroom. She purchased bunk beds for one room and a full-size bed for the other. Sabre, of course, pulled the longest straw, which entitled her to her own room.

"I thought you were going to room with me." Sky sat on Sabre's bed gazing at the comforter with matching drapes and posters on the wall. Sabre had gone to the paint store, picked out an antique rose paint, and painted the walls by herself.

"I'm not sleeping in a bunk bed." Sabre sat in front of an antique dressing table she had found at a yard sale around the corner.

"But it's not fair. Everyone's rooms look so nice but ours." Sky and Shawntay pouted as they watched everyone putting their rooms together.

"I bought those bunk beds on purpose—to keep you guys hungry and working so you'll make enough money to buy your own houses." Charetta paused in the doorway. "You did a nice job in here, Sabre."

Charetta had purchased herself a waterbed and Toni a canopy bed. They both had income from sources other than So Fine's project, so the portion of the advance designated for living expenses went to the girls. The teenagers had a separate phone line and two-way pagers instead of cell phones. The record company leased a PT Cruiser for the group and arranged for them to take driving lessons so they could drive themselves to appointments.

"Y'all got it goin' on up in here." Xtreme was their first house guest and Toni was giving him the grand tour. "I'm moving in. It's a perfect location. You're not far from the office. It's not far from Jamil."

"Where does Jamil live?" Toni asked casually. She had cooked up one of her Mexican fiestas. There was sangria—red wine with slices of orange and lemon and crushed ice—with chips, salsa, guacamole, and tacquitos for appetizers. She had used fruit from trees on the property. Before anyone could think of being full Toni served tacos, enchiladas, refried beans with cheese and onions, and a huge salad. They ate outside by candlelight next to the pool.

"In Encino. Damn, girl." Xtreme unbuttoned his pants and stretched out on the grass. "I didn't know you could cook like that. You're the first woman I ever met who could cook. I'd take you home to meet my mother but she lives in Chicago. I'm going to marry you, Toni."

Everyone laughed as they watched him lying in the grass. Toni sat down next to him and he pulled her into his arms.

"Come on, you guys. Let's take everything inside and give them some privacy." Charetta picked up the pan of remaining enchiladas and the teenagers brought in the other things.

"That would be tight if Xtreme marries Toni. Then we'd have another wedding to go to." Sky smiled as she dumped the disposable plates in the garbage.

"Who else is getting married?" Charetta covered the leftovers with aluminum foil.

"India . . ." Sabre stepped on Sky's foot hard as Shawntay poked her in the ribs.

"India? Who's India marrying?" Charetta rearranged things in the refrigerator in order to accommodate all the leftover food.

"Nobody. We're going to watch Queen Latifah's movie." Sky and the others disappeared out of the kitchen.

"Your mouth is so big," Sabre scolded once they were in the family room. "I'm never telling you any of my secrets."

"Yeah, Sky." Shawntay put the DVD in the player and turned on the TV Charetta and Toni had purchased. "After we promised we wouldn't tell."

"I didn't say who she was marrying, and I've never told any of y'all's secrets," Sky declared.

"Only because we got you out of the kitchen before you told it," Sabre whispered loudly.

Charetta stood in the doorway listening and tiptoed back into the kitchen when she ascertained the teenagers were no longer talking.

Toni and Xtreme had gone into Toni's bedroom. She turned on some salsa music, and they were having a great time while she tried to teach him to dance the salsa. They couldn't stop laughing because he either turned the wrong way or mixed up what foot stepped where. When Xtreme tripped her trying to do a turn, they both fell onto her bed laughing.

"You're hopeless," Toni said.

"You're beautiful." He pulled her into his arms and kissed her.

They lay there in the moonlit room enjoying the music and the aromatherapy candles Toni had lit.

Xtreme sat up and pulled a bag of cocaine out of his pocket. "Now we can really get this party started." He poured some out on a magazine and ingested it.

"Sweetie, why do you do that?" Toni stroked the side of his face while she spoke.

"Do what?"

"That." Toni pointed at the white powder on the magazine.

"Because I like it. I guess. I never really thought about it." Xtreme lay back on the bed. "Why? Do you have a problem with it?"

Toni lay back on the bed beside him and took his hand and kissed it. "Yes. You do a lot of that stuff, and you know it's not good for you . . . and you're an athlete too. You need to take better care of yourself."

Xtreme was silent for a long time. "You're the first girl who ever said anything like that to me."

"That's because I care about you." They both watched the shadows from the flickering candles dancing on the wall.

"I'll stop if you want me to . . ."

"I want, but what do you want?"

"Look at that." Xtreme pointed to a shadow. "It's beautiful, like you."

"You're sweet." Toni kissed him gently on the lips.

Xtreme sat up and looked at her. "I've never known anyone like you, Toni. The others . . . they don't care about me. All they care about is being seen with me, getting high with me, going on trips, or me giving them money and me buying them things. No one's ever cooked for me before or taught me how to dance. . . . Everyone always wants something." His voice faded into the night and he lay back down.

"I don't care about things, Frank Hammond. What I care about and want is you." Toni pulled him closer and they just held each other, and lay there enjoying the patterns of the shadows from the candles as they flickered and danced on the bedroom wall.

Chapter 22

The night is far spent, the day is at hand. Let us then drop the works of darkness and put on the armor of light. Let us walk properly as in the day not in revelry and drunkenness, not in lewdness and lust, not in strife and envy. But put on the Lord Jesus Christ . . .

Nina closed her Bible and sighed. She had been on a fact-finding expedition ever since her conversation with Karla. Toni had called to tell her about the trip to Vegas but there was no reason for her to go because So Fine wasn't performing. She was glad they were away in Vegas. The trip had given her an opportunity to have some much-needed quiet time.

The days were getting shorter and cooler now that it was fall, and it was too chilly for her to sit on Pride Rock any longer. She looked up at the setting sun and decided to adjourn to her office. As she passed Nicki's room she paused to smile when she saw her daughter watching one of her favorite movies.

Nina shared office space with her husband. She was surprised to see Kyle sitting at his desk working on the computer. The room had an ocean view and a huge fireplace. A television and their collection of books lined the walls.

"Can you make me a fire, baby?" Nina set her books on the desk and stood behind Kyle and massaged his shoulders.

"Did you say light your fire?" Kyle pretended to be serious.

"Yes."

"Do you want me to light you up in here? Nicki is right across the hall."

"No. I want you to build a fire in the fireplace with one of those paper logs and that wood over there." Nina laughed.

"That's no fun."

Nina smiled as she watched him build a roaring fire. She stood in front of the fireplace to warm herself. She had been so caught up in her reading, she hadn't realized how chilly it had gotten.

"This is nice." He pulled her onto the loveseat in front of the television. "How's your research going?"

"There's so much to read. I never thought I'd be learning about the music industry out of the Bible."

"The Word is deep. God wants to be involved in every area of our lives." Kyle picked up KRS-One's book *Ruminations* and was immediately engrossed. "I like this brother. If more people in the industry thought like him, there'd be a lot less negativity associated with the hip-hop culture."

"Maybe I should give this book to Jamil." Nina brightened at the thought.

"Does he even read?" Kyle flipped to another section of the book.

"I've never seen him read a book, but Jamil is smart, but not as smart as you." Nina kissed him on the cheek.

"He's definitely a street entrepreneur. All of those guys who run their own labels are phenomenal businessmen. They're multimillionaires and most of them never went to college . . . educated in the streets." Kyle closed the book and handed it to Nina. "You can only try, baby."

"I'm going to try and have lunch with him if that's okay with you. He and the young lady who runs his label are getting married," Nina offered.

"No stuff? Your boy's getting married, and here I thought he was still carrying a torch for you." Kyle was genuinely surprised. "Maybe I had Jamil all wrong. Why don't you invite him and his girl over for dinner?"

"Are you serious?" Nina couldn't believe what she was hearing.

"Sure, why not? He wanted to marry you, he can't be that bad. Actually, I think the brother's pretty smart." Kyle grinned.

"You think Jamil's smart?" Nina had to laugh. "Why?"

"He wanted to marry you."

Nina was just taking the macaroni and cheese out of the oven when the doorbell rang.

Kyle, who had been setting the table, came into the kitchen. "Shall I let the guest of honor in?" He picked up a carrot from the relish tray and snapped it in half before he ate it.

"Yes, but I'm going with you." Nina laughed as she took Kyle's hand and walked with him to the front door. "You did a great job setting the table, baby."

Kyle opened the door, and Jamil and India were standing there without Buffalo.

"Come on in, you guys." Nina gave India a hug as the men shook hands. "India, have you met my husband, Kyle?"

India spoke to Kyle while Jamil kissed Nina on the cheek. She caught a whiff of marijuana he had obviously just smoked and wondered how she had ever smoked the stuff herself as Kyle led them all into the family room.

"Did Buffalo come?" Nina inquired as Jamil and India were seated on the sofa.

"Buff's at the crib. Yo, can I get something to drink?" Jamil demanded.

"What would you like, man?" Kyle met Jamil's eye.

"Y'all got any Hypnotic up in this piece?"

"Naw, playa. We don't flow like that, but I can hook you up with some juice or something," Kyle replied smoothly.

"We'd love some juice," India cut in.

Nina looked at Jamil and then her husband. They were both behaving very strangely. She went into the kitchen for the hot wings and shrimp she had prepared as appetizers while Kyle prepared fruit juice spritzers.

"Your boy is high as a kite," Kyle whispered as he put the drinks on a tray.

Nina and Kyle walked back into the family room with the appetizers and drinks where Jamil and India were on the couch kissing.

"Yo, I'm hungrier than a mother . . ." India jabbed him in the ribs before he could complete the sentence. "Damn, girl, what did you do that for?" Jamil looked at India as he reached for the food.

"We've been laying down some tracks for So Fine's album." India smiled at Nina. "We didn't have time to eat. We left the studio and came straight here."

"The tracks are dope . . . real dope. " Jamil polished off most of the appetizers by himself.

"Well, playa, why don't you come in the dining room so you can really get your eat on?" Kyle suggested. "My girl hooked it up."

"Yo, playa. I thought you was one of them college-boy suit types, but you ah-ight."

Jamil and Kyle traded pounds as Kyle led him into the dining room. Nina was so busy watching them she almost forgot the food.

"Do you need help with anything?" India brought their glasses into the kitchen.

"Thanks. You can grab that bowl of rice." Nina had prepared a seafood gumbo and a large tossed salad. She had made the macaroni and cheese for Nicki.

As if she had heard her name, the little girl came running into the kitchen. "Mommy, I'm hungry."

"You just remembered I made that macaroni and cheese." Nina laughed.

"Nina, is this your daughter?" India lit up like a Christmas tree.

"Yes." Nina could hear Kyle and Jamil having a conversation.

"Nina, she's so cute. Come here, sweetie." India bent down to talk to Nicki. As India stood up, she placed her hands on her stomach. "Nina, I'll tell you something but it's a secret."

"Okay." Nina put down the tureen of gumbo. "What up?"

"I'm pregnant," India whispered. "I just found out today. I haven't even told Jamil." India grinned from ear to ear.

"Congratulations." Nina gave her a hug. "But why haven't you told Jamil?"

"We're getting married next month. I thought I'd tell him then as a wedding present." India was radiantly happy. "But I had to tell somebody so I told you."

"Well, he's going to love that just like he loves you," Nina offered.

Nina was silent as she listened to Kyle and Jamil discussing the business of the biz. Jamil was really impressed with Kyle's financial background and Kyle had to give Jamil his props for running a successful company.

"Yo, playa, why did you choose the name *Suicide* for your company?" Kyle asked as they relaxed in the family room.

Nina had baked a peach-and-mango cobbler, and she served it warm with vanilla ice cream.

Jamil gulped down a spoonful before he replied, "Because the music is so tight you'll go insane listening to it, and if you can't hear one of my tracks you definitely won't want to live without it."

"Don't you think that's a little extreme, man?" Kyle pushed his empty bowl aside and picked up Nicki and set her in his lap.

"No doubt. That's why we gave Xtreme his name." Jamil laughed.

"But the message and the images associated with most of the music aren't very positive."

"Who cares? It's some of the best music around and it sells. My boy's album debut at number one and his CD sold half a million the first week."

"But what about my little girl, man? She loves music and she loves videos. What am I supposed to tell her when she starts trying to dress like a little hoochie because she sees it in the videos?"

"Look, playa. I ain't responsible for what your little girl or anyone else's does. I'm just tryin' to get paid so I can take care of mine, you know?"

"But you are responsible. There's a responsibility that comes with your success," Kyle pointed out.

"I ain't tryin' to be nobody's role model," Jamil blurted out.

"But if you're going to be true to the hip-hop culture, you have a responsibility to the generations behind you." Kyle winked at Nina. She was so proud of him she wanted to shout.

"My responsibility is to give the public some suicidal music."

"You playin' with death, man," Kyle said quietly.

"Man, you straight up trippin'. Ain't nobody playin' with death." Jamil laughed.

"Words are powerful. You can speak things into existence," Nina quickly added.

"Whatever, playa. If people don't like what I'm doin', how I'm livin' f 'em. Haters," Jamil mumbled.

"But what about the babies?" Kyle wasn't backing down.

"What about 'em?"

"Most rappers have no regard for lyrical content or images."

"Look, man. I talk to kids about violence, gangs, and drug abuse . . . I donate money, I always try to hire black people."

"That's great, but aren't you sending out mixed messages?"

Jamil was starting to get a little frustrated. "What are *you* doing for the people?" Jamil folded his arms and looked at Kyle.

"I'm just a brother tryin' to get paid like you. I work with Nina raising money for sickle cell research. I know your foundation was a major sponsor for the Chocolate Affair and I appreciate it. There needs to be more brothers taking care of their own like you."

"Thanks, man." Jamil finally seemed to relax.

"Yeah, Jamil. We really appreciated it," Nina added.

"That's what the money is for . . . to help the people." Jamil looked at India, and Nina sensed he was getting ready to leave.

"Jamil, I have something I'd like for you to read." She handed him a copy of KRS-One's book. "Have you read this?"

Jamil and India looked at the book together. "Naw." He flipped through it and looked at Kyle. "It's been real cool kickin' it with y'all like this. I didn't think I would enjoy myself but I really did. It's been very interesting."

"Cool, playa. You and India are welcome to kick it with me and Nina anytime. Maybe you can come play golf with me and my brother and some of the fellas."

"That'll work. Let me know when." Jamil looked at India. "You ready?"

"I just need to use the rest room." India smiled at Nina who pointed her down the hall. When Kyle took Nicki into the kitchen for ice cream, Nina turned to face Jamil.

"He's ah-ight. He's not me, but he's got your back. I'm happy for you. But I just want to know one thing."

"What's up?" Nina smiled. The evening had been a success. Maybe her husband and the other guys could really influence Jamil in a positive way.

"How long are you going to pass off Topaz's little girl as yours? You livin' a lie. Yo' man wanna be all up in my business, what about the lie all of y'all are livin'?"

"I don't know what you're talking about. Nicki is my daughter," Nina replied coolly as the others entered the room.

"His little girl." Jamil shook his head and gave Nina a sinister laugh. "Yeah . . . right."

Chapter 23

Jamil's Justified Jams Foundation held an annual fund-raiser for at-risk youth at the Teen Center in Compton as part of its gang prevention program. Every year he would gather some of the music industry's brightest and best and hold an outdoor concert and barbecue. There was also a ceremony where the club gave out awards of achievement to individuals who had shown the most improvement. It was a project very close to Jamil's heart because he had been an at-risk youth, and the club had been very instrumental in helping him turn his life around. One of his counselors had noticed Jamil's gift for music and arranged for his first piano lesson.

Some of the neighborhood children had already gathered to watch workers assemble the stage and to catch a glimpse of the celebrities as they arrived. India, of course, was there to ensure that everything ran smoothly and according to schedule. Buffalo lit the charcoal in a huge barbecue pit.

"Look at you, Chef Homeboyardee." India laughed. "Making any ribs today?"

"Just dogs and burgers today, Miss India." Buffalo watched the flames as they leaped through the grate.

"Don't be flirting with the cook." Jamil grabbed India around the waist. "Besides, Buff's not making ribs today anyway."

"He just told me the bad news." India pretended to look disappointed.

"Cheer up, sexy. I'll take you to one of my barbecue spots down here in Compton when everything's over. After that you'll be saying Buffalo who?" Jamil laughed as he pretended to box his enormous friend.

"Your place might be all that, but it'll never make me say Buffalo who?" India stood on her toes and kissed Buffalo on the cheek. Without heels, India was short.

"Hey . . . you made him blush." Jamil looked at India. "No one's ever done that."

"Buffalo's just a big teddy bear." India cuddled up next to him and gave him a hug.

Jamil looked at two of his favorite people hugging and laughed. "Come on, you. I'm getting you away from Buffalo before he burns up the food." He took India by the hand. "I've got some people I'd like for you to meet."

Topaz finished dressing Baby Doll in the denim outfit Jade had made her for So Fine's showcase. She stood next to her daughter in the mirror and smiled. She was wearing a faded denim skirt and Jade had airbrushed a T-shirt with her name and embellished it with rhinestones. She had found a pair of stilettos made out of faded denim that she had bought some time ago. Her hairdresser had twisted her hair and she was wearing a bandanna.

"And where do you two think you're going?" Germain stood in the mirror behind them smiling. "My girls are looking hot."

Baby Doll ran to Germain, and he picked her up. "I told Jamil I'd perform at his benefit for the center," Topaz explained.

"Where is it?"

"Watts or Compton. Somewhere in the hood." Topaz smoothed her eye shadow.

"You're going down *there?*" Germain was surprised.

"Sure, why not? Jamil paid for the entire Chocolate Affair."

"But that was in Santa Barbara." Germain was concerned.

"And this isn't. Jamil helped us when we needed it, and now I want to help him. He's asked before but this was the first time I've been around to do it."

Germain still wasn't convinced.

"I've got my security guys going. We'll be fine, baby." Topaz kissed him gently on the lips.

"Who's going to watch Baby Doll while you're singing?"

"So Fine is performing too. Sabre adores her. She'll watch her for those few minutes I'm onstage."

"I don't know if I like this . . ." Germain began as the telephone rang.

"Baby, answer the phone and stop worrying."

"See if you can talk some sense into your cousin." Germain handed Topaz the telephone. "It's Nina."

"What are you doing now?" Nina laughed.

"Germain's having a hissy fit because Baby Doll and I are going to Jamil's fund-raiser today." Topaz laughed.

"What fund-raiser?" Nina demanded.

"The one he does for the Teen Center in Compton every year," Topaz replied. "Like you don't know."

"I didn't," Nina replied quietly.

"How could you not know? He does it every year and So Fine is performing too."

"I know about the fund-raiser but I didn't know it was today." Nina was trying to remain calm.

"No one told you?" Topaz sat on the edge of the bed.

"No, and I don't think you should go down there." Nina counted to ten.

"Why? I already said I was coming. I can't back out now. Are you having some sort of disagreement with Jamil?"

"Not exactly." Nina had been so busy reading and doing research on the things she had discussed with Karla and Keisha, she hadn't spoken to anyone. And why hadn't Charetta or Toni called to inform her about the event? She hadn't seen either of them since they had taken the girls to Vegas for Xtreme's video. She knew Charetta had been in the studio with Xtreme but why hadn't anyone informed her about today? "Topaz, you really shouldn't go down there. I'm coming over."

"You'll never make it before the limo gets here. Why don't you just meet me down there? Your group is performing and whatever problem it is you're having with Jamil, you need to work it out. I gotta run." Topaz hung up before Nina could say another word.

"I hate when she does that," Nina yelled. "Lord, what am I going to do now?" She ran upstairs to change. "Please protect Topaz, God. And So Fine, Toni, and Char . . ."

Music played and kids swarmed the club eating hamburgers and hot dogs. A soft drink company had donated sodas and bottled water, and there were coolers of drinks everywhere. So Fine had been introduced and they sat at a table signing autographs. Charetta had driven them in her newly leased Land Rover. It sat parked next to Jamil's Escalade and India's black Expedition.

"Have you seen Xtreme?" Toni asked Charetta who had just come out of the club where Jamil was talking to the press.

"No. Lover boy will be here soon," Charetta teased, and Toni made a face.

A motorcycle roared down the street and pulled to a screeching stop in front of the building. It slowly drove onto the grounds, and when the driver removed his helmet everyone began to scream.

"Who is that?" Toni looked at Charetta.

Girls ran behind the driver screaming until he was mobbed. Buffalo left the barbecue grill and pushed his way into the crowd and pulled the young man toward the building.

"Lover boy." Charetta laughed. "He always has to make an entrance. He's gone from helicopters to motorcycles now."

"He told me he had a surprise, but a motorcycle? No way." Toni pushed her way into the building.

"Somebody's in trouble." Charetta laughed. She watched India walk over to the table where the girls were sitting, whisper something in Sabre's ear and all the girls got up and followed her.

"What's going on?" Charetta arrived at the door the same time as they did, and everyone went inside.

"We need them for press," India explained as the girls stood in front of the camera.

"That's my group, and I wasn't informed of any press interviews." Charetta crossed her arms and looked at India who looked too cute in overalls and Timberlands.

"It was on your event sheet. Did you bother to read it?" India looked at Buffalo who indicated he needed to speak with her.

"Some people here want to speak with Char," Buffalo whispered in her ear.

"Are they press or someone connected to the event?" India whispered back.

"No, Miss India. They said they're her brothers," Buffalo informed her.

India looked around the small meeting room that had been set up for press and other VIPs. The place was already overcrowded. "Thanks, Buffalo. I'll take care of it."

India walked back across the room to Charetta who was watching So Fine being interviewed. "Your brothers are outside."

"Oh, let 'em in," Charetta demanded as if India were her servant.

India pulled Charetta away from the interviews. "It's too crowded in here. You're going to have to talk to them outside."

"It's not that crowded," Charetta protested.

"Outside," India whispered through gritted teeth.

"Bitch," Charetta whispered under her breath as she pushed the door open and went outside.

A limousine pulled up in front of the building as Charetta stood outside talking to her brothers.

"That is one fine-ass sista," Charetta's brother Bootsie declared as Topaz stepped out of a black stretch Escalade. "And she knows how to roll. Damn."

The kids started running toward the car, and Topaz jumped back inside.

"Come on. Let's go help her." Charetta led her brothers over to the car and knocked on the window and it slid down. The kids screamed as soon as they saw Topaz's face. "Come on, girl. My brothers will help you inside. There's no backstage entrance here." Charetta smiled.

"You know her?" Bootsie was too impressed.

"Chill," Charetta growled.

India heard all the screaming from inside. She opened the door and saw the limousine parked in front of the building and quickly dialed Topaz's cell phone number.

"Excuse me." Topaz smiled politely and the window closed.

"Topaz, it's India. Is that you out front?"

"Yes, and things are a little crazy." Topaz was almost ready to go back home.

"Don't move," India ordered. "Buffalo's coming out."

Moments later, Topaz saw a man about the size of a buffalo walk up to the car. The kids parted for him like the Red Sea. He walked up to the car and took Baby Doll as Topaz's own security guys got out with her and the small phalanx of men led her inside. Charetta tried to go in with them but she was left outside, and no one else was allowed inside.

"Damn." Charetta smiled at her brothers, trying to cover her embarrassment.

Nina had programmed the location into the electronic navigation system in Kyle's Escalade. She glanced at the directions in front of her and sighed with relief, thankful, she had arrived. It was the first time she had used the system and she wasn't sure if she had used it correctly. Kyle was out playing golf with Sean, Eric, and some of the Lakers. Sean had driven so Kyle's car had been available.

So Fine was onstage performing as Nina got out of the truck. She two-wayed India who came outside and took her where the others were waiting.

"Nini." Baby Doll lifted her arms to be picked up. "You brought her too?" Nina shook her head at her cousin as she kissed the little girl.

"Why are you tripping? Everything is fine." Topaz smiled.

Nina handed Baby Doll to her mother and went over to Toni who was sitting with Xtreme. She politely smiled and pulled Toni to the side.

"Why wasn't I notified about this?" Nina demanded.

Toni's mouth dropped open in surprise. "Char said she told you."

"No one told me anything."

"I'm sorry, Nina." Toni was very apologetic.

"Come on, sweetness." Xtreme pulled Toni away.

"What is up with you?" Topaz demanded.

"We'll talk about it later." Nina took Baby Doll as Topaz went onstage.

India walked over and stood by Nina. "I was wondering where you were."

"I knew nothing about this." Nina was still angry.

"Nothing?"

"Nothing." Nina handed Baby Doll to Sabre who had just kissed Nina and the little girl on the cheek.

"That doesn't surprise me," India replied. "I think success is starting to affect some of us." India glanced at Charetta who was talking to her brothers. "I'll make sure you get every email from now on."

"Thanks, girl." Nina sighed.

"Jamil's taking me for barbecue afterward. Want to go?" India smiled.

"I'll let you know."

"Cool. Got to take care of a few things for my boss." India smiled as she pulled out her cell phone.

Nina joined the girls who were entertaining Baby Doll as Topaz walked offstage.

"Did I tell you that you look fabulous?" Nina gave Topaz a hug.

"No, you were too busy tripping. What is up with you?" Topaz looked at Nina who was wearing sweats.

"It's a long, long story." Nina sighed.

Jamil was onstage receiving all sorts of accolades from the organization. Janice had arrived and he called his mother onstage with him. The kids who had won achievement awards joined them and then all of the performers. Cameras clicked and rolled.

"Where's India, my right hand, the person who made all of this possible?" Jamil grinned from ear to ear.

"Yay, India," Sabre yelled and the rest of So Fine joined her.

"Go, India," Xtreme yelled and Topaz clapped.

Nina smiled as she looked around expecting to see India run onstage any minute.

"You seen India?" Jamil asked Nina after the event ended and everyone had left the stage.

"India's on her cell phone somewhere, and she wasn't able to get off and come on stage. She said she had to take care of something for her boss." Nina smiled.

"You and Topaz going out to eat with us?" Jamil demanded.

"Topaz came in a limo."

"Send it home. Buff's here and a few of my other boys. Y'all Valley girls will be ah-ight in the hood. Y'all rollin' with me." Jamil grinned.

"I'll see what I can do." Nina let out a long sigh as she joined Topaz who was talking with Charetta and her brothers who had finally made it into the VIP area. "Excuse us." Nina pulled Topaz to the side. "Jamil wants us to go with him somewhere for barbecue."

"I didn't really intend to stay. I told Germain I'd be home right after. He really didn't want me to come."

"You should have listened to him." Nina saw Jamil walking toward them.

"Ladies, shall we go?" Jamil smiled at both of them.

"Jamil, I really have to go. I told my husband I'd be on my way home by now. Can we do this some other time?" Topaz fixed her amber eyes on Jamil.

"Sure, but we will be discussing your future with the Suicide family as soon as possible. I want to get started on your CD right away." Jamil smiled at Topaz and then Nina.

Chapter 24

Cleo's Barbecue was located on a lot right by the freeway. Every weekend Cleo would fire up three barrel grills and smoke ribs, links, and chicken. Customers would come from everywhere to purchase dinners or sandwiches bathed in hot or mild sauce and served with a choice of side dishes.

Charetta watched a steady stream of patrons walk up to the trailer where Cleo's wife or son took orders and cash and leave with brown paper bags filled with food. She wondered what Jamil had been thinking when he had chosen Cleo's as the place for them to eat. She was only minutes away from where she had grown up and had been to the lot many times before with her brothers or girlfriends for food. She felt out of place in the Land Rover, and as much as she loved the old neighborhood, she would have preferred eating on the other side of town.

She sat in the car for almost an hour, waiting and watching for the others to arrive. If she had known it would take so long for the Suicide family to gather, she would have never sent her brothers home. She saw a black Escalade drive up, and moments later there was a sharp tap on the window. In the darkness she saw the silhouette of a large man, and she let down the window for Buffalo.

"Boss wants to know if you want something to eat. We're taking food back to the house."

"I'll have whatever he's having." Charetta smiled. She could hardly contain her excitement. She had never been invited to Jamil's estate in Encino. Toni had been there with Xtreme but Charetta had never had the privilege. She bit into her full bottom lip as she carefully put the SUV into drive a few minutes later and followed Jamil's Escalade to the freeway and out to the San Fernando Valley.

She followed the Escalade up a winding hill and watched as a massive black gate rolled open. It seemed like forever before the house came into view. She watched as the five-car garage opened and gasped when she saw Jamil's stead of cars. He was definitely living the diamond life. Jamil came out of the garage and indicated he wanted her to get out of the car.

"I don't know where the others are, but we may as well get the party started." Jamil grinned as Buffalo opened the front door and went inside first with several large grocery bags. Charetta could smell the savory barbecue sauce, and she was immediately hungry. A couple of Jamil's boys appeared from nowhere. There was always someone on the premises to make sure the estate was secure.

Buffalo emptied the contents of the bags on the counter, made himself a plate and took it out to the guest house where he lived.

"That's the last we'll see of him." Jamil watched Buffalo make his way across the expertly manicured grounds to a two-story house. He turned around to face Charetta who was making a plate.

"I'll make your plate," Charetta offered. "What would you like?"

"A little bit of everything." Jamil looked at his watch. "Where is everybody?"

"We're here." Charetta smiled as she handed Jamil the plate. "And that's all that really matters."

"I was thinking we might go down into my studio and lay down some tracks for this song that's been going through my head all day." Jamil tapped out a beat on the counter.

"That's tight." Charetta listened for a few minutes before she joined in with an alternate beat.

"Oh yeah." Jamil sang a melody in his falsetto. "Let's go."

"Hold up, maestro. That melody and those beats ain't goin' nowhere." Charetta grinned as she held up a small tape recorder. "I got it all right here. All work and no play makes Char very boring."

"So what did you have in mind?" Jamil smiled as he met Charetta's eye. He loved working in the studio with her, and together they had created some of his best work.

"I saw a pool table in the other room. I'd hate to come over your house and kick your ass on your own table but what must be will be." Charetta smirked.

"You think?" Jamil grinned.

"I know."

"We'll just have to see about that."

Charetta picked up her plate and followed Jamil into the game room. "Rack 'em." She went over to his bar and scanned the bottles. "Can I get a shot of this Hypnotic?"

"You think you're tough." Jamil laughed. "Get over here and break."

"I am tough." Charetta poured some of the blue alcohol into a glass and downed it before she carefully chalked the end of a pool stick and aimed it at the cue ball. She gave it a good whack and the balls scattered all over the table with a few of them falling into the pockets.

"How do you like me now?" She gave him a triumphant grin as she called out pockets and sank every ball on the table.

"Beginner's luck," Jamil teased. He laughed and poured himself a shot of Hypnotic and downed it before he broke and started sinking balls.

When he missed Charetta doubled over with laughter. "We should have played for money." She grinned as the eight ball thundered into a corner pocket. "Got any other games you want to play?" She was being very suggestive but she didn't care. The alcohol had taken control, and she was enjoying herself.

"PlayStation 2."

"You don't even want to go there." Charetta laughed.

"I'll take you there," Jamil sang as he poured each of them another drink.

"You think you're gonna win by getting me drunk?" Charetta shook her head. "You'll have to do better than that."

He picked up the bottle and gave her a gentle push toward the television. He handed her a controller and they sat on the floor and began to play.

"I can't do this." Charetta laughed as she tossed aside the controller and lay on the floor. Her head was spinning as she stared up at the ceiling.

"And you thought you could hang." Jamil sat up and pulled an extra-large blunt out of his pocket and lit it. He took a hit and passed it to her.

"I still kicked your ass in pool." Charetta looked at Jamil who looked very peaceful lying on the floor beside her.

"I wonder what happened to everyone." Jamil stared at an invisible spot on the ceiling.

"Do you think I really care?" Charetta laughed.

"Probably not. We're doin' our own thing anyway." Jamil fingered one of her braids.

Charetta was silent as she thought about what it would be like to kiss Jamil. Although Toni had only recently said that she thought Jamil and Charetta would make a great couple, Charetta had nursed a major secret crush on Jamil ever since she laid eyes on him the night of Suicide's launch party. She knew right then she had to get close to him. Nina had come close to blowing her entire plan when she tried to get So Fine signed to another label. Then there was India who was always trying to make her look like an idiot as So Fine's manager. But Charetta's songwriting skills had squashed that ploy and now they were together and alone for the very first time.

Charetta had never been that forward with a guy, and if there was ever a time, this was certainly it. She leaned over and kissed Jamil softly on the lips. She could always blame her behavior on the drugs and alcohol if he objected. But much to her surprise he pulled her closer and kissed her back.

Toni and Xtreme walked barefoot along the beach in front of his Laguna Niguel home. It was cold but they barely noticed.

"I can't believe this is your house, Frank. Why don't you ever stay here?" Toni smiled.

"Look at this place." He turned to face the fabulous waterfront estate located in an exclusive area of Orange County. "It's a barn."

"It's wonderful." Toni looked at the moonlit beach with its smooth sand. It was one of the most beautiful beaches she had ever seen.

"It's big, empty, and very lonely." Xtreme sighed.

"So why didn't you get something smaller?" Toni paused to roll up her pants legs and Xtreme knelt down and rolled them up for her.

"Because this is what's expected." He stood and took her hand again and they continued walking.

"I don't understand. What do you mean what's expected?"

"I'm the star pitcher for the Angels. We just won the World Series. I'm also a star rapper . . . baseball's first bad boy. People expect me to live a certain way," Xtreme explained.

"So how does Frank want to live?" Toni met his eye.

"I like your house. There's life there. You with the girls . . . you guys are like a family."

"So do you think you'd like this place better if you had a family? Some babies to occupy all those rooms?" Toni laughed.

"Maybe . . ."

"So what do you want?"

"Xtreme shrugged. "I don't know anymore."

"What *did* you want?"

"To become a professional baseball player. And then I got bored so when Jamil said he could make me a star in hip-hop, that was cool."

"And now?"

"I want to be happy."

"So none of this stuff or none of your accomplishments have made you happy?"

"Not really . . . nothing ever really takes away the pain."

"What pain?"

"The emptiness . . . I can't describe it."

"Is that why you do all the drugs?"

"I guess so. But when the high wears off the pain comes right back," Xtreme replied quietly. "And they're also part of what's expected."

"The motorcycle . . . is that part of doing what's expected?"

"I like riding my bike . . . . Maybe it is expected. I don't know."

"What do you know, Frank?"

"Damn, Toni, what's up with all the questions?"

"I'm just trying to understand you."

"I know, baby. I'm sorry."

There was a long silence as they sat back-to-back on a rock.

"You're making me realize that I don't know who I am or why I do anything anymore." Xtreme sighed with frustration.

"I know who you are." Toni smiled as she turned to face him.

"Oh yeah? Who am I?" Xtreme smiled.

"You're kind, sweet, sensitive, not a very good salsa dancer, a wonderful kisser, a passionate lover, extremely handsome, and . . ."

"And what?" Xtreme laughed. "Don't stop now. I'm enjoying this."

"I don't know if I should tell you."

"Tell me," Xtreme pleaded.

"I don't think I should tell you."

"Why not?" He laughed.

"Because you might stop talking to me." Toni was very serious.

"There is nothing you could ever say to me that would make me stop talking to you," Xtreme informed her. "Now tell me."

"You're the man that I love," Toni whispered softly.

Charetta and Jamil lie in bed together in one of the downstairs guest rooms. Charetta smiled as she watched him sleeping. She couldn't believe they had actually made love. He was the most wonderful man she had ever been with and his boyish good looks made him irresistible. She gently stroked the side of his face and he opened his eyes.

"I was knocked out. I guess you were right. I can't hang." Jamil smiled.

"You can hang with me anytime, Jamil Winters."

"You ready to hit the studio now?"

"Now?" Charetta had hoped they would spend more time in bed.

"Now." Jamil laughed. "Unless you can't hang."

"I can hang." Charetta sat up in bed.

"Cool. I'll meet you downstairs in a few. I'm going upstairs to take a shower."

Charetta went into the bathroom to shower and wondered why Jamil hadn't suggested they take a shower together. "He probably needed to regroup after what happened between us," she rationalized as she finished dressing.

It was just about three in the morning when she found her way into the kitchen for a soda. She glanced at the ceiling above her and decided to go upstairs with Jamil. When she arrived at the staircase, Buffalo was sitting there reading a magazine.

"Hey, Buffalo," Charetta said with a smile.

He nodded in reply.

There was no way for her to get around the enormous man to go upstairs unless he moved. "Excuse me," Charetta finally said, wondering why he was unable to understand the obvious.

"Boss said for you to go in and get started." Buffalo led her outside to the other side of the house and opened the door to the recording studio.

Charetta couldn't understand why she hadn't been allowed upstairs but she turned on the power, took out the tape recorder, and began playing the melody Jamil had sung earlier on one of the keyboards.

"You go, girl." Jamil was grinning when she looked up. He came inside and hooked up a few keyboards so they could begin recording.

"Jamil, Buffalo . . ."

Jamil kissed her before she could say another word. "My little studio honey got it goin' on. Now let's get busy."

Charetta smiled in response. She and Jamil were finally together, and there were no Ninas or Indias around to get in her way this time.

Chapter 25

Nina mindlessly followed Topaz's limousine as it exited the 405 freeway and headed west on Sunset toward Pacific Palisades. She barely noticed Brentwood, one of her favorite places to shop and dine as they drove through the small village. She could see Baby Doll waving out the rear window and wondered why Topaz hadn't strapped the little girl into her seat.

The stretch limo pulled into the driveway, and Nina waited for it to depart so she could pull Kyle's SUV into the driveway and park. Topaz stood in the driveway holding Baby Doll, and Nina couldn't help thinking yet again how much her cousin had changed. There was a time when Topaz would have never held one of her children when she was so dressed up. Was this really the same person who had left her son when he was barely a year old to pursue a singing career?

"Don't you guys look cute?" Nina smiled as Baby Doll reached for her.

"Did you see Mommy sing?" The little girl was still excited over her mother's performance at the center.

"I sure did." Nina kissed Baby Doll and put her on the ground. "You need to walk, Turkey. You're too big and too old to be held now. You're a big girl." Nina spanked her lightly on her behind.

"I'm not a turkey. My name is Baby Doll."

Nina tried not to laugh. "What do they call her in school?"

"They started out calling her Turquoise but she changed that quickly," Topaz whispered as they all went into the house.

"You have got her so spoiled." Nina watched Baby Doll run through the house looking for her brother.

"I had nothing to do with that. Chris and Germain spoiled her while we were in London." Topaz laughed.

"I know. I know." Nina looked around the house. "Where's Germain? I saw his Porsche in the driveway."

"He's probably upstairs reading since little Miss Thang wasn't here to distract him." Topaz pulled a rose out of a huge floral arrangement and sniffed it.

"Big Miss Thang wasn't here to distract him either so he probably got a lot of reading done," Nina pointed out.

"Oh, be quiet. Come upstairs with me so I can change and then we'll see where he is," Topaz demanded.

"While you two suck face? No thanks. You'll probably even try to have a quickie. I'll wait for you downstairs in the playroom."

"Just for that, I will have a quickie." Topaz laughed.

"Oh, please." Nina held up a hand. "You were going to do that anyway. This is Nina you're talking to, remember? Just hurry up so we can talk and I can go home and see my husband and daughter."

"Call Kyle and have him come over. We can all go out for dinner," Topaz suggested.

"He spent the day with the guys. They went to play golf. I don't know if he's back yet." Nina headed toward the small flight of stairs that split the house into several levels. She paused to glance at the beautiful family portrait on the wall.

"You mean you left my Nicki at home all day by herself?" Topaz paused on the stairs and waited for Nina's reply.

"Yes, I left *my* Nicki at home with Rosa. She's fine. I hadn't planned on going out to Compton until you told me you were going."

"That's right. Why were you tripping so hard?" Topaz sat on a stair and unfastened her shoes.

"Go handle your business, girl. We'll talk about it when you come down," Nina replied.

"Okay. I'll send Baby Doll down to keep you company while I change." Topaz picked up her shoes and disappeared up the stairs.

Nina made herself comfortable on the sofa in the playroom. She kicked off her Nikes and poured oil and popcorn into the machine. Within minutes, Baby Doll and Chris were in the room.

"Hi, Nini." Chris pulled a couple of DVDs off the shelf. "Want to watch *X-Men?*" He gave Nina a wink and smiled.

"Who are you trying to charm little boy?" Nina grabbed him in a headlock and they fell onto the sofa laughing.

Baby Doll jumped on Nina and began tickling her. "Don't mess with my brother."

"Two against one?" Nina was still holding on to Chris. "That's not fair. I thought you were going to help me, Turkey."

"I'm Baby Doll," the little girl reminded her. "And I have to help my brother."

"Okay, truce." Nina let go of Chris and he put on the *X-Men* DVD. "You're just like every other brother on the planet. Always trying to see Halle Berry."

"She's fine. We can watch her as Jinx the Bond girl next." Chris patted the DVD case and smiled.

Topaz came into the room and dumped the popcorn in a bowl and handed it to Chris. "Your dad's ordering pizza. You'd better go help him so he orders it the way you like it."

"Yeah, I'd better. Dad always forgets the pineapple." Chris stopped the DVD and took the popcorn and headed out of the room.

"Nina was watching that." Topaz shook her head as she dumped more popcorn seeds into the popper. "Kids . . ."

"I'm sorry." Chris walked back over to the DVD player.

"Leave it." Nina laughed. "Then Miss Halle will be waiting for you. Right where you left her."

"Thanks, Nini." A beautiful smile lit up Chris's face. "I'll be right back."

"I bet you will." Nina laughed.

"You go too." Topaz looked at her daughter. "Daddy and Chris might need your help with the pizza."

Nina and Topaz smiled as Baby Doll ran out of the playroom.

"I didn't have to tell her twice." Topaz laughed. "Miss Baby Doll loves herself some pizza. She has to eat whatever her daddy and brother are eating."

"They are too much." Nina laughed.

"Tell me about it." Topaz agreed. "I ordered Thai for us. So what did you want to talk about?"

"Has Jamil mentioned anything to you about signing with Suicide?" Nina poured popcorn into a bag and tossed a few of the kernels into her mouth.

"Not officially." Topaz ate a handful of popcorn a piece at a time.

"Well, you can't do it, and I don't think we should be hanging out with him either," Nina offered.

"What?" Shock registered on Topaz's face. "Why not?"

"Because Jamil's into some stuff that's totally not cool. Remember how we didn't like the name *suicide*?"

"Yeah . . . what kind of stuff?" Topaz grabbed another handful of popcorn.

"Keisha can probably explain it a lot better than I can. But it has to do with the Bible. Jamil's doing some evil stuff."

"What kind of evil stuff?"

"It has to do with his music and his company."

"Nina, please. You don't expect me to believe that. There's nothing evil about all my platinum albums. That's crazy." Topaz shook her head and laughed.

"I don't think Jamil's doing anything evil intentionally, but it has to do with the power of words. You can speak things into existence and the name of the company is about death," Nina tried to explain. "And I don't want to be involved with anything that's evil or about death."

"Girl, you're crazy." Topaz laughed. "You've been watching too many scary movies."

"I'm serious. The same day I signed the deal, my sister-in-law Karla called me from New Jersey. She knew all about the deal and told me not to have anything to do with it."

"Yeah, she knew because Kyle told Kirk." Topaz was still laughing.

"Kyle never said anything," Nina replied solemnly. "And it's definitely not funny."

"You're serious, aren't you?" The smile slowly faded from Topaz's face.

"Very. Jamil also mentioned our secret to me."

"He didn't."

"He did."

Topaz got off the barstool and started pacing. "What did he say?"

"You don't want to know."

"Did he say he was going to tell?" Topaz's eyes grew wide.

"No. But he might."

"Oh, that's just great." Topaz was still pacing. "I knew we should have never gone to that launch party."

"It's a little late for that, ya think?"

"Jamil won't tell. He signed that confidentiality agreement, remember?" Topaz pointed out.

"Yes, he did, but I don't know if we're dealing with the same Jamil. He took me in a room with Xtreme the night of the party. I never saw so many drugs in my life. For a minute, I thought they were going to rape me." Nina sat on the barstool while Topaz continued to pace.

"You thought *Jamil* was going to rape you?" Topaz looked at Nina.

"Yes. I was really scared," Nina whispered loudly. "I wonder if Xtreme has anything to do with this strange behavior."

"I told you Jamil still had a thing for you." Topaz, in a world of her own, wrung her hands in desperation. "You should have just married him and then we wouldn't be having this problem."

"Oh, right. Let Nina sacrifice her life so Topaz can be with Germain and solve all of *her* problems. I almost forgot how selfish you are," Nina exploded.

"I'm sorry, Nina. You know I didn't mean that. You've done enough for me already. This thing is just making me really crazy." Topaz massaged her temple. "Now what are we going to do?"

"I don't know. But we both need to stay away from Jamil."

"How are you going to do that when you just signed So Fine to his label?" Topaz demanded.

"I'll think of something . . . And he doesn't still have a thing for me. He's marrying India." Nina pushed a piece a popcorn across the counter.

"He is?"

"On Thanksgiving," Nina added.

"Then what the hell is his problem?" Topaz shouted.

"Girl, would you be quiet? Do you want Germain to hear us?" Nina looked at Topaz like she was crazy.

"Germain's gonna find out, and my marriage will be over," Topaz wailed.

"Girl, would you get a quick grip?"

Topaz opened a small refrigerator and took out a bottle of Cristal.

"Good idea." Nina took a healthy sip. "I told you Jamil was into something evil."

"If he tells our secret that's most definitely evil." Topaz was still pacing.

"Tell me about it."

"How come you're just now telling me all of this?" Topaz demanded.

"I was trying to protect you . . . waiting to see how the situation would play itself out. But you can't be running all over the place with Jamil and taking Baby Doll with you. I don't trust him, and I wouldn't want anything to happen to one of the kids."

"I still can't believe Jamil would do something to hurt us." Topaz shook her head.

"He's not the same person, T. I definitely know that."

"And you knew him better than anyone." Topaz looked at Nina.

"India's pregnant." Nina had a blank expression on her face.

"What has that got to do with this?"

"She hasn't told Jamil yet."

"So what is she waiting for?" Topaz was about to explode. "And I still don't understand what her being pregnant has to do with us."

"She wants to surprise him on their wedding day." Nina finished her champagne. "He really loves her, so I'm hoping when she does tell him, he'll chill out and really get into being a daddy and forget about us. He told me that he wanted kids when he asked me to marry him, but I thought he was joking. India's really sweet, and she's good for him."

"I hope he chills out too." Topaz sighed. "All we need is for him to start blabbing his mouth now when things have gone so well."

"Tell me about it." Nina sighed. "All we can do is pray and stay away from Jamil."

"You don't have to tell me twice," Topaz said as Germain walked into the room with their takeout order.

Germain put the bag on the counter and smiled at the cousins. "Tell you what twice, pretty girl?"

Chapter 26

Jamil sat in his bedroom staring out of the window at the placid aquamarine swimming pool. It was late Sunday afternoon and he hadn't seen or heard from India since the barbecue at the Teen Center and it was really starting to bug him. He quickly typed into the two-way yet again, WHERE ARE YOU? and dialed her cell phone, which rang until it kicked over to voice mail.

"Where the hell are you, India?" he yelled as he two-wayed Buffalo to meet him in the kitchen.

Jamil was waiting when Buffalo walked in the back door. "You heard from Miss India yet?"

"Naw, man."

"Let's roll." Buffalo led the way out to his Escalade which Jamil had 310 Motoring customize for him. There was additional space in the front, and the seats were covered with the fabric used to make Louis Vuitton bags and purses. The truck was painted a special shade of chocolate and the rims and grills had been dipped in gold.

Buffalo headed for the Ventura Freeway and then south on the 405 toward Compton. "Y'all have a fight or something?"

"Naw, man. Everything was cool. I bought all that barbecue for her but she never showed up. I thought it was strange that she didn't call and say something but she's been doing a lot of secretive stuff for the wedding."

"She never came on stage either when you gave her that shout-out," Buffalo reminded him.

"That's right. She didn't." Jamil took out his cell phone and dialed a number. "What up?"

Nina bristled at the sound of his voice. "Hey, Jamil."

"Yesterday at the Teen Center what did my girl India say to you?" Jamil demanded.

"She said a lot. Why?" Nina chose her words carefully as she wondered about the purpose of his call.

"Did she say she was going anywhere or doing something special?"

"No. Why?"

"Because I haven't seen her since the barbecue. She's not answering her two-way or her cell phone, and that's not like her."

Nina didn't know what to say. She really didn't know India that well. "I'm sure India's fine. She's probably working on something for you guys' wedding."

"Yeah . . . that's what I thought." He just about to hang up when his cell phone beeped. "Hold on a minute." He clicked over to the other line. "Holla."

"Is this Jamil Winters?" a voice asked.

"Who wants to know?" Jamil barked.

"This is Cedars-Sinai ER. We have a young lady here who's been very badly beaten. We've been trying to notify her family but all of her identification has been stolen," the voice replied.

"So why did you call me?" Jamil asked.

"Some neighborhood kids found her in an alley not far from the Teen Center in Compton. They told the police they had seen her there yesterday. We were finally able to get in touch with the director. He came over and told us she was your business partner and he gave me your number."

"We'll be right there." Jamil forgot about Nina and closed his cell phone. "Somebody beat up India, Buff. She's at Cedars."

Buffalo exited the 405 and headed back to the Santa Monica Freeway. They were both silent as he drove toward the hospital. Jamil's cell phone rang again. "Holla."

"You hung up on me, Jamil. Is everything okay?" Nina asked softly.

"No. Somebody beat up India. I'm on my way to Cedars." He clicked off without another word.

Nina, in shock, just sat there holding the telephone until Kyle took it from her and hung it up. "What's up with you?" Kyle said and laughed.

"Somebody beat up India, Jamil's fiancée," Nina slowly explained.

"That pretty little thing who came to dinner with him?"

Nina nodded.

"Is she okay?"

"I don't know. She's at Cedars."

"Get your coat and let's go," Kyle said as he grabbed a jacket and headed for the door.

Buffalo drove right up to the entrance of the ER. Jamil jumped out of the car before he could stop and ran into the hospital. "I'm here for India Summers." They used to joke about their surnames Summers and Winters. Jamil always said it was a match made in heaven.

"She's in our intensive care unit." A nurse took out a clipboard and directed him to the elevators. Jamil charged down the hall like a madman and pressed the up button until an elevator finally arrived. It stopped on every floor, and he was climbing the walls by the time it finally delivered him on the fifth floor and the doors slid open. He got the creeps when he saw patients hooked up to machines and wondered what in the world had happened to India to land her in here.

"India Summers." He found his voice somewhere when he arrived at the nurse's station.

"And you are?"

"Her fiancé."

The nurse led him into a room right across from the station and when Jamil saw her, he wanted to cry. Her body was so swollen she was about three times her normal size. Her eyes looked like two slits, and her neatly braided hair was matted. Jamil could see dried blood in the few braids that hung from her bandaged head. There was a tube up her nose and one in her mouth. She was also being given a blood transfusion. He gave the nurse a look that demanded an explanation.

"Your fiancée lost a lot of blood. The doctor's ordered eight units. She's holding on barely."

"Is she going to die?" Jamil managed to whisper.

"The next twenty-four hours are crucial. I'm sorry about the baby."

"Baby?" Jamil repeated.

"You didn't know?"

Jamil shook his head.

"She was three months pregnant. It was a girl." The nurse put a hand on his shoulder for encouragement. "Why don't you try talking to her?"

"Can she hear me?" Jamil felt his throat closing up.

"She's been given a lot of pain medicine. That's a morphine drip." The nurse touched a bag of clear liquid that was being administered through an IV. "We tried to make her as comfortable as possible."

"Thanks." Jamil walked over to the bed and sat down by a body that in no way resembled his beautiful India. "India." Amazingly his voice was strong and clear. "Baby, I'm here."

She gave him no indication whether she had heard or not. The only sound in the room was beeping machinery.

"Baby, why didn't you tell me we were going to have a baby?" Tears squeezed out of his eyes and spilled down his cheeks. "We were going to have a little girl, and I know she would have been beautiful just like you. But we'll have others after you get better."

Buffalo walked into the room, took one look at India, and walked out. He stood in the hall shaking his head.

"And don't worry about work," Jamil continued. "I'll take care of everything."

Janice Winters rushed down the hall and into the room. Buffalo had phoned her. You could hear her heels clicking on the linoleum before she was in sight. "Oh my God." She clasped a hand to her mouth and broke into tears. "Baby, what happened?"

"I don't know," Jamil whispered. "She was making some phone calls at the Teen Center. I didn't hear from her but I thought she might have been working on some stuff for the wedding. Me and Buff were on our way to Compton when the hospital called. Some kids found her near the Teen Center."

Janice pulled Jamil into her arms, and mother and son cried together.

"She's gonna be fine, Mom. She has to get better." Jamil was whispering again.

"I know, baby. I know."

Nina and Kyle arrived on the floor. Buffalo took them into the waiting room and told them what had transpired.

"Oh no," Nina said, sobbing.

"How's Jamil holding up, man?" Kyle asked as he held Nina.

"His moms is with him."

"Cool." Kyle leaned back in his seat. "Who would do something like that?"

"I don't know. But I *will* find out." Buffalo wasn't known for emotion but determination burned in his eyes.

Janice walked into the waiting room. "Hi, baby."

Nina got up to give her a hug. "Hi, Janice." Nina sniffed. "How is she?"

Janice cried a fresh set of tears. "Somebody tried to kill that girl. India is so sweet. Who would want to do a thing like that?"

Buffalo pulled out his cell phone and left the room.

"But she's gonna be alright?" Nina was hopeful.

"Only the good Lord knows." Janice searched her bag for a tissue. Nina took one out of her purse and handed it to her.

"How's Jamil?" Nina asked quietly.

"Why don't you go sit with him for a minute, baby? He's not about to leave her side," Janice said.

Nina looked at Kyle who nodded his approval. She tiptoed down the hall to India's room, trying to think of something to say. "Hey, Jamil."

He turned around and looked at Nina and refocused his attention on India. "Hey."

"How is she?" Nina asked.

"We have to wait and see. She lost a lot of blood," he replied flatly.

"Do you have any idea of who did this?"

"No, but it's definitely gonna get ugly when I do." He spat the words out like venom.

"Jamil . . ." Nina knew that his anger was talking.

"Don't Jamil me," he growled. "She was three months pregnant. We were going to have a little girl."

"I thought she was going to surprise you at the wedding," Nina said softly.

"So that's why she didn't tell me. When did she tell you?"

"The night you guys came over to dinner. She was so excited. She said she had to tell somebody so she told me."

Jamil turned around and looked at her again but said nothing.

"Boss, 5-0 is here. They want to take a statement," Buffalo informed them.

"Later," Jamil barked.

"Why don't you try talking to her?" Nina finally suggested.

"I already did."

"Try again."

"You talk to her."

"Okay." Nina went around to the other side of the bed. "Hey, Miss India. How you doin', girlfriend? Jamil's here, and he really needs you to talk to him, babe. You know how men are with things like this." Nina managed a smile that disappeared immediately when she saw the dried blood in India's hair. She had never experienced anything as horrible as the sight of India lying there, and she wanted to ran out of the room as fast as she could but she knew she had to be strong for Jamil. She offered a silent prayer.

"Hold her hand," Nina commanded.

Jamil looked at her like she was crazy.

"Take her hand," Nina repeated.

Jamil slowly took India's swollen hand into his and held it. "Where's your ring, baby?"

"I'm sure they removed all her jewelry when she came into the ER," Nina informed him.

Jamil bent his head down and kissed the swollen hand, and he felt her squeeze it ever so slightly. "Nina, she squeezed my hand. She squeezed my hand," Jamil repeated excitedly.

"She's going to be fine, Jamil." Nina smiled happily. "Just fine."

India passed on late that night . . . to heaven or not, Nina never knew. India's brother took her body back to Barbados. Nina helped Janice arrange a memorial service for India's friends and Suicide personnel. Several days later Jamil finally went back to work. India's assistants had already divided her duties and cleaned out her office but Jamil could still smell her signature fragrance.

Jamil sat in his office staring out at the traffic on Olive Boulevard. He had never felt so alone.

"Jamil." Anita knocked at the door and entered. "We need you to decide what songs you want to use on So Fine's promotional tour. And then we'll need some DATS and CDs."

"I'll take care of it." Jamil opened a drawer and pulled out a couple of CD covers. Something caught his eye, and he pulled it out of the drawer. It was the framed photograph of him and Nina. He had forgotten it was there. He carefully studied her beautiful face and then his own, which was plastered with a smile. It had been taken after Topaz's first performance at the Soul Train awards, when they first fell in love. He threw it across the room and the glass shattered into pieces, then he put his head down on his desk and sobbed.

Chapter 27

Everyone was deeply depressed by India's death, even more so because it was sudden and totally unexpected. Xtreme and So Fine were scheduled to do a ten-city promotional tour and no one wanted to go. Xtreme couldn't go because the Angels were in the world series, and So Fine just wouldn't exert any energy.

"You think someone wants to buy a CD by someone who sounds the way you girls do?" Charetta barked. "I'm sorry India's gone but life goes on. And we really need to have it together for JW."

"JW?" Sabre look at Charetta and then the others.

"Jamil." Charetta glared at Sabre.

"India would really want you guys to sing." This was Nina's first appearance at the girls' rehearsal. She had been so devastated by India's tragedy that the best she could do was to drag herself out to Pride Rock where she had sat for hours watching the ocean and crying, trying to make some sense out of India's death until Kyle forced her to come inside. She had been so cold her teeth were chattering so he made her tea, gave her warm baths, combed her hair, and then he held her.

"Nina." Sabre led the way as all the girls ran up to her and hugged her.

"How you guys doing?" Nina prayed quickly over each girl as she gave her a hug.

"We miss India," Sabre wailed.

"I know. I miss her too." Nina smiled as Toni gave her a hug. "But she would really want you guys to be at your best. The label was very important to her, and you guys are a part of it." Nina couldn't even say the word *suicide* anymore and admitting the girls were still a part of the label was a hard reality to face.

"Okay, Nina. We're gonna do this for India." Sabre took her position in front of the mirror.

"Could you start the music, Toni?" Shawntay asked.

Toni restarted the CD and their performance was one thousand percent better. Charetta walked across the room and stood next to Nina.

"You were at the hospital. Why didn't you call us so we could have been there for Jamil too?" she demanded.

"Char, I was there purely by accident. Jamil had called me. I was on the other line when he got the call from the hospital," Nina explained.

"What did he call you for?" Charetta looked Nina up and down.

"He wanted to know if I had spoken to India." Nina watched the girls as they continued to rehearse.

"You and India were friends?"

"Yes, we were." Nina focused her attention on Charetta. "Why?"

"No reason in particular." Charetta was surprised that India would befriend Jamil's ex-girlfriend. "You still could have called us. We just really wanted to show our support."

"I can understand that but Jamil was a mess. He really didn't want anyone around."

"Are you coming on tour with us?" Charetta asked.

"Not the entire tour, but definitely New York City. My in-laws live in Philly and New Jersey, so Kyle and I are going to bring Nicki and spend some time with them." Nina smiled as the girls executed a tight dance routine. She was glad she had listened to Kyle and come out to their rehearsal.

"Hey." Jamil walked in the rehearsal hall with Buffalo. "What up?"

"Hey, JW." Charetta couldn't contain her smile when she saw him. "How ya doin'?"

"I'm cool." He walked to a spot in the studio where he could get a full view of the girls. "What up, So Fine?"

Nina was happy to see the smile that graced his face. When the music stopped, all the girls ran over to give Jamil a hug.

"We're so sorry about what happened to Miss India," Sabre whispered in his ear. "We knew you guys were supposed to get married. She told us when we were in Las Vegas."

"Thanks." Jamil planted a kiss on each of their cheeks. "So y'all ready to turn out this promotional tour?"

"Yes," the girls chorused.

"Cool." Jamil gave them a sly grin. "Now I want to see everything from the top."

Toni restarted the music as the girls began to dance. She ran over to Charetta and whispered in her ear, "It's a good thing he didn't get here five minutes earlier or he would have cancelled the entire thing. Thank goodness Nina showed up when she did. She perked them right on up."

"She did." Charetta glanced at Nina who was talking to Jamil.

"Thanks for coming to the hospital." Jamil gave Nina a hug.

"I'm glad I could be there for you." Nina smiled, hoping for the courage to say something she had thought about saying during her days of solace on Pride Rock. "Jamil."

"Yeah?" He was really enjoying So Fine's routines. "I love the choreography, Toni," he yelled over the music.

"Jamil, did you think about any of the things Kyle and I spoke to you about the night you guys came to dinner?" Nina heard herself say.

"What things? We talked about a lot of things that night." Jamil stopped watching the girls and focused all of his attention on Nina.

"You know how we talked about the power of words and the repercussions of naming the company Suicide?" Nina sighed with relief. She had finally said it.

Jamil was silent for a long time. "I thought about it."

"India's death was a repercussion, and it was very violent."

"You crazy." Jamil looked Nina up and down with a wild look in his eyes. "India didn't die because I named the company Suicide. She died because somebody beat her down, and when I find out who did it, there gonna be some repercussions."

"India wouldn't want that," Nina said quietly.

"How the hell do you know what she would want?" Nina had never seen him that angry. "Somebody cut her life short and our daughter's."

"But even if you did find out who did it, it won't bring India back," Nina pleaded.

"If . . . ? I will find out who did it and when I do . . ." Jamil was raging with anger.

"Jamil, just think about changing the name of the company before something else happens, please?"

"Hell naw. Nobody else is gonna get hurt. India was the victim of a violent crime. It happens all the time, every day, everywhere. I only wish I had never taken her in that part of the city, but stuff happens . . . even in Beverly Hills and Malibu."

"That's true. But why India and why now? All of us were down there and nothing happened to anyone else."

"I thought about that, and I'll never forgive myself for taking her down there but it could have been any of us. Everybody loved India, so I know it was nothing personal, but she was going to be my wifey." Jamil choked when he said *wifey*.

"But no one knew you guys were getting married."

"You knew."

"Because you told me and you know I would never tell—"

"I know you would never tell but I have increased security around all the artists, the office, my mom's house, and mine just in case it was personal and somebody was trying to get at me. I wish somebody would try something, he'll get smoked. . . . And I ain't changing the name of my company. India came up with that name and that's the way it's going to stay."

"But, Jamil . . . it's the spirit behind it and the name is associated with death. You can't fight a spirit with guns."

"That spirit stuff is a bunch of crap. I don't believe that." His laughter was cold and cynical.

"Just because you don't believe something doesn't mean it isn't true," Nina insisted.

"Whatever. Look I'm 'bout to bounce up outta here because I can't stand all your yakkin' in my ear. Peace." Jamil left the rehearsal without saying another word to anybody, and Nina could only hope he would think about the things she had said.

"I'll see you guys in NYC," Nina called out as she left the building. "At least he didn't mention anything about Topaz." Nina sighed with relief.

* * *

Toni didn't have much to say as they packed up and headed to the airport. She had been unusually silent and with everything going on no one had really noticed.

"You've been extra quiet lately," Charetta pointed out once they were airborne. "Is it the India ordeal or is it because Xtreme couldn't come on tour with us?"

"He stopped talking to me. I should have never told him that I was in love with him." Toni sighed unhappily and looked out of the window.

"You told him you were in love with him?" Charetta repeated.

"I did it like a fool . . ."

"You are not a fool. He should be glad to have someone like you in love with him."

"Whatever." Toni brushed a tear from her eye.

"Toni, are you sure that's the reason he stopped talking to you? He's in the playoffs and you know how men are—only able to think about one thing at a time. He probably just needs to focus."

"That's not it. I called him three times and he barely spoke to me at the memorial service."

"He didn't call you back once?" Charetta closed the *Billboard* magazine and looked at Toni.

"Nope."

"Call him again."

"I will not. I knew I shouldn't have told him. But he told me there was nothing I could ever say to him that would stop him from talking to me."

"Ha!" Charetta shook her head. "Men are some strange creatures. He's probably just scared."

"Scared? Scared of what?"

"Scared of how he feels." Charetta glanced around the area where they were all sitting to make sure no one was listening to their conversation. All of the girls were asleep. "Jamil and I made love."

A smile lit up Toni's face. "Stop."

Charetta could only smile.

"You really did. When did it happen?"

"The night after the program at the Teen Center."

"You little skank . . . and you didn't even tell me. I want details."

"It was just the two of us at his house playing pool and drinking Hypnotic, and it just happened." Charetta grinned happily. "And it was da bomb."

"For real?" Toni still couldn't believe it.

"For really real." Charetta laughed. "So I know how guys can trip when something they can't handle goes down. I've seen my brothers do it when they were really into some girl."

"Has he said anything to you about India?"

"No."

"That's really interesting, Char, because you know he was going to marry India."

"Really?"

"They were getting married on Thanksgiving."

"So that's what those little heffas were talking about."

"What are you talking about, Char?"

I overheard the girls saying India was getting married but they didn't say to who. So how did you know?"

"Frank told me. He was going to be Jamil's best man. The wedding was going to be in Barbados."

"Wedding or not, we sure did the wild thang."

"That's still kind of deep that he would sleep with you, but men are such dogs. So you guys were upstairs in his bedroom. Isn't it fantastic?"

"We never went upstairs. Buffalo . . ." Charetta stopped speaking.

"Buffalo what?"

"It's nothing important." Charetta couldn't tell her best friend that Buffalo never allowed her to go upstairs to Jamil's fantastic suite.

"It's going to take him a while to get over India, but he's going to want to be with someone eventually, so maybe you guys will hook up."

"I could see myself as Mrs. Jamil Winters." An easy smile graced Charetta's face, and her eyes were sparkling.

"I bet you could. You guys really clicked in the studio."

"He called me his little studio honey. We worked on some songs that night." Charetta was grinning again.

"I always thought you guys would make a cute couple. I'm just sorry that his relationship with India ended the way it did."

"I know," Charetta agreed. "But life does go on."

Chapter 28

VH1 was producing one of its noted *Divas* musical specials, and Topaz was going to be a part of it. The concert would be in New York City. Coincidentally, it was the same week that So Fine would be in the city on their promotional tour, so Jamil, through his many connections, was able to get them on the show singing with Topaz. The girls couldn't have been more excited to share the stage with their friend and mentor, but they were elated over their appearance on BET's *106 and Park* with Free and AJ.

Jamil joined them in New York for rehearsals for the concert. Topaz had brought along Chris and Baby Doll; and Nina and Kyle were there with Nicki. Mary J. Blige was rehearsing when Jamil walked in with Buffalo and Anita. Even though Jamil was wearing sunglasses, Nina knew the moment she saw him he was high.

"What up, black people?" Jamil kissed Topaz first and then So Fine, Nina, Toni, and Charetta.

The girls were all over Jamil with words of gratitude, hugs, and kisses as all three of them talked at once telling him about their adventures on the road.

"That has to do wonders for a brother's ego," Kyle said so only Nina could hear.

"Don't hate the playa, hate the game." Nina laughed and kissed him on the cheek.

"Do you always know the right thing to say?" Kyle looked at her with smiling eyes.

"Just to the man I love." Nina looked at Jamil as she continued talking. "He's really buzzed."

"It's going to take him a minute to get over India."

"How you doin', boo?" Topaz smiled at Jamil.

"Ah-ight. How you doin'?" Jamil fingered one of Topaz's long golden locks.

"This show is gonna be off the hook." Topaz smiled as she watched Ashanti take the stage.

"Ho-ney dip." Jamil grinned with pleasure as his eyes followed Ashanti. "I'm gonna do a couple of tracks on her next album."

"Really?" The smile slowly faded from Topaz's face.

"Fo' sho. I know she's a little younger than you, but you don't have anything to worry about, beautiful, as long as you cut a deal with Suicide." Jamil called Sabre over. "Sit down, gorgeous."

Sabre smiled warmly at Jamil as she cuddled up next to him.

"If you gonna lose sleep over any female in this room, this is the one. I'm gonna sign her to a solo deal in a few years, and she's gonna blow up. Sabre is a diamond." Jamil planted a kiss on her cheek and laughed as Topaz got up and walked away.

"Are you really gonna sign me to a solo deal?" Sabre turned wide, innocent eyes on Jamil.

"Most definitely, but we'll keep that on the down low 'cause the other girls might get jelly." Jamil smoothed Sabre's hair as he spoke. "And I want Nina to be your manager."

"What about Char and Toni?" Sabre fingered the diamonds in Jamil's Rolex.

"Bling-bling." Jamil grinned.

"Cha-ching. Cha-ching," Sabre replied.

"Char and Toni will manage So Fine and Nina will take care of you. I'm gonna set you up with your own TV show like *The Fresh Prince* and *Moesha,* movies like J.Lo. Your own clothing line, and some phat endorsements. We gonna do some real fly stuff," Jamil promised.

"What is up with you?" Nina asked as Topaz dragged her out of rehearsal and into her dressing room. It was decorated with vases of her favorite flowers. There was also a nice spread of Thai food and her favorite Cristal. In her rider, she had also requested a separate room for Baby Doll and a PlayStation 2 for Chris. Baby Doll and Nicki were taking naps while Chris played video games.

"Baby, you've played long enough. You know how your daddy feels about those video games. Turn that off and go in the other room and do your homework," Topaz said.

"I already did it, Mom." Chris didn't take his eyes off the TV set as things continued to crash and explode.

"Then read one of your books. I need to talk to Auntie Nina right now."

"Okay." Chris turned off the game, picked up his backpack, and went into the other room.

"Thanks, baby. I love you," Topaz called after him. She took out a bottle of champagne and opened it while Nina sat down on a beautiful rose-colored sofa that Topaz had also requested for her dressing room.

"My career is over, washed up, I'm a has-been." She poured the bubbly into two glasses and handed one to Nina.

"You are not. Don't tell me you're tripping over the other people on the show because you're only here 'cause the industry considers you a diva. And you will always be a diva." Nina set her glass on the table and got a bottle of juice out of the refrigerator.

"Thanks, Nina." Topaz sighed and leaned back on the sofa.

"What brought all this on?" Nina dipped a skewer of chicken satay into peanut sauce.

"Jamil."

"What did he do now?" Nina looked into her cousin's amber eyes.

"I thought he was giving me a compliment until he called Sabre over and said she was going to be my competition."

"Oh, please." Nina laughed. "Jamil's talking crazy. And I wouldn't take him seriously right now."

"Why not?"

"One, because he's buzzed and two, because Sabre is not as good of a singer as you. And three, because she's not you." Nina got up and made herself a plate. "Girl, this food is da bomb."

"I'm not really hungry right now." Topaz poured herself another glass of champagne.

"Topaz, don't start tripping. You have a show to do tonight, and you don't need anything messing with your head."

"You're right." Topaz sighed. "I guess Jamil was really trying to get to me when he told me he's doing several cuts for Ashanti's next album. He told me I'd have nothing to worry about as long as I was with Suicide."

"He didn't say anything about Nicki, did he?" Nina's face clouded over with concern.

"No."

"Praise God." Nina sighed with relief. "Are you done with rehearsals?"

"Yes."

"Then let's get out of here and go back to the hotel so you can get your head together before the show."

Nina sat in the dressing room with Topaz while a hairstylist worked on her golden mane with a blow dryer and then a flat iron.

"We haven't done this in a long time." Topaz smiled at Nina. "I didn't realize how much I missed my career until I did this show."

"You've only been off the scene for a few years. When people see you all the time, they get sick of you. By the time you record your CD and drop that first single, everyone will be ready and waiting."

There was a cloud of mist as the stylist sprayed Topaz's hair.

"You just put another hole in the ozone layer with all that hairspray." Nina coughed and poured herself a glass of water. She had on the perfect little black dress, and she had pinned her hair up.

"This diva has a lot of hair." Topaz's stylist laughed as he had Topaz stand and continued spraying her hair. "Besides, there aren't any fluorocarbons in this." He read the tall white can of hairspray just to be sure.

"I was just teasing," Nina said. There was a knock at the door and Nina got up to answer it. She opened it and was surprised when she saw Kyle and Chris with the two girls. "What are you doing here?" Nina laughed. She had left the hotel earlier so she could accompany Topaz while she dressed for the concert. The little girls were supposed to remain at the hotel with the nanny.

"Hi, Mommy." Nicki, who was in Kyle's arms, reached for Nina.

"Look at you, beautiful." Nina smiled at her daughter who was wearing a black-and-pink taffeta dress, and her hair was brushed up into a bun.

"I know how you guys like to do that mother-daughter thing so I did the best I could with her hair." Kyle kissed his wife on the cheek. "You're looking very beautiful tonight."

"Look at you, you tall drink of water." Nina winked at Kyle as she looked at Nicki. "Did you thank your daddy for making you look so beautiful?"

"Thank you, Daddy."

Nina and Kyle laughed until Baby Doll pulled on Kyle's jacket. "What about me?"

Kyle picked her up. "What about you, Miss Baby Doll?" He tried not to smile as he looked at the little girl.

"Nini, Uncle Kyle did my hair too. Don't I look beautiful too?"

Baby Doll was dressed in gold taffeta. "You certainly are beautiful. In fact, you and Nicki are the real divas of the night." Nina smiled at both little girls.

"Baby divas." Kyle shook his head.

"That's what you get for being such a ladies' man. Now you're surrounded by women and we're all divas," Nina pointed out.

"Tell me about it." Kyle sighed as if he bore the weight of the world on his shoulders.

"And you men say we're drama. Y'all are the kings of drama." Nina laughed.

Topaz entered in a splash of gold. She lit up the room like a spotlight as she swished across the floor in her designer gown. Everyone was speechless as they watched her check her flawless glamour makeup in the mirror.

"What's wrong? Do I look okay?" Topaz walked over to the full-length mirror to look at her dress. "I don't look fat or anything do I?"

"Tell me you're joking." Nina set Nicki on the sofa.

"Pretty, Auntie." Nicki fixed her amber eyes on Topaz and smiled.

"Thank you, sweetheart." Topaz bent down and kissed the little girl.

"Me, too, Mommy." Baby Doll puckered up her lips.

"Mother, you look so beautiful, we couldn't speak." Chris smiled at Topaz.

"Spoken like a true playa," Kyle said as he and Chris traded pounds. "You rendered us all speechless."

"Really?" Topaz looked into the smiling faces of the ones she considered her nearest and dearest.

"Really." Nina smiled at her cousin. "You're going to turn it out."

* * *

The concert was fabulous. Topaz received a standing ovation on her solo number. So Fine joined her to perform Topaz's rendition of "For the Love of Money." Topaz almost lost it when she saw Sabre. She quickly collected herself as So Fine did their part of the song and finished like the consummate professional she was.

"You guys were wonderful." Jamil, Charetta, Toni, and Nina couldn't say enough about the performance.

Nina looked at Topaz who was like a volcano about to erupt. "What's wrong?"

"Sabre," Topaz fumed.

"Sabre what?" Nina waited for an answer.

Without saying another word Topaz marched over to Sabre and snatched the earrings off of her ears and pushed her. "Take it off. Take it all off before I kick your ass." Topaz was so angry she couldn't see straight.

"What's going on?" Toni walked over to the two of them.

"Stay out of this." Topaz's eyes were like daggers when she looked at Toni.

Sabre was so frightened, her hands were shaking and she could barely undo the catch on the necklace.

"No, we won't stay out of this." Charetta was in the conversation now.

Sabre handed her the matching topaz necklace and the topaz-and-diamond tennis bracelet. She reached down to her ankle and removed the bracelet and dropped it into Topaz's extended hand.

"I want my dress back, too," Topaz demanded.

"Here?" Sabre, who usually had too much attitude, was very intimidated by Topaz's presence. She had never seen Topaz look so beautiful nor so angry.

"Right here and right now." Topaz was shaking with anger.

"What's going on?" Charetta asked again.

"Tell her." Topaz didn't blink as she stared at Sabre.

"I'm wearing her dress and that's her jewelry," Sabre answered quietly.

"I thought you gave her those things." Charetta looked at Topaz.

"I gave her a lot of things, but not *those* things. That dress is one of a kind and the jewelry came from Tiffany's. It was a gift from my daughter's father, and it belongs to Baby Doll."

"You gave a child jewelry from Tiffany's?" Charetta's face registered shock.

"What business is it of yours if I did?" Topaz looked at Charetta who threw her hands up into the air.

"I allowed you free reign of my house, I let you use my dance studio, and I gave you shoes and clothing. I tried to be a friend but that's what I get for helping out a bunch of hood rats."

Topaz stormed out of the backstage area and into her dressing room and Sabre burst into tears.

"What the hell did you do that for?" Charetta yelled at Sabre.

"I didn't know it was real," Sabre said, sniffing.

"Your ass is lucky 'cause if it had been me I would have kicked it all over this building," Charetta barked. "And if you stole those things why would you wear them in front of her?"

Sabre just sniffed as she wiped her eyes with the back of her hand.

Charetta shook her head. "You's a stupid, silly-ass little heffa."

Tears continued to spill out of Sabre's eyes and down her cheeks.

"Sabre, the only reason Topaz didn't kick your behind all over this building is because she had on that designer dress." Nina wanted to laugh.

Jamil, who had been talking during the all the drama, was unaware of what had just transpired between the divas.

"Why is Sabre crying?" Jamil demanded. "She just sang and danced her heart out and she looks fine as hell in that red dress." He pulled her into his arms where she cried like a baby, and Charetta slowly counted to ten in her head.

"That's Topaz's dress and Sabre had on Topaz's jewelry. We were at Topaz's house and she gave us some of her things except she didn't give Sabre those things," Toni explained.

"Look at me, Sabre," Jamil demanded. "Look at me." He held her away from him but she wouldn't hold up her head. "Sabre, look at me." Jamil's voice was softer as he lifted her head and looked into her eyes, which were still filled with tears.

Charetta was ready to explode with jealousy.

"You are a star. And I don't ever want you to steal anything again because you're my diamond."

Sabre's antics had stolen the spotlight from Sky and Shawntay, and they all were a little jealous of all the attention she was getting, especially from Jamil. Nina, who had gone to check on Topaz in the press-room, rejoined the small group.

"What are you, Sabre?" Jamil asked softly.

"I'm a star and I'm a diamond." Sabre finally smiled for the first time since she had been confronted by Topaz.

"And don't you ever forget it." Jamil kissed her gently on the lips and Charetta went back to So Fine's dressing room. Jamil took Sabre by the hand. "Come on, y'all. Let's bounce. We need to hit the press-room and there are some after-parties we need to do."

As the group began to disperse from the backstage area, Jamil saw Nina. "This is all your fault for letting this thing get out of control."

Nina opened her mouth and closed it. She had nothing to say.

The next day Jamil took So Fine shopping on Madison Avenue. He took them to the best stores and spent money like water. Before they left the city, and unbeknownst to the others, he took Sabre to Jacob the jeweler and ordered her a small diamond-encrusted pendant on a platinum filigree chain. Bling-bling.

Chapter 29

Jamil put his hands in his pockets as he looked out of his office at the traffic on Olive Boulevard. He was spending a lot more time there than usual. Xtreme's *Xtremely Xtreme* CD stayed at the top of the charts and had already sold more than five million copies, and So Fine's first single was blazing the charts. Business couldn't be better but Jamil was totally uninterested. There was music and reels of video footage awaiting his approval. New talent had recently been signed to the label but he could have cared less.

He stood there for several more minutes and then he walked over to his desk and picked up the telephone and summoned Anita. No one had mentioned filling India's position but someone needed to make decisions.

"Anita, get Topaz on the phone for me. Her number should be in my Rolodex. If it's not current, call Nina Beaubien and get it from her."

Jamil had sent Topaz several two-way messages but there had been no response. He picked up his two-way and typed in a message to Charetta and returned to the window. Several minutes later the intercom buzzed.

"I have Topaz on the line," Anita informed him.

"Cool." A little smile eased its way onto his face as he picked up the phone. "Superstar."

"Hi, Jamil," Topaz replied coolly.

"Do I sense a divatude?"

"I'm really busy right now."

"Too busy for an old friend?"

Topaz's sigh was long and deep. "No, Jamil. Never."

"That's my girl." Jamil smiled knowingly. "Meet me at L'Ermitage for drinks. Say five-thirty?"

"I can't, Jamil. That's family time."

"Family time?" Jamil laughed. "Are you serious?"

"Yes."

"How do you think you're gonna stay at the top of your game neglecting important meetings for family time? Get a nanny like everybody else."

Topaz was silent as she thought about what Jamil had just said.

"You need to drop a bangin' CD. It's time. You turned it out at that *Divas* concert and people are ready for more. You need to come back right, and I'm just the one to make the delivery."

"I definitely want you involved in the project," Topaz began.

"Your contract is up with Latrell, isn't it?" Jamil cut in.

"Yes. But we're going to—"

"Good. Latrell used to be the man, but he's fat in the pockets now and his game is weak."

"What do you mean?" Topaz asked.

"He doesn't have the juice to get who you need if you want to be a diamond. I can do that for you. You got the pipes and you definitely got the look. I can make that happen. I'm gonna get you in some movies too. When I'm finished, you'll blow J.Lo out of the water."

"Can we do a lunch meeting?" Topaz was excited.

"Sure, sweetness. We'll do the Ivy. Anita will get back to you after she's made the reservations." Jamil hung up the phone and grinned as he leaned back in his chair. "Everybody has a price, and I just bought Topaz."

Anita walked into his office. "Char Jackson is here to see you."

"She sure got here fast." Jamil laughed.

"What?" Anita looked blank.

"Nothing. I have a few phone calls to make. I'll buzz you when I want you to bring her in." Jamil flipped on the television and channel surfed. His two-way beeped nonstop and he typed in responses. Thirty minutes had gone by when he finally had Charetta come in.

"What up, girl? How's my favorite songwriter and producer?" He gave her one of his best smiles.

"I'm cool. What up with you?" Charetta flopped down on the sofa. She was wearing stretch denim and her hair was braided.

"Work. See all this? " Jamil pointed to all the tapes stacked on his desk.

"You got a serious backlog there." Charetta got up and picked up a tape.

"That's new music I need to listen to and some video footage from a couple of our other acts. I was wondering if you could help a brother out." Jamil smiled and Charetta melted.

"Sure, JW."

"Cool. You take care of the music and I'll look at the tapes. You can use India's—no you can work in the conference room. Anita will show you where everything is."

Nina sat in the playroom with Topaz. When Topaz phoned her to tell her about her conversation with Jamil, Nina had jumped in the car and driven right over.

"I don't believe you." Nina shook her head and looked at her cousin like she was crazy. "You promised me you weren't going to have anything to do with Suicide and now you're taking meetings with Jamil?"

"He wants to sign me. He said Latrell's game is weak and he could deliver. He said I was a diamond and I'd blow J.Lo out of the water."

"You already are a diamond and you're not in competition with J.Lo."

"Nina, I haven't had a CD out for years."

"Your last one is still being played and so is the first one," Nina reminded her.

"That's true, but I have to come back strong. There's a lot of competition out there. Jamil said he'd put me on top." Topaz was really excited. "He's talking about giving me all the things I want, and he has my vision."

"Jamil's got you hyped and you're feeling the vapors. Jamil isn't God."

"I know that," Topaz snapped.

"Then act like it. There are other labels out there who can do the same thing for you."

"I don't want another label." Topaz met Nina's eye.

"Oh, Lord. Not you too." Nina put her hands on her head. "What is wrong with you people?"

"Nina, don't start that death stuff again because I don't want to hear it. I thought about what you said, and I don't believe it."

"Oh, so you gonna go cut a deal with a label that stands for death? That's real smart," Nina yelled.

"It's just hip-hop."

"That is not hip-hop," Nina yelled.

"It is too. And stop yelling. It's just an edge, an image. It's part of the business." Topaz smiled. "Don't take everything so seriously, Nina."

"You weren't there. You didn't see India. Somebody tried to kill her. It's a miracle she was still breathing when they brought her to the hospital, and you tell me it's just hip-hop?"

"I'm sorry about what happened to India. Very sorry, but it was an accident, and accidents happen. You don't see Jamil closing the doors and saying he's not going to do hip-hop anymore because of what happened to India."

"He needs to," Nina said softly.

"Earth to Nina. Come back to the real world." Topaz laughed.

"It's not funny, and I don't even know how you could trust Jamil after the things I've told you and even the things he's said to you."

"What are you talking about?"

"Do you have rocks for brains or is it selective memory? Let's start with what he said when we were in New York. Didn't he tell you Sabre was your competition?"

"Yes, but we both said he was just messing with my head."

"So how do you know he didn't mean that? Maybe he just wants you at Suicide so he can tie up your career while he blows up Sabre."

"Jamil would never do that," Topaz replied quickly.

"How do you know? We both said he's not the same person."

"Because I'm worth too much money. He's not going to sign me for peanuts. We're talking millions here, baby. Lots of them. Jamil can't afford to throw away that kind of money and not recoup it."

"You have a point there, but I still wouldn't trust him."

"Nina, it's business. Lighten up." Topaz opened the refrigerator and took out a bottle of champagne and placed two flutes on the counter.

"None for me, thank you."

"Fine." Topaz put away the second glass and looked at Nina as she sipped at hers. "I didn't want to say this but you've changed since you married Kyle."

"I have not."

"Yes, you have."

"How?"

"Do you still keep your stash in that little red metallic box?"

"I don't do that anymore. And how do you know what was in my box unless you were snooping?"

"And this . . ." Topaz continued. "You used to always have a glass of champagne with me."

"So. Just because I don't want to have a drink in the middle of the day, that's a problem?"

"No, but I know it's because of Kyle."

"We have a glass occasionally but no, we don't drink the stuff like water."

"I don't either, but I don't like stress and it helps me to relax."

"Prayer and reading your Bible can do that."

"And all this God stuff . . ."

"All this God stuff was fine when you wanted Germain back, so now that you've got him you feel you don't need the Lord in your life anymore?"

"I never said that."

Nina got up and put her hands on her cousin's shoulders and looked into her eyes. "Topaz, I love you and you're closer to me than my own sister. These are serious times. Jesus is coming back, and I don't want to see anyone I love left behind."

Topaz smiled and kissed Nina on the cheek. "I love you, too, Nina, but it's just hip-hop."

Charetta brought all of the tapes into Jamil's office. She had logged all of her comments on index cards and numbered them and the tapes accordingly. She was surprised to find him staring out of the window at the evening traffic.

"All through, JW." Jamil was startled by her presence. He hadn't heard her entering his office. "You've got some really great tracks here."

"Cool." Jamil flipped through the stack of cards with Charetta's comments. "I've got some other things you can help me out with too. Can you spare the time and work with me in the office for a minute?"

"Anything for a friend." Charetta smiled happily.

"Cool. I'll make it worth your while. So you want to go eat or something?"

"Or something." Charetta didn't know where the girly attitude and the words came from. Jamil drew things out of her that she didn't know were there.

"I feel like burgers and fries. How 'bout you?"

"I like burgers and fries."

"Did you park in the garage?"

"Yes."

"Leave your car and we'll take the Hummer."

Charetta was so excited she could barely speak. She was actually going to ride with Jamil. By the time they got to the reception area, Buffalo was waiting.

"Let's roll, Buff. Char's one of the guys tonight."

Charetta didn't know if she cared for being labeled one of the boys but she could see where her dream of running things with Jamil was coming into fruition. Buffalo got behind the wheel and Jamil sat in the back with Charetta.

"Powder or trees?" Jamil pulled out a bag of drugs.

"Both." Charetta laughed and Jamil laughed with her.

"My kind of girl." Jamil gave her a blunt to smoke. Charetta watched him spread lines on the cover of a magazine.

"Y'all need to chill with that while I do the drive-through." Buffalo was never a man of many words. That was the most Charetta had ever heard him say.

"Ah-ight, Buff. What do you want to eat?" Jamil asked Charetta.

"A cheeseburger, and super-size it."

"Super-size it." Jamil was practically on the floor. "Home girl got jokes, Buff."

They devoured the food and the drugs on the ride home.

"You down for some pool?" Jamil asked as they entered the house.

"You want me to kick your ass on your pool table again?" Charetta laughed.

"You just got lucky."

"I sure did." Charetta smiled. "The day I met you." She kissed him before she broke.

Charetta won three games straight. She gave Jamil a smug grin when she sank the last ball.

"Damn, girl. How you gonna come up in my house and kick my ass like that?" Jamil looked at her like a sad little puppy. The male ego hated to lose.

"Tell you what." Charetta walked over to the bar and found a bottle of tequila. "Let's do some body shots. Buff's not coming back in here, is he?"

"Nope."

"Cool." Charetta pulled her T-shirt over her head. She poured several shots of tequila and began lining them up on the bar

Jamil was immediately turned on when he saw she wasn't wearing a bra. He hadn't really looked at her the first time they had sex but he was pleased when he saw her tightly toned body.

Charetta poured a shot and drank it and then she handed him one. "Ah-ight. Go for it."

Jamil licked the alcohol off her smooth skin and reached for another.

"Not so fast, baby. Char gets a turn too." Charetta pulled his shirt over his head and poured her tequila on his chest. By the time she was finished removing the alcohol he was dragging her toward the downstairs bedroom.

"How come we can't do this upstairs in your room?" Charetta asked. She was thinking about what Toni had said when she told her they had done it.

"Don't you worry about goin' upstairs. Just shut up and kiss me, ho," Jamil commanded, and Charetta promptly obeyed.

Chapter 30

It was an unusually warm day in December even for Southern California and it was even hotter at the girls' house in Van Nuys. The temperature was in the nineties and it felt like summer. For once there was no business, school, or lessons, so after breakfast, everyone had dispersed in different directions. The teenagers to the mall to do some Christmas shopping, and Charetta had offered no explanation of her plans . . . not even to Toni.

Toni was glad to have the house to herself. It was rarely, if ever, when she was completely alone, and she relished the quiet and peacefulness in the empty house. She placed her hands over the small bulge in her stomach and wondered how much longer she would be able to keep her pregnancy a secret. There was no question of who the father was . . . it was Frank. She hadn't been with anyone else, and she still hadn't seen or heard from him since the night she had told him that she loved him.

Toni went into the kitchen and jumped when she bumped into Charetta on her way out of the kitchen. "Char, you scared me. What are you doing here? I thought you were gone." She put a hand over her breast and felt her heart racing.

"I just ran out to do an errand."

"Oh." Toni looked at Charetta whose recent behavior had taken a strange turn. She was staying out all night and paying very little attention to the needs of the girls. And for some reason, Nina rarely came around, so all the management responsibilities of the group fell on Toni.

"Are the kids here?" Charetta looked around for some sign of their whereabouts.

"No. You know they went to the mall."

"That's right." Charetta laughed as she lit a blunt. "I forgot."

"Don't do that in here." Toni made a face as Charetta puffed away. "That stuff stinks."

"Since when?"

"Since forever. Go outside, Char. Please." Toni got up and turned on the ceiling fan. She didn't want to inhale any secondhand smoke, and she didn't want anything to affect her unborn baby.

"Ah-ight, chica. Chill. I'll put it out. Just don't have a hissy fit on me." Char carefully extinguished the marijuana.

"I can't believe you would do that in here."

"I said I was sorry. Damn, girl. Kill the drama."

Toni knew without asking that Charetta had been hanging out with Jamil. "Char, be careful."

"Be careful of what?"

"Jamil. It's too soon for him to be serious about anyone yet, and I don't want to see you get hurt. You have to give this thing time."

"I'm not going to get hurt. And did you ever think that maybe Jamil wasn't really in love with India? Guys always *think* they're in love until something better comes along."

"That could be true but you still need to take it slow. Jamil probably doesn't even know what he's feeling. Men aren't as emotional as women. He needs time to process his feelings," Toni offered.

"I'm cool, girl. But thanks for having my back."

"Always." Toni smiled. "Always. You're my sister."

"Have you heard from Xtreme yet?"

"No." Toni gently rubbed her stomach.

"Don't feel bad, girl. I don't think Jamil has either. He hardly ever mentions him unless he's talking about his CD. You must have did a number on his head because the brother disappeared."

"Really?" Toni was amazed. She thought Xtreme and Jamil were inseparable.

"Did you try calling him again?"

"Yes, and he didn't return the call. I'm done. I thought he was different but I guess I was wrong."

The telephone rang and Charetta picked it up. "Toni, it's him."

"Char, stop teasing."

"No, it's really him." Charetta looked too serious as she held out the receiver.

"Frank is on the phone?" Toni was shocked. It had been weeks since they had spoken.

"Yeah. Is that weird or what?"

"I don't believe you."

"Girl, would you take this phone and talk to the man before I kick your ass over this house?"

Toni had to smile as she took the receiver.

"Hey, Toni." It really was Xtreme.

"It's really him, Char," Toni whispered loudly.

"I told you," Charetta whispered back. "I wouldn't joke about something like that."

"I'm sorry I haven't been around or returned your phone calls."

Toni made no comment as she rolled her eyes.

"I was wondering, if you weren't doing anything if I could come over and maybe we could go to the beach or something so we can talk."

"So you don't call since who knows when, and all of a sudden you do call and I'm supposed to jump up and go to the beach with you? Are you crazy?" Toni's voice rose an octave. She was so livid, she began to speak in Spanish.

Charetta covered her mouth to contain the laughter that wanted so badly to escape.

"Yeah, I'm crazy, crazy about you. I love you, Toni," Xtreme replied softly.

Toni was ready to continue her tirade when his words finally sunk in. "What did you say?"

"I said I love you."

"I love you, too, Frank."

"Ahh." Charetta smiled. "The lovebirds made up."

Toni hung up the phone all smiles. "He's coming over."

"Cool. I'm gonna head out so you guys can have the place to yourselves."

"You don't have to go. I'll make dinner." Toni ran into the kitchen to look in the refrigerator. "We don't have anything. I need to go shopping."

Charetta walked into the kitchen and closed the refrigerator door. "You aren't cooking anything. That man hasn't called you or tried to see you for weeks. Go out to dinner or order something. I listened to you earlier, now you listen to me."

"You're probably right." Toni looked longingly at the refrigerator. She loved to cook and she loved cooking for her man.

"I mean it, Toni. He's a brother and sometimes they need a kick in the head. I grew up with five of them. You gotta keep a black man in check or he will get way outta control."

"Okay, Char." Toni was laughing for the first time in weeks. "I won't cook. At least not today."

"Good. I'm gonna bounce before your man makes one of his grand entrances. Stick a note on the door and tell the kids to go see a movie."

"Char . . ." Toni put her hands on her hips.

"I'm out, girlfriend. Have fun," Charetta called as she went out the door. Toni smiled and ran into her room to change clothes.

Charetta took Ventura Boulevard all the way to Jamil's house. Since the day was so warm they had made plans to go swimming. She had gone to Fashion Square to purchase a new bathing suit and cover-up so she could look especially good for Jamil. She pulled her Land Rover up to the gate and pressed the button on the squawk box.

"Holla."

Charetta smiled as soon as she heard his voice. "It's me, JW."

"Who?"

"It's me."

"Who the hell is me?"

"Jamil, it's Char. Stop playing and open the gate."

"Stop playing? Girl, you betta recognize."

Charetta let out a long sigh. He was killing the mood. She hated when he put her through changes like that. "Are you going to let me in or what?"

The black wrought-iron gate slowly rolled open, and she drove on the property and pulled up next to a black convertible Mercedes with the top dropped. She glanced at the Benz as she got her things out of the truck and went inside where Jamil was in the kitchen drinking Hypnotic.

"What up?"

"Why you trippin' with the gate?" Charetta demanded.

"Because I felt like it." Jamil took a sip out of a tall glass filled with ice and liquor that resembled blue Kool-Aid. "You want a drink?"

"Yeah, I'm gonna need something if you expect me to put up with your silly ass." She reached for his drink, but he held it out of her reach.

"Go make your own."

She rolled her eyes at him as she stormed into the billiard room and made herself a drink and Jamil followed her laughing.

"Come here." He pulled her into his arms and kissed her and she felt herself melting. "You know I was just playing."

"You play too much."

"Wanna play some pool?" Jamil picked up a cue stick.

"I always beat you. That's no fun." Charetta finished her drink and made another.

"Did it ever cross your mind that I might be letting you win?" Jamil aimed at the cue ball and sent it flying across the table.

"No."

"Why?"

"Because you always act like a punk when you lose." Charetta looked at him and laughed. "I need some real competition."

"Oh, you must want to go home 'cause you don't come to my house and talk to me any kind of way."

"Jamil, I was just playing. Can't you take a joke?"

"I was just playin', too, but you want to come up in my house with an attitude. Don't you know I could have anybody over here?"

"You said you wanted to spend time with me."

"Not with an attitude."

"Okay, no attitude. See, I'm smiling." Charetta grinned from ear to ear.

"That's more like it. So what do you want to do?"

"Go for a drive in your convertible Mercedes and then go for a swim."

"No." Jamil sank balls in the pockets.

"No what?"

"No, we ain't goin' for a drive in my Benz but we can go swimming."

Charetta walked out of the room and went into the downstairs bedroom and sat on the bed. She thought about going home and then she remembered Toni was at the house with Xtreme. She thought about what Toni had said earlier about Jamil not being in touch with his feelings and decided he needed some help. She put on her new bathing suit, a red thong bikini, and walked back into the room.

"Damn, girl. I see you're ready to go swimming." Jamil followed her outside to the pool and watched her get in.

"Are you coming in? The water feels great." Charetta laughed as she watched him pull off his shirt and dive in. She swam to the deep end of the pool and watched him swim up to her. They were both laughing as they tussled in the water. He pulled off the top of her suit and flung it out of the pool and laughed so hard he had to hold on to the edge of the pool.

"Jamil."

"What?" He could barely speak because he was still laughing.

Several of his boys walked by the pool. "West Coast." They threw up some gang signs and then they saw Charetta.

"Damn, J. Is this one of your new hoes?" one of them asked. Their eyes practically popped out of their heads when they spotted her in the pool topless.

"That's just Char," Jamil offered.

Charetta was mortified. She had no towel, her top was lying by the side of the pool, and all of the men's eyes were glued on her.

"Jamil, I don't believe you. Get them out of here while I get out of the pool," Charetta commanded.

"Attitude. That girl got too much attitude." Jamil laughed and his friends joined in.

Charetta swam to the opposite end of the pool, climbed out, and ran into the house. She could hear them all outside laughing while she found a towel and dried off. A few minutes later, as she was throwing her things inside a beach bag, Jamil came into the room.

"Where you goin'?"

"Home."

"Come here."

He tried to pull her into his arms and she pushed him on the bed.

Charetta was strong for a girl and used to defending herself against her brothers. Jamil jumped back up and she pushed him down again.

"Oh, it's on now," Jamil declared. They tussled around the room slamming into furniture and against walls and picture frames. She had wrapped a towel around herself and he pulled that off her. They were both out of breath when he wrestled her down on the bed and fell out beside her.

"Damn, girl. You tried to kick my ass."

"I will if you ever do that again."

"It wasn't like I did it on purpose. I didn't know they were coming over."

"You didn't do anything to help either. Just laughed with your boys."

"Don't be mad." He kissed her until she finally gave in.

"I'm getting a drink. Do you want one?" She pulled on the cover-up to her bathing suit.

"Hook me up with some Hypnotic."

Charetta slipped something out of her bag and went to make the drinks. She dropped a small pill in his glass and splashed his favorite blue alcohol into it along with ice and stirred the drink. She placed a pill in her glass, too, and poured in cranberry juice and carried both glasses back into the bedroom.

"Here." Charetta handed him his drink and sat on the bed.

"Get in," he ordered.

"No. I want to go upstairs." She looked at him as she sipped her drink, and for the first time, he noticed she had light eyes.

"Are you wearing colored contacts?"

"No."

"Your eyes are that color?"

"Yes."

"They're pretty."

"Thanks." That was the first personal compliment he had ever given her. "I want to go upstairs."

"What is it about you and upstairs?"

"I want to be with you in your room, not down here."

"It ain't going to be any different."

"You never know. Now let's go before I kick your ass again." Charetta pulled him out of the bed and pushed him toward the stairs.

"Ah-ight." He led her upstairs to his bedroom, decorated in black, charcoal, and silver. The marble bath was done in the same colors.

"Look at that." Charetta climbed into the bed and scooted over until she was in the middle and stared up at the flat-screen monitor fastened on the ceiling. "Do you actually watch TV this way?"

"Sometime." He climbed in the bed next to her and looked up at the ceiling. The ecstasy she had slipped him was already starting to take effect.

"I want to try watching television this way. Where's the remote?"

"Look in the nightstand."

Charetta rolled over and pulled the drawer in the nightstand open. She was shocked when she saw a box of jewelry—bracelets, rings, necklaces. A ring box was on top of the other stuff and she opened it.

"Damn." She was shocked when she saw the five-carat diamond engagement ring. "Jamil, what's this?"

"What's what?" He was half-asleep.

"This." Charetta held up the ring in the box so he could see.

He sat up, opened his eyes, and looked at what she was holding. It was the engagement ring he had given Nina and never taken back. "What the hell are you doin' with that? See, that's why I didn't want to bring your nosy ass up here."

Charetta took it out of the box and tried it on. It fit perfectly and didn't need to be sized. "Can I have it?"

"Yeah." He laughed sarcastically. "You can have it."

Charetta was all smiles as she continued her search through the drawer until she finally located the remote and turned on the television. "Come on, boo. Char's gonna love you right."

Later, as soon as he fell asleep, Charetta picked up his used condom and carefully packed it in a container of dry ice and sneaked it downstairs with the rest of her things. She tiptoed back up the stairs and climbed into bed beside Jamil and fell asleep until Buffalo knocked on the door.

"Boss, Toni just called. She's at the hospital. Xtreme had an accident on his motorcycle on the way to her house, and he's in a coma."

Chapter 31

Nina was relieved when she pulled into the driveway and saw that Kyle's Escalade was missing. She had been Christmas shopping and she didn't want him to see his presents. She didn't know who was worse—Kyle or Nicki—when it came to birthdays and Christmas. She took the bags containing his gifts and dashed upstairs and stashed them inside Nicki's closet just in case he came home while she was taking things out of the car. She had just taken the last Toys R Us bag out of the car and closed the door when he pulled into the driveway beside her.

"Let me help you with those, baby." Kyle was already out of the car. He grabbed all the shopping bags and kissed his wife before she had a chance to say anything.

"You are too smooth." Nina laughed until she remembered she had purchased Kyle a train set for his birthday and it was inside one of the bags he was carrying.

"What's wrong?" Kyle's face registered his concern.

"Oh, nothing. I think I may have left something at the store."

"Something you already purchased?" Kyle set the bag with the train set down and Nina snatched it up.

"No. But I don't want to go back to the mall. It was really crowded." She picked up a few of the other bags and disappeared. Topaz had taken the girls to a Christmas party so she didn't have to concern herself with Nicki trying to see what was inside the bags too. A colonial-style dollhouse was still in the Range Rover with a hand-painted china tea set.

"Let's go see a movie." Kyle pulled Nina onto the sofa beside him.

"Okay." Nina took the entertainment section out of the *Los Angeles Times* and opened it. "Do you want to go out here or to the Beverly Center so we can go to P.F. Chang's for dinner?"

"Do we have to pick up Nicki tonight?"

"No. Topaz said Germain would bring her home tomorrow evening," Nina offered.

"Cool. Then let's go to City Walk," Kyle suggested.

"Oooh." Nina grinned. "We haven't been there for a while."

"We can get some dinner and catch a midnight showing and see two movies."

"Sounds like a plan to me." Nina took Kyle's hand in hers. "But you know your daughter's favorite karaoke place is there." Nina smiled. "Aren't you going to feel a little guilty for going without her?"

"No because I got her a karaoke machine for Christmas." Kyle headed through the canyon toward the Ventura Freeway.

"A toy or the real deal? "

"The real deal. Nothing but the best for my princess." Kyle smiled proudly.

"Why did I even ask?" Nina laughed. "She's going to love it and you."

"Don't be jelly," Kyle teased.

They were both laughing when a cell phone rang.

"Is that you or me?" Nina searched through her bag for her phone.

"That's you." Kyle watched Nina flip the phone open just before it went to voice mail.

"We'll be there as soon as we can," Nina replied quietly. "We were on our way to the movies."

"What is it? Is something wrong with Nicki?"

Nina sighed and shook her head. "Xtreme was in an accident on the 405 on his motorcycle. Some metal containers that were chained to a flatbed rolled off the truck and onto the freeway. One of the containers hit Xtreme and he was thrown into the air."

"Dang." Kyle was speechless. "Is he okay?"

"He's unconscious."

"What hospital?"

"Long Beach. He was on his way to see Toni."

Toni nervously paced the floor in the intensive care unit. Highway patrol had identified Xtreme as the star pitcher for the Angels and located the team's owner who had phoned Xtreme's parents in Detroit. On a hunch, the patrolman had dialed the last number called in Xtreme's cell phone and reached Toni. The nurse had come and gone so Toni was back by his bedside. He looked as though he was sleeping peacefully. He had crushed his entire right side when he was thrown into the air. He had broken an arm, a leg, and crushed several fingers on his right hand. There was a cut on his forehead that ran across his scalp, which had required seventy-two stitches. The doctor said he was young and strong, but he was unable to ascertain the extent of the damage that had been done to Xtreme's brain or why he was still unconscious.

Toni jumped up and began pacing again. She just couldn't be still. She heard voices and looked up to see the teenagers arriving.

"Toni." The girls rushed toward her, and she embraced all three of them at once.

"How's Xtreme?" Sabre asked.

"He's unconscious, but he's holding his own." Toni wiped a tear from her eye.

"Holding his own?" Sky peered at him over Toni's shoulder.

"He doesn't need any of those machines to help him breathe," Toni replied.

"That's good, right, Toni?" Sabre looked hopeful.

"I think so. I've already been to the chapel to say a prayer for him." Toni left the girls in the waiting room and went back to Xtreme.

Nina and Kyle appeared in the waiting room next. Sabre said very little, pretending to be absorbed in a magazine. They went into Xtreme's room and spoke briefly with Toni.

"I can't go through this again," Nina said once they were seated in waiting room. "This thing is turning into a nightmare."

"I know, baby. We can leave if you want." Kyle took Nina's hand.

"I don't want to leave Toni here by herself."

"She's not by herself. The girls are here."

"Like, I said, I don't want to leave Toni here by herself." Nina got up and went to speak with the teenagers. "Where's Char?"

"I don't know. We were at the mall. Toni two-wayed us and told us to come to the hospital," Sky replied.

"You want to take the kids and go see a movie or something?" Kyle whispered in her ear.

"Yeah, after Char gets here. Good idea. Thanks, baby."

Charetta arrived within the next half hour. She had gone home to change clothes. She barely spoke to anyone as she passed through the waiting area on her way into Xtreme's room.

"How's he doing, sweetie?" Charetta hugged Toni who began crying. "Buffalo said he was in a coma."

"He's unconscious," Toni corrected with a sniff.

"What did the doctor say?" Charetta sat down in a chair.

"Nothing really. Char, I'm pregnant," Toni whispered.

"You are?" A huge smile covered Charetta's face. "Congratulations."

"I never had a chance to tell him." Tears spilled out of Toni's eyes.

"You'll get a chance to tell him." Charetta put her arms around Toni. "I'm pregnant too." She thought about Jamil's condom that was on ice.

Toni sniffed and wiped her eyes with a tissue. "You are?"

"Yes." Charetta smiled.

"Congratulations." Toni smiled again as she gave Charetta a hug.

"I wonder what those two are hugging about," Nina whispered to Kyle.

The elevator doors opened and Jamil and Buffalo walked in. "What up, black people?" Jamil looked terrible. He reeked of marijuana and his eyes looked tired. His clothes looked like he had just picked them up off the floor.

"Jamil? Are you okay?" Nina couldn't remember when, if ever, she had seen him look so bad.

Sabre was in his face before he had a chance to respond. "Hi, Jamil." She pressed herself against his body and into his arms.

"Hi, gorgeous." Jamil kissed her on the cheek as the other teenagers ran up. "How are my fine-ass girls?" He looked into Xtreme's room and saw Charetta and Toni watching him so he turned away.

"Poor Jamil. He looks awful." Nina observed the entire thing while she rested her head on Kyle's shoulder. "He's not ready for this again either."

"Maybe he'll think about what we said now." Kyle stroked his wife's hands. "Let's go. Char's here now."

"Maybe we should hang out a little longer." Nina's eye followed Jamil.

"Xtreme has lots of people here. His teammates. His mom and dad are on the way. See if the kids want to go see a movie and let's go." Kyle spoke softly in her ear.

"How you doin', Miss Nina?" Buffalo stopped to speak.

"I'm doin' okay, Buffalo. How are you?" Nina had never heard him say more than a few words.

"Not expectin' to be in nobody's hospital again."

"Yeah. Me too. How's Jamil doin'? I know Xtreme is his boy." Before Buffalo could reply, Charetta came out of the hospital room and into the waiting area.

"Hey, Buff. How ya doin'?" Charetta butted into the conversation, making a lot of unnecessary movements with her hands until Nina spotted the diamond on her finger.

Buffalo grunted and went to see So Fine.

Nina took Charetta's hand. "Char, that's a really nice ring. Where did you get it?"

"It was a present from a very good friend." Charetta pulled her hand away from Nina.

"That's really nice." Nina tried to keep a straight face as she went to speak to Toni. "Kyle and I are going to take the girls to my house. This is no place for them."

"That's a good idea, Nina, thanks." Toni smiled warmly. "Girl, when Frank gets better, we need to have a long talk."

"We will." Nina smiled and kissed her on the cheek. "And you don't worry. Xtreme's going to be just fine."

"He has to be, Nina. I'm pregnant," Toni whispered in Nina's ear.

"Oh my God." Nina heard herself saying the exact same words to Jamil that she had said about India. It was as though history was repeating itself. She ran out of the room and ran smack into Jamil, grabbed him by the collar, and began shaking him. "Change the name of the company, Jamil. Get rid of that name before someone else dies."

The room was silent as everyone turned to look at Nina who was crying hysterically. Kyle rushed to her side but she didn't see her husband. All Nina could feel and see was death. It was all around her . . . the pain, the loss, the emptiness, and the darkness. It was all over the waiting room, in Xtreme's room. It was like the movie *Ghost*. Her eyes were opened and she could see in another world. She felt like it was trying to swallow her up and then she was angry.

"Nooooo," Nina screamed with every once of energy she had.

Buffalo picked her up and headed toward the elevator.

"Baby, what's wrong?" Kyle was terrified. He had never seen Nina that way.

"She needed to get out of there, man. I felt like doin' the same thing." Buffalo put Nina in the car where she continued to scream.

The girls just stood around.

"Y'all get in the car and follow them home," Buffalo barked at the teenagers. "I'm gonna call y'all in half an hour, and I better hear some ocean breezes."

Nina was asleep by the time they reached the freeway. Kyle led the group back out to Malibu. Before they reached the house, Nina opened her eyes.

"Everything the water touches is our kingdom." Kyle smiled as he continued down the last stretch of the highway.

"I know, Simba." Nina leaned on his shoulder.

"Are you okay?"

"Yeah, why?"

"You were a little upset at the hospital."

"I was?"

"You don't remember?"

Nina shook her head as her cell phone rang.

"I'll answer that. I don't want anyone upsetting you again."

"Ah-ight." Nina smiled and handed him the phone. She watched her husband listen intently.

"That was Buffalo. Xtreme opened his eyes and asked for a cheeseburger and French fries right after you had your screaming fit. Jamil went out and bought him an In and Out burger and the doctor said he's going to be fine."

Chapter 32

Jamil's publicist had managed to keep the circumstances surrounding India's death out of the press, although there had been a lot of gossip in the industry. He looked at the Angels front office personnel talking with a local sportscaster about Frank Hammond's condition. According to them, Frank would probably miss spring training but be as good as new by the time the next season began. Suicide's legal counsel had advised Jamil to allow the Angels to handle everything. Two accidents would definitely raise a few eyebrows.

Jamil turned off the television set and went to look out of his office window. His two-way beeped but he ignored it. He had been receiving messages all morning about Xtreme. He knew the industry was buzzing, and he had to do something. He picked up the telephone and dialed a number.

"Superstar." Jamil's face lit up as he continued talking. "We need to finalize our plans for signing you to the label. "

"Jamil, I'm in the middle of something and I'm going to have to call you right back." Topaz hung up the telephone before Jamil could say another word and dialed her cousin.

Kyle answered the telephone. "Nina's been through a lot and she's not talking to anyone today." Kyle looked out the window at Nina who was walking on the beach.

"But I need to ask her about Xtreme," Topaz protested.

"What about him?"

"Does she think his motorcycle accident has anything to do with that stuff she was talking about?"

"What do you think, Topaz? You know, it's really time for you to start thinking for yourself and stop depending on Nina all the time."

"I can think for myself."

"Then do it." Kyle hung up the phone as Nina came inside.

"Enjoy your walk, baby?"

"Yes. Who was on the phone?"

"Wrong number."

Topaz called her lawyer and asked him to inform Jamil that she would not be signing with Suicide.

"Not?" Her counsel repeated just to be sure he had heard correctly.

"That's right. I'm not signing any deals."

"It's a very lucrative offer."

"Just do what I told you to do," Topaz barked and hung up.

One hour later Anita informed Jamil that Topaz's attorney was on the line. Jamil picked up the phone happy because the moment Topaz signed, a press release would be issued immediately informing the media of her association with the label and hopefully offset the news of Xtreme's accident. Jamil picked up the telephone grinning.

"Jamil, my client has asked me to inform you that she's passing on your offer."

"She's doing what?" Jamil had been reclining in his desk chair. He sat up straight and gave his caller his full attention.

"She's not interested. Thank you very much."

Jamil stared at the phone, trying to figure out what had gone wrong. "Oh, hell no." He called Topaz first and the phone rang through to her answering service. He slammed the receiver down and speed-dialed Nina and was immediately angry when Kyle answered.

"Let me speak to Nina," Jamil commanded.

"She's not available." Kyle was overly polite as he delivered the message.

"This is important. I really need to talk to her right away."

"I said she's not available."

"Where is she?"

"She is not available. Do you understand the words that are coming out of my mouth?" Kyle and Nina, who had been listening to the entire conversation, were practically on the floor laughing.

"He's going to be mad at us." Nina wiped a tear from her eye. "Jamil's not used to being told no."

"So." Kyle pulled his wife into his arms. "He'll get over it, and I get tired of everyone calling you when they have a problem."

Jamil was furious. He wanted to tear up something but he couldn't destroy his own office. Charetta walked in with a stack of tapes.

"Not now." Jamil was almost whispering.

"This is a really good song. I think it would be great for So Fine," Charetta continued.

Jamil took the box of tapes and threw them against the wall. "I said not now, bitch. Do you understand English?"

Charetta looked at the tapes all over the floor and then Jamil. "Did I do something?"

"No."

"Is something wrong?"

"Everything's wrong," Jamil yelled.

"What is it, baby?"

"Topaz was going to sign and now she won't. I know Nina has something to do with this." He used to talk to India whenever he was having a bad day.

"Topaz was going to sign with Suicide?" Charetta sat down on the sofa.

"Yes." Jamil sat there looking at his two-way, which had just beeped.

"That's interesting."

"Why?" Jamil couldn't help wondering why Charetta who always had something to say, suddenly had nothing to say.

"It just seems that signing her could be a slight conflict of interest with So Fine. You put her on the label and everyone's going to forget about the girls."

"Now that's real interesting because Nina is one of So Fine's managers and she thought signing her cousin would be great for the label." Jamil knew Nina hadn't said any such thing. He just wanted to make Charetta angry.

"That bitch is so two-faced," Charetta fumed.

"You know she's going to always look out for her cousin," Jamil pointed out. "She would never let one of the girls get more shine than Topaz."

"There are other labels. Why does she want Topaz here?" Charetta was up and pacing.

"I guess she wants to keep everything in the family." Jamil typed in a message to Nina telling her to phone him at the office as soon as possible.

"She needs her ass kicked," Charetta barked. "How is she going to mess with people's livelihood like that?"

"You always talkin' about kickin' somebody's ass." Jamil smiled as he pushed Charetta on the couch and kissed her. "You think you're tough."

"I kicked your ass, boo." She laughed and he pushed her away.

"I ain't your boo," he grumbled.

"That's not what you said last night." Charetta laughed. "You know you love me."

"Jamil, you have a phone call," Anita buzzed through the intercom.

"Who is it?" He picked up the telephone so he could speak privately.

"That call you asked me to put through."

"Wait for me in the conference room," Jamil barked at Charetta.

In the conference room, Charetta phoned Toni who was still at the hospital with Xtreme. "Toni, how's Frank?"

"Still eating cheeseburgers." Toni laughed happily.

"Did you tell him about the baby yet?"

"No. I thought I'd wait until he gets out. I've been spending time with his mother too. I think she likes me."

"That's a good thing since you're gonna be her grandbaby's momma." Charetta laughed.

"Char—"

"Don't Char me. Are the girls home from Nina's?"

"Kyle sent them home to go to school. They're going back later."

"Squash that. I just found out that Nina's doin' shady business. She's been pushing Jamil to sign Topaz."

"So . . ."

"So that's a conflict of interest. Do I have to spell it out for you? Damn, girl. Your precious Nina will never allow the girls to be bigger than Topaz."

"I don't believe that," Toni began.

"Would you believe it if Jamil said it?"

"Yes."

"Good, because that's where I got my information. So call the girls and tell them to go home after school. They don't need a baby-sitter. Sabre's been uncomfortable with them ever since New York. I should have kicked both of their asses, especially Topaz's for goin' off on her like that. Who the hell do they think they are?"

"The rich and the beautiful?" Toni was still skeptical.

"The rich and the about to be broke. I'm gonna draw up some papers and take Nina to court for conflict of interest. She wants to deal dirty . . . I'll beat her at her own game."

Charetta hung up without realizing Jamil had been on the phone listening to the entire conversation. He was able to listen in on anyone's conversations at anytime. The only people who knew that was India, who had the phones installed, and Buffalo. It was an added security feature. Jamil had never listened to anyone's conversations—until now.

Jamil sent Nina another two-way message. She had ignored all of his previous ones, and Jamil hated to be ignored. CALL ME. YOUR GIRL IS ABOUT TO SUE YOU AND I'M GOING TO START TALKING TO THE PRESS IF YOU DON'T CALL ME RIGHT NOW ON THE CELLY.

His cell phone rang within minutes and he smiled. "Holla."

"What is it, Jamil?" Nina was very much in control.

"How you feelin'?"

"As if you really cared."

"I care about you, Nina. I'll always care about you."

"Who's getting ready to sue me?"

"Char." Jamil managed to say her name without laughing.

"She's not my girl. So what are *you* talking to the press about?" Nina cut straight to the chase.

"Your girl was all set to sign the paperwork and she reneged on the deal. What up with that?"

"What are you talking about, Jamil?"

"Topaz. She's not signing with Suicide. Got all siddity and had her lawyer call me. She didn't have the nerve to call me herself."

"I don't know what you're talking about, Jamil."

"Sure you do. You two have no secrets, but I'm about to shout one of them out to the press unless I get a signed contract by the end of business tomorrow."

"I thought you cared about me."

"I do. That's why I'm givin' you another day to get that contract signed all sweet and pretty."

Nina hung up on Jamil and called Topaz.

"Are you sure it's okay for you to talk to me?" Topaz obviously had an attitude. "You better ask Kyle's permission first."

"What are you talking about, Topaz?" Nina counted to ten.

"I never pictured you to marry the controlling type."

"Topaz, talk to me before I hang up on you too. Between you and Jamil, I have a really bad headache."

"Me and Jamil? How dare you even put me in the same sentence with him?" Topaz fumed. "Did Kyle tell you I called?"

"No."

"That just proves he's controlling. I don't even know why I expected him to tell you after the things he said to me." Topaz was nearly in tears.

"What things?" Nina demanded.

"He said I needed to learn how to make decisions for myself and not run to you with everything."

"Kyle said that?"

"Yes."

"He didn't mean it. He was upset."

"Well, I did what I had to do, so why are you calling now?"

"Jamil's making threats again. He said you have by the end of business tomorrow to sign or he's going to the press with our secret."

"He didn't."

"He did."

"Xtreme's accident . . . I'm beginning to think you were right, Nina."

"Xtreme's gonna be fine, Topaz."

"I know that but I may not be."

"I tried to tell you but you wanted to be a diamond. Miss Bling-Bling."

"All right, so I got a little caught up. What are we going to do?"

"I like the way *you* always becomes *we*."

"Nina, it's not like this doesn't affect you too."

"That's true, but my husband already knows all my business."

"I wonder what Kyle would think about you kissing Jamil."

"I never kissed Jamil. Jamil kissed me," Nina shouted.

"I might as well face it. I'm going to lose Germain." Topaz started crying and Nina softened.

"Don't cry, T. You know I'm gonna help you. We've still got twenty-four hours to come up with something." Nina hung up the phone and saw Kyle standing in the doorway. "Hi, baby. I didn't know you were standing there."

"I wanted to know what you wanted to do for dinner but I guess you couldn't hear me with all that yelling you were doing."

Nina smiled and patted a spot on the bed next to her. "That was just Topaz and her drama, baby. You know how she is."

"So, you kissing Jamil? Was that about Topaz and her drama too?"

"Baby, I can explain that. I should have told you when it happened."

"When did it happen?" Kyle spoke so softly he frightened her.

"Midsummer Night's Magic. It meant nothing, baby." Nina tried to pull him toward her and he backed away.

"If it didn't mean anything, why didn't you tell me?"

"Because I was afraid you'd stop me from working with the girls because of Jamil."

"You're right about that." Kyle sat on the edge of the bed. "I should have stopped you."

"I wish you had," Nina replied quietly. "None of us would be in this mess now. It's all my fault. I dragged everyone into this, and now I can't get them out."

"It's not your fault."

"But if I hadn't tried to help Char and Toni, the girls wouldn't be out here and I wouldn't be trying to get everyone away from Suicide. Jamil wouldn't be trying to blackmail Topaz. Char wants to sue me. And now you're mad at me. I don't know how much more of this I can take." Nina looked at Kyle with tears streaming out of her eyes.

"Jamil isn't a threat to me. He's an idiot. I don't know what you saw in him. What bothers me is that you felt you couldn't come to me . . . and after everything we've been through."

"I'm sorry, Kyle. Do you forgive me?"

"Of course, Nina. I'll always forgive you."

"Topaz said I should have told you," Nina managed through her tears.

"Nina, I don't ever want our relationship to be like hers."

"It won't be, because I'm not like Topaz."

"I don't know how she sleeps at night."

"I don't know how we do either, sometimes," Nina said softly.

"I'm not making excuses for us but we just came in and did the right thing for Nicki. I wanted to help you. I guess that's one of the reasons God put us together so I could help you save the world and clean up the mess."

Nina crawled across the bed and into Kyle's arms. "I love you so much, baby. I don't know what I'd do if you weren't around to rescue me."

"I love you, too, baby." Kyle stroked her face while he held her. "Man, if I had known a girl as fine as you was going to have so much drama, I would have run and never looked back."

"Kyle," Nina said, finally laughing, "I can't believe you said that."

"Why? I ran right into your arms, didn't I?"

"Oh, baby. That was so sweet."

They sat in the moonlit room listening to the ocean.

"I promise I'll try to stop making such a mess of things."

"What? And stop the drama?" Kyle finally laughed. "Life wouldn't be the same."

"Daddy"—Nicki came into the bedroom covered from head to toe with fingerpaint—"Daddy."

Nina and Kyle looked at each other and laughed.

"Come here, you messy little girl." Kyle picked her up and sat her on Nina's lap. "I'm a happy man. I've just got one big messy family."

Nina looked at her husband and daughter smearing fingerpaint on one another, and for the moment, forgot about Jamil and every other problem Suicide Records had brought into her life.

Chapter 33

Charetta stood by the laser printer in Suicide's conference room and watched the pages of her document slide out of the printer one by one. She perused them quickly, inhaling the scent of the freshly dried ink as she signed and folded them into an envelope with a Suicide Records logo.

"Have these messengered to Nina Ross." Charetta dropped the envelope on Anita's desk as she headed for Jamil's office. She opened the door and found him in his usual place staring out of the window. "Why are you always looking out of that window?" She stood beside him trying to ascertain why he held such a fascination for the view.

"Because I like it," he replied coolly.

"What you need is a change of venue. A room with a view."

"What the hell are you talking about now?" Jamil left the window and went to sit behind his desk.

"A vacation. We need to go on vacation," Charetta declared excitedly.

A vacation? Ain't nobody goin' on vacation."

"Sure we are," Charetta continued. "Remember how much fun we had in Vegas? A vacation would be the perfect thing to get everybody back on top for the New Year, especially after all the drama that's been going on around here."

"How much is all this going to cost?" Jamil seemed somewhat interested.

"I'll do some research on the Internet and put a budget together. This is going to be so much fun."

She went back to her spot in the conference room. It bothered her that India's office was still off-limits but she had to take her territory slowly. Jamil fought her on practically everything she tried to do, but eventually he always gave in.

"Hey, Toni. How's Xtreme? I always try to say Frank but it seems so corny." Charetta laughed to prove her point.

"Complaining about the casts on his leg and arm and acting like a spoiled brat, but otherwise he's doing great." Toni smiled as she watched his mother serve him lunch in bed. "His mother is here cooking all his favorite foods."

"And what are you doing?"

"I'm going to make dinner tonight. He told his mother he wanted some Mexican food."

"Did you tell him about the baby yet?"

"No. I wanted to wait until we have some privacy. His parents are going home after Christmas."

"Do you think he's able to travel? I'm planning a vacation for everybody, and I'm sure you two could use one."

"That sounds like fun, Char. I'll talk to him about it and let you know. Where did you want to go?"

"I was thinking about the Caribbean, but it's such a hassle to fly now, with the holidays. I wish there was somewhere nearby with a beach and lots of sun."

"Did you check out the Mexican Caribbean?"

"Mexican Caribbean?"

"Oh, yes. Cancun is da bomb and they've got some other spots like Playa del Carmen and Islas de las Mujeres. It's gorgeous. We used to go every year when I was a little girl."

"I almost forgot you were part of the rich and the beautiful, Toni, but you ah-ight with me. You ain't phony like that chickenhead Nina."

"Char."

"Don't Char me. I sent her the paperwork. We're about to be rid of her ass forever."

* * *

Kyle signed for the envelope from Suicide Records and brought it upstairs to the bedroom where Nina was relaxing. "I wonder what the idiot wants now." He dropped the letter onto the bed next to his wife.

"I don't even want to open it." Nina looked at the envelope with the Suicide logo and shivered. "I should have burned the first one that came to the house and we wouldn't be in this mess now."

"But you didn't and there's no turning back now. I'll open it." Kyle picked up the envelope and ripped it open and read it quickly. "I think you may be very interested in this."

"What?" Nina picked up the letter and read it and looked at her husband. "Char's suing me for conflict of interest unless I sign over my interest in the group."

"God just gave you your walking papers. You can walk away from this thing finally. Merry Christmas, baby." Kyle grabbed his wife and kissed her but she didn't seem as enthusiastic. "Okay, what's wrong now?"

"I don't know. Char feels like she's won something here, and I want her to know she didn't."

"Nina, you can't save the whole world. Let's take this for what it is. Settle with her and walk away clear."

"You're right, baby." Nina picked up the papers and looked at them again. "I wonder if I can use this thing to get Jamil off Topaz's back. We don't have that much time left before he goes to the press."

"He's bluffing." Kyle looked at his wife. "I wouldn't sign anything."

"But what if he does go to the press? He can really cause some serious damage to all of us. And what about the kids? Topaz isn't the only one who would suffer."

"Didn't you say he signed some sort of agreement?"

"Topaz had one drawn up before we went to London. But Jamil knows he signed that agreement."

Kyle fell onto the bed laughing. "I told you the man was an idiot. Call Topaz and tell her to come over here with a copy of that agreement. We're gonna see what your boy is really made of."

Charetta walked back into Jamil's office and was surprised to find So Fine sitting on the black sofa. Jamil was like a new man, excited and lit up from head to toe with renewed energy as he chatted with the girls and gave them sodas from the small refrigerator in his office.

Her eyes fell on the small diamond pendant around Sabre's neck and she knew immediately that Jamil had given it to her.

"What are you guys doing here?" she barked. "I thought you had school."

"We're on Christmas vacation," Sabre offered. "Nobody was home so we just came by here to say hello."

"Y'all enjoying that little PT Cruiser that Ind—that we hooked for you?" Jamil sat behind his desk and Charetta followed his eyes as they rested on Sabre.

"It's real cool," Sky answered.

"So who does all the driving?" Jamil asked.

"We all did at first," Shawntay offered, "but Sabre is the best driver so we let her drive."

"And that's cool with you?" Jamil smiled and Charetta wanted to slap the silly grin off his face. She couldn't believe he was making a fool of himself over some teenagers.

"Yeah, it's cool. But they always get jelly 'cause I catch all the guys."

"Scrubs." Sky laughed.

"And bug a boos," Shawntay added.

"Yeah, that's why I give them to you." Sabre grinned.

"Y'all gonna let her play you like that?" Jamil laughed.

"Okay. Y'all need to bounce. We got work to do," Charetta cut in.

"I'm gonna take them to lunch first." Jamil picked up his jacket and opened his office door. "After you, ladies. We'll see you later, bug a boo." Jamil laughed and the girls joined in.

Charetta managed a smile as they went out the door. Charetta couldn't help noticing how Sabre was always snuggled right under Jamil's arm and next to his heart. She thought about the expensive diamond that he had especially designed for Sabre and wondered what the girl had done to deserve such an expensive gift until she remembered the large diamond on her own finger and smiled.

Toni browned ground beef in a large cast-iron skillet. She and Virginia Hammond, Frank's mother, had gone on a major shopping spree. There was absolutely nothing to cook in or eat off in the kitchen. There were no linens for any of the beds, nor towels for the bathrooms—none of those major accessories that personalized a house and made it a home.

During Xtreme's initial days home from the hospital, Virginia did the cooking and Toni decorated while Frank, Senior, spent time with Junior. Toni wanted to laugh every time his parents called him that. The thing she found even more interesting was that his dad was the pastor of a small congregation in Detroit. His parents had really blown his image as the bad-boy rapper and superstar pitcher for the Angels but Toni didn't mind.

"That smells wonderful, darling." Virginia Hammond took a seat in the kitchen and watched as Toni prepared dinner. "My son keeps telling me you're an excellent cook."

"I love to cook." Toni rolled the last of the beef into a corn tortilla and sprinkled the casserole with cheese. She took out several avocados and peeled them so she could make Xtreme's favorite guacamole.

"You don't look like you're a stranger to the kitchen."

"My grandmother made all the girls in the family learn how to cook. Whenever we stayed at my grandfather's ranch we had to cook, even if we were on vacation."

"Girls these days want husbands and they know nothing about being wives. I will never understand a young lady not knowing how to cook."

Toni poured a glass of lemonade for each of them and sat down at the table with Xtreme's mother. "You know I still can't believe Frank's dad is a pastor. He never mentioned it to me."

"We know all about that." Virgina laughed. "But Junior's dad and I never gave up on him. We knew he was out here involved in some things we didn't approve of, but we had to trust Jesus. I warned Junior about all that Suicide stuff when he first mentioned it, but he wasn't listening to me."

Toni got up to make the refried beans.

"You were definitely an answer to my prayers."

"Me?" Toni turned around to look at Virginia. "What did I do?"

"You made him think. He called home and told me all about this beautiful dancer girl who he really liked. Junior has never called home to tell me about anyone. I was concerned until he said you made him rethink everything he had ever done with his life."

"He told you that?" Toni was shocked. "Did he tell you that I told him I loved him?"

Virginia smiled as she finished her lemonade. "I heard all about that too. Toni, what did you put in this lemonade? It's delicious."

Toni poured more lemonade into her glass and smiled. "I put in some oranges and limes."

"So that's your secret." Virginia sipped on the glass of lemonade, enjoying the medley of citrus fruits on her tongue. She was a very attractive woman, somewhere in her early fifties. It was more than obvious that Xtreme had inherited his good looks from his mother.

"Does Junior know you're pregnant?"

Toni almost dropped the pan of beans covered with grated Monterey Jack cheese that she was about to put in the oven. "No," she finally managed to answer.

"Why haven't you told him?"

"When he stopped talking to me, I didn't know how he felt. I didn't want him to think I was trying to trap him with a baby. He called the day of the accident. I was going to tell him then but he never made it over."

"Well, I'm not going to be an interfering mama. You tell him when you think the time is right."

"I will," Toni agreed happily.

"And see if you can get him refocused on baseball and away from that Suicide stuff. I wasn't happy about that at all."

"I'll do my best," Toni promised. "Mrs. Hammond?"

"Virginia," she politely corrected.

"How did you know I was pregnant?"

"Mothers always know. Now give me some more of that lemonade and whatever it is you have in the oven, Toni, because as good as this kitchen smells, I know you can cook."

Chapter 34

It was late afternoon when Kyle opened the door for Topaz and led her up to their bedroom. The days were getting shorter, and it was already dark. Topaz was surprised to find Nina lying on the bed underneath a comforter.

"Nina, what's wrong? Are you sick?" Topaz sat on the bed next to her cousin and looked into her eyes.

"No, I'm fine. I'm just chilling. Kyle confined me to my room for a few days, that's all. He'd better be careful because I'm beginning to enjoy this." Nina smiled at Kyle.

"Did you bring the agreement?' Kyle looked at Topaz.

"Yes, but I don't know what good it's going to do." Topaz sighed unhappily. "I don't want to sign with Suicide and I don't want Jamil telling my business."

"You aren't going to have to worry about either." Kyle laughed after he read over the document. "Jamil is an idiot. I gave him too much credit. Now who's going to give him the news?" Kyle was excited as he looked at Nina and Topaz.

"You call him," Nina suggested. "That'll really make his day." She picked up the phone and dialed Jamil's cell number.

"Holla," Jamil barked into the phone. He was in the Hummer on his way home with Charetta.

"He is so tired," Nina whispered as she handed the phone to Kyle.

"Jamil," Kyle began.

"Holla."

Kyle shook his head and laughed. "This is going to fun," he whispered so only the girls could hear. "Jamil, this is Kyle Ross, Nina's husband. I'm calling on behalf of the ladies."

"Yeah," Jamil was immediately interested.

"I'm looking at a copy of a confidentiality agreement signed by Jamil Winters regarding a trip to London, England."

"Quit stalling, man."

"You agreed to keep a certain matter between you and the ladies confidential, and now I understand you want to disclose this information to the press."

"I'm about to make a phone call, man."

"You do that and Topaz will take you and Suicide to court and sue you for every cent you own and then some. You utter one word to the press and we'll sue you for breach of contract, blackmail, and a whole lot of other things those high-priced suits are paid to come up with. Then, we'll have you inside a courtroom so long, you'll forget what the inside of a studio looks like."

Jamil was silent as he thought about what Kyle had just said.

"My man, are you still there?" Kyle smiled as he looked at the girls.

"Look, dog, I ain't got no issue with you."

"I didn't have one with you either, but you're playing around with my family and I'm not having that," Kyle fired back.

"Yo, it's cool. Topaz ain't all that. She's getting too old for the business anyway. I've already got the next real superstar."

Kyle hung up the phone and looked at Nina then Topaz. "I knew he was bluffing."

"What did he say?" Nina demanded.

"Nothing important. But most importantly, y'all are free."

Nina and Topaz screamed with joy.

"Thank you, baby." Nina kissed Kyle.

"Yes, thank you, Kyle." Topaz smiled.

"No problem. Family looks out for family," Kyle replied.

"Let's celebrate. I want a big cheese pizza and a forty of Coke." Nina laughed. "And then I want to watch a movie with my husband and my sister."

Kyle had bought a stack of new DVDs for Nina and they were trying to decide which one to watch when the front doorbell rang.

"Wait. Did you hear something?" Nina quickly hushed everyone as the doorbell rang again. "Someone's at the door," Nina whispered.

"Why are you whispering?" Topaz laughed as Kyle went to check the security monitor. "You ordered a pizza, silly girl."

"It's Sabre," Kyle informed them.

"Sabre?" Nina repeated. "I wonder what she wants." The doorbell rang several more times, and Kyle looked at his wife.

"Send the little thief home." Topaz continued looking at the DVDs.

"I wonder what she wants and why she drove all the way out here without calling first." Nina looked puzzled. "Especially on the day that Char sues me."

"Char sued you? Oh no, I wouldn't even let her ass in here," Topaz offered.

Kyle headed toward the stairs. "I already know, baby, you want me to let her in."

Nina smiled proudly as she looked at Topaz. "He knows me so well."

"And so do I. Why would you even let her in?"

"For the same reason I always help you." Nina threw the comforter on the bed. "Stay up here, Baby Doll. And stay out of trouble."

Nina arrived downstairs as Kyle ushered Sabre into the living room. It was obvious the girl was shaken and something was definitely wrong.

"I'm sorry I didn't call first, Nina, but I had nowhere else to go." Sabre was still shaking as she followed Nina and Kyle into the family room where a fire crackled and sputtered in the fireplace.

"What is it, Sabre?" Nina asked.

"I was in Char's room. We were going to the movies with some guys from school." Sabre paused to look at Nina and Kyle before she continued speaking. "Char had some earrings I wanted to borrow. She's never at home anymore so I went into her room to get them."

"Sabre, when are you going to stop taking things that don't belong to you?"

"Let her finish, Nina."

"I was looking through her jewelry and I found India's ring. You know the one she always wore?"

"You found India's ring?" Nina looked at her husband. "Sabre, are you sure?"

"Yes, She let me try it on. It was so pretty. I could never forget that ring."

"India's ring was in Char's jewelry box. Oh my God." Nina clasped a hand over her mouth and looked at her husband. "That means—"

"That means you need to go home and bring us that ring, Sabre," Kyle cut in. "Does anyone else know you're here?"

"No. I told Sky and Shawntay I wasn't feeling well and to go on without me," Sabre explained.

"Did you tell anyone about the ring?" Kyle asked.

"No. Sky and Shawntay are Char's cousins. I'm not. I was afraid she might do something to me too." Sabre was terrified.

"Just because Char has India's ring doesn't mean she did something to her," Nina finally said, and Kyle and Sabre both looked at her.

"But it does mean she knows who did it," Sabre pointed out.

Kyle looked at Nina. "The police were never able to solve India's murder. Finding her ring is a major clue."

Nina felt sick all over. Did Charetta actually have something to do with India's death? She sat down on the sofa and massaged her temples.

"Sabre, go home and get the ring and bring it back here," Kyle demanded. "Even better, we'll go with you."

"You will?" Sabre looked relieved.

"Kyle we can't go over there. That would really look suspicious. What if Char's there? And what about the lawsuit?"

"We won't go all the way to the house. We'll follow Sabre and wait somewhere nearby while she goes and gets the ring. Boom. We all come back here and call the police." Kyle made everything sound so easy.

Within minutes Nina and Kyle were headed through the canyon to the Ventura Freeway and Topaz went home.

"Just when I thought it was safe to go back in the water," Nina mumbled while Kyle followed the girls' PT Cruiser.

After what seemed like forever, they finally made it to Van Nuys. Sabre pulled into the parking lot of a nearby Ralphs supermarket. She looked like a frail child when she knocked on the window.

"I'm going home now. I'll be right back."

Nina and Kyle watched her drive away.

"Do you think this is a set-up?" Nina looked at Kyle.

"We're sure about to find out."

A short while later, they watched Sabre drive into the lot, park the car in a nearby space, and run over to the truck.

Kyle unlocked the back door. "Did you get it?"

Sabre shook her head with eyes that were as big as saucers. "It's gone. I couldn't find the ring anywhere."

"What?" Nina was shocked. "You're not playing games with us are you, Sabre?"

"No."

"Was anybody there?" Kyle demanded..

"No."

"Do you think Sky or Shawntay took it?"

"I don't think so."

"Where are Toni and Char?" Nina fired the questions.

"Toni's at Xtreme's house, and I think Char's still with Jamil. At least she was when we went by there earlier and Jamil took us out to lunch," Sabre replied.

"Dang." Kyle looked confused. "I wonder what happened to that ring."

"I don't know." Sabre was still shaking her head. "I swear it was there when I left, but now it's gone. Even the jewelry box is gone."

"You mean all of her jewelry is missing?" Nina was horrified.

"Char keeps everything in this silver engraved box with her name on it, and it's gone too."

"I wonder who took it," Nina thought out loud.

"Somebody who knows more about this than we do," Kyle finished. "Sabre, you've got to go home and act like nothing happened."

"I can't do that. I'm afraid. What if Char knows I was in her jewelry box and saw India's ring?" Sabre was in tears.

"Do you want to find out who did this to India?" Kyle handed her a tissue.

"Yes." Sabre sniffed and blew her nose.

"Then you have got to go home and act like nothing happened. You can't make any phone calls from the house either. Leave the house and only use your cell phone," Kyle instructed.

"You can use your two-way but delete the message as soon as you send it and make sure you delete any messages from me," Nina added.

"If you feel like you're in danger, call the police and come to the house," Kyle further instructed as he unlocked the back door.

Nina gave Sabre a hug before Sabre drove away. "Do you think we did the right thing?"

"We don't have enough evidence to go to the police without that ring. We'd all be in danger if we did."

"Do you really think it was India's ring?"

"Sabre's got a thing for the bling-bling. That was some rock Jamil gave India."

Nina clasped a hand to her mouth. "Did I tell you Char was wearing my old engagement ring the other night at the hospital?"

"You're kidding?"

"No, she kept waving her hand in front of my face. She wanted me to see it."

"Char certainly has a thing for engagement rings." Kyle laughed. "Do you think she knew it was your ring?"

"Who knows what Char thinks? She's changed since high school."

"She didn't change. You're just seeing the real Char."

Nina sighed long and hard and looked up at her husband. "Do you think Sabre will be able to handle this?"

"I sure hope so for her safety and ours, but I'm still not convinced it's not some type of set-up."

Chapter 35

When Jamil opened his eyes he could hear voices downstairs in his house. He put on his robe and was surprised when he went downstairs and found his mother in the kitchen having a yelling match with Charetta.

"Mom, I didn't know you were coming over." He kissed Janice on the cheek and headed toward the refrigerator.

"I'll get it for you, baby." Charetta took out a bottle of fresh-squeezed orange juice and poured some into a glass for Jamil.

He picked it up and drank the entire thing within seconds and placed it on the counter, and Charetta immediately refilled it. "Now what were y'all making all that noise about?"

"I came over to discuss the details of our annual New Year's Eve party with you, and she informs me that the you two are engaged and everyone's going to Cancun for some big party. Now I know that isn't true." Janice glared at Charetta.

"It's true," Jamil replied softly.

"Oh, hell no. I don't believe for one minute you're in love with this tramp."

"Tramp?" Charetta was clearly insulted. "I ain't nobody's tramp."

"Baby, she's not even your type." Janice was on the verge of tears.

"Come on, Mom. Don't start crying." Jamil led his mother out of the kitchen and into the living room where they could speak privately.

"Have sex with her, go to Cancun. But don't marry her. You haven't had enough time to get over India yet."

"Mom, India's gone, and I had to move on with my life. Char's a lot of fun and she's really smart. She may not be as beautiful as the other women in my life, but I really care about her."

"Care? Baby, you're supposed to be in love. I don't see that little sparkle you had in your eyes when you were with India or Nina." Janice found a tissue and wiped the tears from her eyes.

"Mom." Jamil stood and Janice pulled him back down on the sofa beside her.

"Baby, I love you. You deserve the very best. I've always been so proud of you. I want you to be happy but not with this girl. She's not for you."

Jamil focused on something on the other side of the room. He was trying really hard not to cry. "I love you, too, Mom, but I want to do this. I gotta do this."

Janice stood and took Jamil's face in her hands and kissed him. "Alright, baby. You know I've never interfered in your life. If you say she's the one, she's the one. But don't ask me to support this."

"Mom, why don't you bring some of your friends and come with us to Cancun? We can have the New Year's party down there."

"I don't think so, baby, but you have a good time." Janice kissed him again and left. She took out her cell phone and scrolled through it looking for a number as she got into the pearl-white Escalade Jamil had given her for Christmas.

Nina heard her two-way beeping in the office where she had left it. She was in Nicki's room coloring with her in one of the oversized coloring books her daughter had received for Christmas. Nicki's favorite Donnie McClurkin CD was playing and Nicki sang along.

"No weapon," Nicki sang in perfect pitch.

Nina loved to hear her little girl sing. Every week Nicki had a new favorite song and this week it was Donnie McClurkin again. The two-way continued beeping so Nina got up and went to answer it.

"Hurry, Mommy."

"I will." Nina dashed across the hall and picked up her beeper. With all the excitement of the holidays, she had pushed Sabre and India's ring out of her mind until she saw Sabre's two-way number.

Nina swallowed hard and considered not answering it. She took a deep breath and read the message.

EVERYONE IS GOING TO CANCUN FOR JAMIL AND CHAR'S ENGAGEMENT PARTY. WHAT SHOULD I DO?

"Engagement party?" Nina said out loud. "What is Jamil doing?"

Nina went to check on Nicki who was still coloring and singing and dashed downstairs into the family room where Kyle was reading a book. "Kyle, Jamil and Char are engaged. Sabre just two-wayed me. They're all going to Cancun to celebrate."

"No way." Kyle put down the newspaper.

"Sabre wants to know what she should do." Nina could see the large Christmas tree in the foyer with Kyle's train set laid out around it. "I knew things had been a little too quiet." The telephone rang and she got up to answer it.

"Nina, this is Janice Winters. I really need to talk to you."

"Do you want to come over here?" Nina didn't know what else she could say. She could hear the frustration in the woman's voice.

"Could I?"

"Sure, Janice." Nina gave her directions and responded to Sabre's message. HOLD TIGHT. MORE INFO COMING IN.

SKY AND SHAWNTAY ARE PACKING. WE'RE SUPPOSED TO LEAVE TOMORROW, Sabre sent back almost immediately.

THEN YOU START PACKING TOO. THEN LEAVE AND SAY YOU HAVE TO GO GET SOMETHING AND CALL ME.

WHAT IF THEY WANT TO COME WITH ME?

DITCH 'EM. Nina closed her two-way and shook her head. "Jamil's mom is on her way over. She sounded really upset. I didn't know what else to tell her, and she may have more information."

"You did the right thing," Kyle reassured her.

"I still think we should call the police."

"And tell them what? We still don't have any evidence."

Jamil took Charetta shopping to buy new things for their trip. She had been so envious when he had taken the girls shopping in New York. He even purchased a set of luggage.

"Nina was always trying to get me to do more traveling. The first time I ever went out of the country, I went with her. We went to the Cayman Islands. Topaz and Gunther, me and Nina.

"You mean Gunther Lawrence, the film director who died of a heart attack?" Charetta was very interested.

"The one and only."

"That's right, Topaz was married to him. You were traveling with them?"

"I told you we were like family. Those were some really great times," Jamil reminisced.

"I don't know what you ever saw in Nina." Charetta watched a waiter pour more champagne into their glasses. They were having an early dinner in Beverly Hills.

Jamil only smiled. "Nina's cool. She was my first love."

"And I'll be your last." Charetta kissed him softly on the lips. "What is it with you and Nina? I know you two have some sort of big secret."

"You'll never know," Jamil fired back.

"You know she kicked you to the curb because you were from the hood."

"You don't know what you're talkin' about. Nina's not like that."

"And you sound like you're still sprung. Just like my brother. He thought Nina was so cool and so beautiful, but she kicked him to the curb too."

"Which one, Bootsie?" Jamil laughed.

"Yes." Charetta was a little defensive.

"He was way out of his league." Jamil laughed.

"And obviously you were, too, because Nina married Kyle and not you," Charetta fired back.

"You need to shut up, bitch, because you don't know what you're talking about." Jamil paid the check and they left.

"I'm sorry, baby. I don't want to fight with you. We're engaged now so let's keep everything from the past in the past. Besides . . . I'm pregnant." She smiled at Jamil. "Happy New Year!"

"Pregnant?" Jamil stopped cold in his tracks. "When did that happen? I used protection every time."

"I guess one of those condoms had a little hole in it." Charetta laughed.

"Did you put a hole in it?" Jamil demanded.

"No. And why are you so upset anyway? We're getting married."

"Who said I even want kids?"

"India was pregnant," Charetta said quietly.

"That was India, and this is you. I'm in a different place now. I want to focus on the label and launch Sabre's solo career."

"Sabre's solo career?" Charetta spat out the words like poison. "I didn't know anything about her having a solo career."

"You don't have to know everything, and you won't, bitch. That's the way it is and if you're going to be with me you'd better get used to it."

Nina opened the door for Janice Winters. Nina could smell alcohol and marijuana when the woman came into the house.

"What a beautiful home, Nina. And a beautiful tree." Janice looked around the house still beautifully decorated for Christmas and burst into tears. "I'm sorry, Nina. I shouldn't have come here, but I had nowhere else to go."

"That's okay, Janice." Nina took her into the family room. "You remember my husband, Kyle?"

"Who could forget that tall drink of water." Janice managed to smile between the tears.

"What's wrong, Janice?" Nina handed her some tissues.

"Jamil, he's engaged to that girl, Char. I tried to talk him out of it but he won't listen to me."

"What do you want me to do?" Nina asked.

"You two have always been friends, and you were there for him when India died. He'll listen to you."

"I don't think so, Janice. Jamil's been acting strange every since he started the label. I told him to change the name but he's not listening to me."

"Change the name? What's wrong with the name?"

"Suicide . . . it's associated with death. India died. Xtreme almost died. That's too many coincidences for me. Words are powerful. You can speak things into existence. There's a lot of things going on with Jamil that I never saw when we were together."

"Death . . . I never thought about it like that. This girl, Char. She sure seems to have him under some kind of spell. She's not even his type, and I think he's still in love with India. He's just moving so fast."

"So I take it you don't like Char?" Kyle asked.

"Hell no. She's the kind of girl I worked three jobs to get him away from." Janice took the bottle of water Nina gave her.

"I still don't know how I can help. I don't even know anything about their engagement."

"I told you and now you know."

The telephone rang and Kyle went to answer it.

"I don't feel comfortable talking to him about this when he hasn't said anything to me. I'm sorry." Nina explained.

"Excuse me, baby." Kyle handed Nina the telephone. "It's Jamil," he whispered loudly.

Nina took the phone and swallowed hard. "Hey, Jamil."

"Happy New Year, gorgeous."

"Happy New Year, Jamil." Nina was amazed that she had any speaking voice.

"I want you to come down to Cancun. There's going to be a celebration. Char and I are engaged, and I want you there to thank you personally for bringing this wonderful woman into my life." Jamil planted a kiss on Charetta's cheek.

"You and Char are engaged?" Nina looked at Janice.

"Yes, and you've got to be there. We've got some nice beachfront villas picked out. So, bring my boy Kyle along so we can play some golf. And just to show you there's no hard feelings, I even reserved a villa for Superstar. Her loss is Sabre's gain."

"Jamil, don't you think you're rushing things just a little? You haven't had enough time to get over India and you barely know Char. What's the big hurry?"

"Life moves on. And I'm tired of everyone telling me I'm rushing things. I know what I'm doing. I've found a good woman. And she just told me she's pregnant, so we've got a lot to celebrate for the New Year."

"Char is pregnant?"

"Oh hell no." Janice was up on her feet. "Over my dead body. I definitely want a paternity test."

"Yeah, my boo's got a little sumpin,' sumpin' in the oven." Jamil laughed and Nina made a face at the thought.

"You've got to go down there and talk him out of it, Nina. Please," Janice pleaded.

"What is my going down there going to change?" Nina whispered.

Kyle wrote SABRE on a notepad and held it up behind Janice.

"Okay, Jamil. We'll be there," Nina agreed reluctantly.

"Bet. There's an open reservation with the airline in your name. Char's gonna fax over all the information."

Nina hung up and looked at Janice and then Kyle.

"Did Jamil know you were here?"

"No way." Janice smiled and gave Nina a hug. "He's reaching out to you, Nina. I knew you could help. Now go down to Cancun and be a friend to my baby boy."

Chapter 36

Charetta, Jamil, and Buffalo picked up the girls in a limo and headed for Los Angeles International. They were all too excited as they chatted away about the trip to Mexico. None of the girls, including Charetta, had ever been out of the country. Sabre was a little less talkative than the others.

"What up with my little diamond?" Jamil asked during the ride to the airport.

"She had a fight with one of her boyfriends." Sky laughed.

"You got more than one?" Jamil smiled.

"She sure does," Shawntay joined in.

"That's because she's a diamond." Jamil looked at the others. "And y'all just tryin' to keep your stuff on the down low. The name of the group is So Fine."

Sabre relaxed somewhat when she saw that Charetta was more interested in Jamil than the girls. And the fight with her boyfriend had served as a wonderful excuse to explain her mood to the girls.

Toni and Xtreme were waiting for them at the gate when they finally made it through security screening.

"Xtreme." The girls were careful of his leg and arm, which were still in a cast. He was sitting in a wheelchair and Toni was holding his crutches.

"Hey, little sweeties." Xtreme grinned as they covered him with kisses.

"Who let you out, playa?" Jamil grinned at his boy then he gave him a hug. "No more motorcycles, dog."

"No more motorcycles. Between Mom and Toni, I'm glad to even be out of the house."

"The doctor said it was okay for him to travel. Can you believe that? And his mother said she never could get him to be still, so here we are." Toni smiled happily.

"I was about to go stir crazy up in that house."

"Oh, it wasn't that bad. You are such a drama king." Toni was still smiling.

"I would have gone crazy if I didn't have you." Xtreme kissed her in front of everyone and Jamil looked away.

"We're getting married." Toni snuggled up to Xtreme. "So we had to come celebrate too."

"Congratulations." Charetta kissed them both. "This is so cool. Two engagements."

Xtreme held Toni's hand. "I still have to get her a ring but we already have a date in mind."

"When?" Charetta and the girls chorused excitedly.

"We're thinking June. I'll be all healed by then and able to walk down the aisle." Xtreme smiled and So Fine swooned. They still found him extremely good-looking. "And . . . Toni will have had the baby by then."

"Baby?" Jamil almost choked.

"Yeah, man." Xtreme couldn't contain the smile that lit up his face. "She's got one in the oven, and I'm going to be a daddy."

"And we're getting married at Frank's church. Did you guys know his dad is a pastor?" Toni looked at Jamil.

"I didn't know all that, playa. How come you never told me?" Jamil demanded.

"Guess it never came up in none of our conversations. I was really out there. But thanks to the Lord and Toni, I've got my head back on straight. God knew I needed help and he sent me an angel." Xtreme kissed Toni again and Jamil stood.

"This plane should be boarding soon. I'm going to check on getting my boy on first."

"I'll check into it, boss," Buffalo cut in.

"How come you didn't tell them about our baby?" Charetta asked Jamil as they boarded the airplane.

" 'Cause I ain't ready for everybody to be all up in my business yet."

* * *

Nina and Kyle were getting out of a limo when Topaz, Germain, and the kids pulled up next to them.

"Baby Doll, Chris." Nicki rolled down the window and waved. It was a sunny day and she was wearing her star-shaped sunglasses.

"Hi, Nicki." Baby Doll looked at Germain. "Daddy, get out of the car."

"Hold up, Miss Thang." Germain laughed as Kyle took Nicki out of the car, kissed her, and handed her to Nina.

"Now I want you to be a good little girl for Uncle Germain and Auntie." Nina kissed her and handed her to Topaz who was also wearing a pair of sunglasses.

"With those glasses on you guys look just alike." Germain pulled Nicki out of Topaz's arms.

"Daddy, put Nicki in the car," Baby Doll demanded again.

Nina tried not to laugh as she kissed Germain on the cheek and pulled Topaz away from him. "Are you sure you won't come with us? Jamil made a specific request for the superstar."

"I think it'll be better if I stay here with Germain and the kids. You know you don't have to go either. And I can't believe Char had India's ring. That's some scary stuff. Do you really think she had something to do with India's death?" Topaz's hair was pulled back into a ponytail like Nicki's, and the resemblance between them was unexplainable.

"I'll call you when we get back." Nina blew kisses at the kids and joined Kyle who was checking their luggage with the skycaps.

Everyone was excited when the airplane began its descent into Cancun and they were able to see cobalt and aquamarine water smack the shores of powder-white sand beaches.

"Just what the doctor ordered." Xtreme smiled at Toni.

Jamil was silent as he caught a glimpse of the boats and Jet Skis skirting up and down the Caribbean Sea.

"Isn't it wonderful, boo?" Charetta looked at Jamil with sparkling eyes.

"Yeah, Char. It's da bomb." Jamil smiled.

Everyone was already at the beach when Nina and Kyle checked into the villa complete with its own private swimming pool.

"Look at this." Kyle smiled at Nina. "We can just stay in here and skinny dip."

"Any other time, that would be great, but this doesn't feel like much of a vacation." Nina wrapped her arms around Kyle and looked up at him.

"I know, baby. But we're here. So let's just make the best of it." Kyle looked out at the water. "That beach looks kind of right. Look, you can even see the coral reef. Up for some diving?"

"Okay," Nina agreed. "But tomorrow."

They woke up the next morning and made their way down to the beach where the girls practically ran them over on the way out to the water.

"Excuse you?" Nina put her hands on her hips and pretended to be mad.

"Hey, Nina. Hi, Kyle." Sky and Shawntay paused to say hello.

Sabre said nothing but her eyes spoke volumes. She gave them each a hug as she ran off behind the others.

"What do you make of that?" Kyle looked at Nina.

"I'm glad you're here?" Nina replied thoughtfully.

"Let's do this." Kyle followed the path he thought the girls had taken down to the beach and found the others.

"Nina." Toni jumped up and greeted her. "I didn't know you were coming."

"We came down to celebrate with Jamil." Kyle kissed Charetta lightly on the cheek as he reached for Jamil and gave him a pound. "Congratulations, playa."

Jamil was wearing sunglasses and chilling under a colorful umbrella. There was a light buffet of grilled lobster, fresh salads and fruit, and champagne. "Thanks, playa. Eat, drink, and be merry."

Nina bent down in the sand next to Xtreme and gave him a hug. "I am so glad to see you." A few tears collected in her eyes, and she quickly brushed them away.

"Thanks, darlin'. I know you were at the hospital and everyone seems to think you have something to do with my sitting here." Xtreme shook hands with Kyle.

"Me?" Nina finally laughed. "What did I do?"

"Yo, Kyle. Toni said your dad is a pastor." Xtreme looked up at Kyle who sat in the chair next to him.

"That's right, man."

Charetta groaned and threw off her cover-up. "I'm going in the water before they start testifying up in here. Come on, boo." She extended a hand to Jamil who followed her out to the beach.

"Hey, Miss Nina." A gentle breeze played with Buffalo's partially unbuttoned tropical-print shirt while he flipped through a copy of *Sports Illustrated.*

Nina wanted to say something but she didn't know what to say. "Hey, Buffalo. Gorgeous day, huh?"

"Absolutely." Buffalo returned to his magazine, and Nina and Kyle found empty seats under the umbrellas.

Jamil and Charetta returned and quickly finished off a bottle of champagne. The teenagers screamed for everyone's attention as they flew by on Jet Skis. Charetta jumped up and ran in to the water and climbed on behind one of her young cousins.

"Jamil, I need to talk to you," Nina heard herself say.

"Sure," Jamil agreed.

Buffalo carefully eyed the two of them.

"Not here. Let's go for a walk," Nina suggested.

They strolled up the beach where they were out of sight but could still see the activity on the water.

"What up?" Jamil smiled at Nina.

"What is up with you marrying Char?"

"Life goes on."

"You're making a big mistake."

"That's your opinion. I don't tell you how to run your life. You don't tell me how to run mine."

Nina sighed heavily as she looked at the ground and then Jamil. "I don't know how to say this, so I'm just going to say it." Nina looked out at the water. "We think Char had something to do with India's death."

"I know," Jamil replied quietly.

"You know?" Nina's eyes grew wide with horror. "How long have you known?"

"A few days after India died."

"How did you find out when the police don't even know?"

"Five-0 is weak. They don't care nothin' about black people, especially in Compton. I've got money and I know people. Everybody has a price."

"I don't believe you." Nina shook her head.

"So how did you find out?" Jamil demanded.

Nina watched Sabre racing with the others on a Jet Ski. "I'd rather not say, but it has something to do with India's ring."

"Her engagement ring? It's in Char's jewelry box, in a safe place."

"You have the ring? Are you going to turn Char in to the police?"

"Nope."

"Tell me you're not still going to marry her."

"Hell no."

Nina sighed with relief. "So what's this engagement party stuff about?"

"Part of a plan."

"What kind of plan?"

"You'll see."

"Jamil, what are you up to?" All of a sudden Nina was very frightened.

"Look, gorgeous. I loved you. Things didn't work out. Old boy is cool. I like the way he looks out for you. Kyle's a good brother."

"Jamil . . ."

"You know you always did talk too much." Jamil laughed. "Look, for the record, I wasn't ever going to tell Superstar's little secret. Y'all are my little Valley girls. Stuff happens. But now I expect you to return the favor and keep mine."

"What are you talking about, Jamil?"

"India, that was my heart. After you broke it, she came along and fixed it." Jamil watched the girls on the Jet Skis.

"Life isn't over, Jamil. You'll find somebody new who will love you even more." Nina felt herself perspiring in the hot sun.

"No life ain't over, but Char's sure is." Jamil watched Charetta zip past the others on Shawntay's Jet Ski.

"Oh my God. Jamil no."

"I told you that night at the hospital what I was gonna do. Now this will be our secret." Jamil ran toward the water and flagged Shawntay down. She gave Jamil her life vest and he climbed on the Jet Ski in front of Charetta. He revved the motor a few times and roared past the others. Nina ran down the beach to find Kyle as Jamil headed away from the beach straight for the horizon.

"Kyle." Nina's face was covered with tears. Toni and Xtreme had gone inside, and Buffalo was calmly eating a lobster.

"What is it, baby?"

"Jamil knows everything and he's going to kill Char," Nina whispered.

Chapter 37

Jamil haphazardly drove the Jet Ski way out on the sea, driving very fast and then suddenly stomping on the brakes. He drove out past a coral reef and the divers where the waves were very rough and choppy.

"Hey." Charetta laughed. "Where did everybody go?"

Jamil just kept driving like a madman.

"Baby, do you think it's okay for us to be out this far?"

"I'm not your baby."

"Sure you are." Charetta laughed as she held him tighter.

"You must be crazy, bitch."

"Baby, what's wrong?"

"How could you think I'd ever want you to have my baby or that I'd even marry you, skank?"

"Jamil."

Nina was frantic on the beach. "We have to stop him. We have to stop him before he does something crazy."

"He told you, Nina?" Buffalo had a wild look on his face.

"Yes."

"I was hoping you could talk him out of it. He wouldn't listen to me. I wanted to let the authorities handle it. I've got the ring in her jewelry box right here." Buffalo patted a leather bag.

"Come on, you guys, we've got to stop him," Nina yelled.

The three of them charged down the beach and flagged in the girls.

"We need your Jet Skis." Kyle jumped on one and Nina climbed on behind him. Buffalo zipped off in the direction where they had last seen Jamil.

"You killed India." Jamil screamed over the roar of the Jet Ski. "And now I'm going to kill you."

"I didn't kill her. It was an accident. I only wanted her out of the way so you and I could spend some time together. She was always in the way. Somebody was always in the way," Charetta cried.

"You're only sorry because you got caught."

"No, really. They were only supposed to take her car and leave her stranded, but something went wrong. Terribly wrong."

Buffalo and Kyle kept driving but there was no sign of Jamil.

"Just like something terrible's gonna go wrong out here." Jamil tried to unhook his jacket from the key so he could jump off of the Jet Ski and it would run out of control and crash onto the rocks. Charetta saw what he was trying to do and fought with him.

Buffalo spotted them struggling on the horizon. "There they are."

"Hurry up." Nina hung on to Kyle as they drove toward the couple struggling on the Jet Ski.

A huge speedboat was approaching them from the opposite direction but Jamil and Charetta were too busy fighting to see it.

"Look out," Nina screamed as they drove up within shouting distance. Jamil and Charetta turned just as the speedboat roared over the Jet Ski, sending it and them to the bottom of the sea. "Oh my God," Nina screamed as the boat sped on by.

Buffalo and Kyle drove up to where they thought they had seen Charetta and Jamil go down but there was no sign of anyone or anything anywhere. Seconds later, pieces of the broken Jet Ski pressed their way up to the surface of the water and Nina screamed.

"Jamil," Nina cried softly. They sat there for several more minutes hoping that Jamil and Charetta would emerge from the sea just as the machinery had that floated in pieces around them.

Kyle and Buffalo exchanged glances.

"Let's go notify the Coast Guard," Kyle suggested. "Jamil and Charetta might come up somewhere else."

Nina said nothing as they headed back toward land. She constantly looked back over her shoulder, hoping and praying that Charetta and Jamil both would be floating in the sea in their bright orange life vests.

Buffalo and Kyle filed a report with the Mexican Coast Guard but there was no sign of the speedboat, Jamil, Charetta, or their bodies. The only thing that they ever recovered was one of the life vests much farther out from the place where they had the accident in the Caribbean Sea.

Within days, the news was everywhere—MTV, BET, CNN. The industry buzzed with gossip. Janice Winters had a memorial service for Jamil at a church in Compton. People lined the streets to express their grief while others tried to get a glimpse of all the stars who were in attendance.

"Jamil was a son, a grandson, a cousin, a nephew, and a friend, not to mention a very talented artist. We'll feel his loss forever, but his memory will live on through the many songs he wrote. Each time we hear one, we will always remember Jamil."

The minister continued speaking while Janice cried her eyes out. Nina hadn't stopped crying since they left Cancun. "Do you think Jamil's in heaven?" she whispered to Kyle. "I could handle this so much better if I knew he was there."

Keisha and Eric accompanied Nina, Kyle, Topaz, and Germain to the service. Xtreme was there with the girls. Buffalo walked up and greeted everyone after it was over.

"Hey, Buff." Nina hugged the big guy tightly.

"Old J." Buffalo smiled. "Trying to be tough. I tried to tell him but he just wouldn't listen."

"We know." Nina sniffed. "You were a good friend."

"And so were you." Buffalo smiled.

Nina cried a fresh batch of tears.

"I told him not to name that label Suicide and I told him to go to the police when we found out what happened to India," Buffalo continued.

"We know." Nina managed to smile.

"J was as straight as they came. He never even got in a fight when we were growing up. He thought this bad-boy hip-hop thing was a game. Tryin' to live up to some image. I should have kicked his ass a long time ago. I wish he was here so I could kick it now."

"I kept saying from the very beginning none of this was like Jamil," Nina pointed out.

"It wasn't. I saw him changing and when India died, he lost it." Buffalo accepted a tissue from Keisha. "He should have been like you, man." Buffalo looked at Xtreme. "Quit while he was ahead."

"I had to get knocked out. I was already asking myself where my life was goin' and just when I got the answer I had the accident. I wish something like that could have helped Jamil," Xtreme said sadly.

"That's the devil's game plan . . . to snatch you out of here before you see the Light," Keisha offered.

"Yeah, I felt myself floating away and then I heard Nina screaming and I woke up." Xtreme looked at Nina. "Thanks, sweetie."

Nina managed a smile. "I'll never understand how Jamil spent all of that time with Char knowing what she had done."

"I couldn't have done it." Buffalo shook his head.

"Yeah," everyone chorused.

"You do what you have to do," Topaz whispered softly. She took her cousin's hand and squeezed it.

"Jamil almost snatched her a couple of times and so did I. He believed in keeping his friends close and his enemies even closer." Buffalo chuckled.

"What a waste." Kyle shook his head. "What a waste of two lives."

Everyone was reflective as Janice walked up and hugged Nina. "I know you did your best, girl. I had no idea my son was walking around with all of that anger inside of him. But they never found my baby's body, so I'm gonna keep hoping that I get a phone call one day and it'll be my baby boy on the other end of the line." She kissed Nina and smiled at everyone before she walked off to greet other people.

"So Fine." Kyle smiled at the girls. "What are your plans since Toni went to spend some time with her grandparents?"

"We're going back to Brooklyn," Sky replied.

"All of you?" Kyle looked at the girls.

"Me and Sky are, for a little while at least. I've been thinking about going to college," Shawntay offered.

"And I miss going to school with all my friends." Sky shook her head. "I can't believe I just said that."

"What about you, Sabre?" Nina smiled as the young girl nervously fingered the expensive diamond pendant that hung around her neck. For a minute, Nina wished she had the engagement ring that Jamil had given her as a memento of her friend, but the memories in her heart would always be there.

"I'm getting emancipated. Jamil had me signed as solo artist and the parent label wants to keep me, so I'm getting my own place and I'm going to pursue my singing career."

"Good for you." Nina smiled. "Jamil would like that."

"Thanks, Nina." Sabre hugged her and then the others. "Is it okay if I still come around?"

"Sure," Nina replied. "You'd better."

"Okay." Sabre smiled happily. "We're gonna go. I'm taking them to the airport."

"I've got a plane to catch too." Xtreme smiled. "I'm going to meet Toni's grandparents. We're gonna hang out down there until spring training."

"Cool, man. You and Toni give us a call when you get in town. Us preachers' kids have to stick together." Kyle smiled as they exchanged pounds.

"Y'all won't be able to get rid of us." Xtreme waved as he walked away.

"Buffalo, you are welcome at my house anytime." Nina smiled and gave him a hug. "My teddy-bear friend."

"Cool. I'm gonna go see if Janice needs help with anything." Buffalo hugged Kyle and shook hands with all the others.

Nina sighed as she looked at Kyle, Topaz, Germain, Keisha, and Eric. "I need a big old cheese pizza and two forties of Coke." She laughed as they headed out to the limousine they had all come in together.

"You'd better come get your daughter before Germain and Chris ruin her. You know she's a little diva." Topaz smiled.

"I know." Nina smiled.

"I'm gonna say something, and I don't want you to take this the wrong way," Topaz whispered to Nina as they climbed inside the super-stretch limo.

"What?"

"There is one thing positive about all of this."

"And what would that be?" Nina looked at Topaz.

"Nobody else knows our secret," Topaz whispered.

"That's true," Nina replied thoughtfully. "But Jamil was just bluffing. He was our friend and he would have never told."

POSTLUDE

Don't believe the hype
behind this Diamond Life.
You might lose your life
Tryin' to prove that your rhyme is tight.
You'll succeed if the time is right,
But more than the time
Make sure your mind is right
Eyesight focused toward the Light.

You can ball or fall
You can lose everything
Or leave with it all
In this life, fast money, women, and cars
But it cost tryin' to be a Chocolate Star.

All I'm tryin' to do is bring y'all the Light
Cause the King might call tonight . . .

—Xtreme's Rap written by
Scott Smith aka Justified